THE MERSEY MOTHERS

SHEILA RILEY

Boldwood

A CIP catalogue record for this book is available from the British Library.

Paperback ISBN 978-1-83889-332-3

Large Print ISBN 978-1-83889-676-8

Hardback ISBN 978-1-80415-982-8

Ebook ISBN 978-1-83889-333-0

Kindle ISBN 978-1-83889-334-7

Audio CD ISBN 978-1-83889-330-9

MP3 CD ISBN 978-1-83889-674-4

Digital audio download ISBN 978-1-83889-331-6

Boldwood Books Ltd
23 Bowerdean Street
London SW6 3TN
www.boldwoodbooks.com

PROLOGUE
JANUARY 1947

He sat rigid. Fixed on her every move. Each spin revealing a gaudy red suspender holding up black nylon stockings, no doubt supplied by Uncle Sam's finest. He knew the instant she clocked him. Her self-assured expression faltered. She hadn't expected to see him. Her uncertain gaze tracked the journey of the man who went into the gents' lavatory...

Raising his chin, he ignored Bert, the part-time pianist, hammering out a foot-stomping tune. And she twirled when taproom singing cut through the fog of tobacco smoke and bounced off the red papered walls. Revellers clap, clap, clapping in time to the music. Throwing back her head, confidence restored. Laughing. She thought they were over. *She ought to know better.*

The music stopped!

Her ruby lips frozen in a practiced smile. Whooping when a tavern drinker hooked her thickening waist, pulling her to him, nuzzling private words in her ear. Pulling herself free, she ignored an invitation. Nodding to the empty seat. She shook her head. Hesitant, her eyes sneaking a look to the closed door of the gents'. And a fire-breathing dragon reared up inside him. So, the rumour he had heard was true.

Tightly squeezing the glass in his hand, it shattered, spraying glittering shards across the table. She gave him her full attention now. Narrowing the distance between them, she crossed the crowded bar. So close he could see the loathing in her eyes.

Damn you to hell!

'You've no right following me!' She stabbed him with her words and grabbed her handbag, coat and scarf. Her lips dripped venom as she gripped the gleaming brass handle of the Tram Tavern door... In seconds, he was behind her, forcing her outside.

* * *

'Making a show of me like that,' she hissed, shaking his bloodstained hand off her arm, 'you had everybody looking when you broke that glass!' *Bloody lunatic.* She wrapped the hand-knitted scarf round her head and neck, pulling up the wide collar of her coat.

Hurrying now, her heels scraped the cracked pavement as a westerly gale whipped off the River Mersey, pushing her along the dock road. She would take the long way home. Try to shake him off. Knowing what he was after. And not wanting a scene in front of her kids, Jack and Lucy. A torrent of hailstones turned the ground icy white. He pushed her into the doorway of Blackledge's bakery.

Angry, she took out an untipped cigarette and lit it. And, tilting back her head, she blew a straight line of smoke over his shoulder towards the overhead railway, high above the immense granite walls following the docks along the constant surge of river, and flicked ash with measured nonchalance.

'There's a real party atmosphere in the tavern tonight. Cheerful, you know.' *Like the good times when I worked on the White Star Line's finest. Before Cunard took over.* She blinked rapidly, ignoring his intimidating glare. *Then there was the war, of course – the first, not the second. By the second war, I was well and truly anchored.*

'Why don't you leave me alone?' Aggravated, she wondered why she provoked jealous men? She flicked the cigarette into the gutter, her blunt self-confidence giving her an insolent air. 'Piss off! I told you, we're over. I'm taking my kids back to Ireland.'

'We're over when I say so,' he growled. 'And you won't be going to Ireland.'

'You wanna bet?' She made to move out of the doorway, and he put the flat of his hands against the cold tiles above her shoulder. 'I'm going. And you can't stop me!'

Ducking out of his way, her heel caught in the space once filled by a terracotta tile and she stumbled, saved only by his immense bulk. *That last rum's gone straight to my head.*

As did the thundering slap that caught her side on. Her head hitting the tiles with a crack. No time to cry out or retaliate. She gasped a lungful of freezing air that floated round her like a hoar-frost shroud. She put up her hand, failing to fend off a blow that made her eyeballs dance. Tears of shock rolled unchecked down her cheeks. And for the first time in a long while, she prayed. 'Holy Mary, Mother of God...'

His grip tightened around her throat, the throbbing pressure cutting off her words. She gagged. Her mind screaming, *Stop!* The bomb-damaged street spun, and her tongue lolled from swollen lips. As darkness closed round her, he stopped squeezing.

Aware of being dragged, she felt her ankle strap break, and he hurled her shoe over the wall of a derelict house, before pulling her down the narrow back alley. A dark and lonely shortcut that no respectable woman would journey on a night like this...

* * *

Betrayal was not an option. Nobody was allowed to leave him. Drawing his forefinger and thumb along the full length of his razor-thin moustache, his rasping breath came in short bursts, and he spat out the mucous that had gathered in his mouth. Standing on the bank of the canal, the bulging veins in his temple pulsated. She had betrayed him. He wasn't going to stand for that. She had some gall. Moving back to Ireland, she said... That was her first mistake... Leaving him was her second. She was never going back...

The fire-breathing dragon was appeased, and his ice-coloured eyes stared at the water until it stilled. Only then did he turn and walk away.

1

WINTER, JANUARY 1953

Twenty-five-year-old Evie Kilgaren put away the last of the Saturday reports, closed the filing cabinet drawer and sighed. Looking out of the office window across the cobbled yard, she felt as gloomy as the darkening sky, knowing the accounts she had just finished were nowhere near good enough to keep Skinner & Son going for much longer. Focusing on the shapeless black clouds scudding across an ashen sky, she tried to keep such thoughts at bay. But Evie knew that ignoring them would not make her and Danny's troubles go away. Something had to be done. But what?

Turning from the window, Evie put the cover over her type-writer, tidied her desk and made sure all was neat for Monday. Hoping that next week would be better, the scant work she had done this morning didn't merit coming into the office on a Saturday. But her brother, Jack was in Korea doing his National Service, he had been there for the last two years; Lucy, her sister, was working in Madam B's, training to be a hairdresser, and Danny, her fiancé had gone on a long-distance delivery, so there wasn't much point in staying at home on her own.

Locking the office door and securing the huge double gates of the yard, she shivered when the bone-chilling gale whipped up from the choppy River Mersey and snatched at the woollen scarf covering her head. She had to bend forward to catch her breath as the eddying wind clawed at her clothes and whipped swirling papers and empty cigarette packets across the debris and along Reckoner's Row towards the house she had lived in all of her life – except for that time when her mother's lodger threw her out onto the street, and she had to be rescued by Sergeant Danny Harris. The man she was now engaged to marry.

When he left the army, Danny had bought the haulage firm, from his stepfather Henry Skinner, for the grand price of one pound. And since then, Evie and Danny had been working hard to make the haulage business pay, but it was far from easy.

Evie worried about Danny going on the delivery to a firm on the far side of Manchester. He didn't usually go so far from Liverpool, but he was in no position to turn down work of any kind, no matter what day or distance. Since Lenard Haulage opened along Regent Road known the world over as the dock road, a few months ago, business in Skinner's haulage yard had suffered an almost fatal blow. It didn't help matters that Danny had been sent on a number of hoax calls either. The order to go and pick up deliveries from warehouses along the dock road were met with blank-faced foremen scratching their heads, not knowing by whom, or even why, he had been hired, although the dockets looked real enough.

Evie wished she could do something to help build up the business. Danny was doing everything he could to keep his head above water, but with work slowing to a crawl, there was barely enough to go round, and there was a danger that he may have to lay men off who had worked in the yard longer than he had.

'I could put an advert in the paper,' she'd told Danny last night. 'Using my post office box number should bring in new accounts for me to pay bills.' But she hadn't been prepared for the pained look in his eyes, and she knew, when she saw the muscle in his jaw twitch, that he was doing his best to keep a cool head.

'I know you want to do all you can, love, but this is my worry, not yours.' It was the way he had said *love*, which tore at her heart. The word sounded so distant, like something you would say to a stranger. *Thanks, love, do call again.* And Evie feared he might be having second thoughts about their summer wedding. Maybe even having second thoughts about marrying her – full stop. He had always said he wanted to build an empire before he settled down and Evie had told him she would help him. But how could you build an empire on nothing but hopes and dreams – *and* keep a family going? It was impossible, and wasn't helped by the fact that Lenard Haulage had a dozen wagons and drivers, many more than Skinner's did. So why did Lenard want this yard too? They had recently made an offer which Danny had refused. Evie had her suspicions, of course. Skinner & Son was situated in Summer Settle, prime dockland, close to the warehouses and waterfront. It would be the cherry on Lenard's cake.

How could they possibly compete with Lenard's set-up with his motorised wagons? Skinner and Son mostly had horses, which were far slower. They had only one motorised wagon and needed more in order to compete. But to be able to buy wagons, they had to have money. An insurmountable situation, which Evie could see no way out of, and had foregone a proper wage to help sustain the business. She had even taken on *confidential accounts* to supplement her income, like she had done in the far-off days when she was studying to become a certified accountant. Taking on work for a number of businessmen through a post office box address to keep business private on both sides. Men who didn't want their income made available for one reason or another.

So, desperate means called for desperate measures, and with Lenard Haulage taking over a large slice of the road transport cake, she was in no position to be fussy. Especially when, each day, she saw Danny's happy-go-lucky spark diminish a little bit more.

This yard was his life. His stepfather, Henry Skinner, had kept it going through the depression in the nineteen-thirties, then during the war; he'd risked being blown off the dock road in his effort to deliver produce to wherever it was needed.

Danny, a proud man, a good man, who would help anybody in difficulty, could not keep secrets from her. And she wasn't about to let his business go under if she could possibly do something to help it flourish. She had a duty as his fiancée and his bookkeeper to ease his burden. Even suggesting they wait a little longer to marry. Although the thought of it broke her heart, she was ever so thankful when Danny refused to entertain the idea.

He'd told her he would marry her tomorrow if he could. But he knew that preparations were being made for the coming Coronation of the new Queen at the beginning of June, so they decided to marry at the end of June. Her day was going to be the one she deserved, he said, even if he had to work all the hours God sent to earn the money to pay for it. Which was all well and good, she thought, but what if there was no work to be had?

Evie, pragmatic through necessity, was not one for making extravagant gestures and would be happy with a quiet wedding. Just a few close friends, like Connie and Angus who ran the Tram Tavern and their two little ones, and of course Mim, Connie's mother. Then there was the family, Meggie and Henry, Danny's birth mother and stepfather, and Evie's brother Jack and sister Lucy... And what about Ada Harris? And Grace? And Bobby? The family Danny had thought of as his own before Bert Harris blew the whole thing spectacularly out in the open three years ago.

But Danny would not hear of a quiet wedding day. He was determined to make sure she got her big splash. The only question in Evie's mind was how he was going to afford it *and* keep his men in work? The answer was beyond her.

Nothing much had changed round here, the same people lived in the same houses, rarely moving out of the area they knew so well. Some of the young men had gone off to do their National Service, like her twenty-year-old brother Jack, who had been in Korea for the last two years. National Service had been lengthened from eighteen months, because of the Korean war, when troops from North Korea invaded South Korea and the United Nations Security Council had sent armed forces from America and Great Britain to aid South Korea.

The wind howled like a banshee as Evie hurried, head down, along Reckoner's Row, eager to get her front door open. Once inside, she put her backside to the door to close it in the damp, swollen wood, keen to get a good fire going for when Lucy came home from work.

In the back kitchen, Evie emptied her wicker shopping basket of a paper parcel containing scrag-ends of mutton and some cheap chuck beef, which, although it would need a long time cooking in the oven would make a very tasty casserole mixed with the pot-herbs and potatoes she'd managed to buy that morning, and she was looking forward to getting a hearty meal on the go, making a thick crust to go on top.

On a day like this her sister would enjoy a hot meal to come home to and Danny, if he managed to get back from the delivery job out in Netherford, would too when he made his usual after work visit. Evie shivered; those rough, narrow country lanes did not bear thinking about in this weather and she hoped Danny's clapped-out truck that had seen better days years ago was up to coping with this deluge.

* * *

'That's a dark, sinister sky if ever I saw one,' Lucy said to her best friend, fellow apprentice Rachel McAndrew, who was hanging damp towels over anything that would allow them to dry while turning on the hairdryers in the dressing-out cubicles to dry them for the afternoon clients.

'Dark and sinister...' Rachel scoffed light-heartedly. 'Have you swallowed a gothic novel?' Rachel laughed and Lucy pulled back the pink-frilled net curtain draped decadently across the wide window of *Madam Barberry's Coiffure*. A posh-sounding name for the ladies hairdressing salon on busy Stanley Road leading into *town*, as everybody called the centre of Liverpool.

'We're usually mad busy at this time on a Saturday,' said Lucy, who would rather be tending to a client's hair than mopping floors, which is what the senior stylist, Madam Barberry, would instruct her to do if business was slack. 'This horrible weather is obviously putting people off having their hair done today.'

'Would you pay to have your hair done on a day like this, because I know I wouldn't,' Rachel said, and Lucy gave her friend a playful shove.

She and Rachel had both started working at the same time for Madam Barberry, or *Mrs Bouffant* as Rachel called their employer who would not be out of place on the parade ground of the local army barracks. They quickly became friends, even though they were as different as black and white in personality. Lucy and Rachel were the same slender size and shape but there the similarity ended. Lucy daydreamed about owning her own salon one day, while harum-scarum Rachel wanted nothing more than to find a nice boy to marry and get out of her mother's overflowing house of six children and befuddled grandma, who didn't know what day it was half the time.

Rachel and her family were a bit scatty and sometimes raucous, but Lucy loved the hustle and bustle of their house, next door, knowing her own was a bit quiet and sedate with just her and Evie rattling around, especially now that their Jack had been posted to Korea. The McAndrews had only moved in last year and Lucy thought they were a breath of fresh air in the small row of houses opposite the canal.

'D'you think a lemon rinse would brighten this up?' Rachel asked, flicking her high, ponytail.

'I think it would,' Lucy answered, 'but I can see two problems there, three if you count your dad.' Lucy ignored Rachel's raised eyebrow, knowing her friend would not have a bad word said about her boisterous family. 'First, it's nowhere near summer, so we've got no sun to help the lemon juice along. And second, you can't buy a lemon for love nor money!'

'That's true.' Rachel's shoulders slumped, and she twisted her fringe into a small curly sausage.

'Why don't you just comb some peroxide through it?' Lucy asked.

'I combed peroxide through my fringe when I first started here, and when Dad asked what happened, I told him the sun had lightened it.' Rachel pulled a face in the mirror, safe in the knowledge her employer was in the staff room having her lunch while she and Lucy continued to hang up the towels. 'The next morning Dad gave me half a crown and told me to ask Mrs Bouffant to take the sun out of my hair.' Both girls laughed at the thought.

'Half a crown?' said Lucy. 'I'd have done it for free.'

'I spent the half crown and rubbed black boot polish on the front.' Rachel could hardly get the words out for laughing. 'I looked like Al Jolson by the end of the day!'

By the time they had stopped laughing, all thoughts of the driving rain and howling wind had disappeared.

'It's not that me da's old-fashioned,' Rachel said as the laughter ebbed away, 'it's just that he doesn't like me messing with me hair.'

'Highly unlikely when you are in this profession,' Lucy teased, noticing her pal's ash blonde hair had grown dull over the winter.

'I wish I was born with your titian-coloured hair,' Rachel said. 'Redheads are impulsive, irrational, quick-tempered, passionate and revolutionary.'

'That sounds more like you than me,' replied Lucy, pulling a face in the mirror at her mane of glossy auburn curls. 'Maybe you should have been a redhead.'

'Yes,' Rachel sighed, talking through the mirror, 'I could just see myself with a golden mane of tumbling tresses.'

'Now who's swallowed a book?' Lucy laughed. 'Our Evie doesn't mind what I do to my hair, although she's not as particular as me about her looks.'

'Oo, go on, now, don't let her hear you say that.' They both laughed again, but not for long when they heard the click of Madam's heels on the linoleum covered floor next door.

'You sound like my parents,' Rachel moaned, 'you don't know how lucky you are not having a mam and dad laying down the law,' Her tactless words sounded harsher coming from her lips than they did in her head and Rachel's face suddenly suffused with a deep red tinge. 'Oh, Lucy, I am so sorry, I didn't mean that the way it came out!'

'I know you didn't,' said Lucy, who knew her friend's thoughts usually came into her head and went straight out of her mouth like a helter-skelter ride. 'Our Evie's like a mam since our own mam...' Lucy didn't want to think about how her mother had been found dead in the local canal, six years ago, and her da – her good shepherd – had been wrongly locked away in a *hospital,* accused of her demise.

The laughter died, as always when she thought of her father. For, as much as she was sure she would have loved her mam had she known her better, the truth of the matter was, Lucy hardly knew her at all, having been evacuated to Ireland as a baby with her brother, Jack, at the beginning of the war in 1939. She didn't see anything of her mam, Rene, for years. Not until two years after the war ended. Rene had evicted the lodger, Leo Darnel, at Christmas, so she could bring her and Jack back to Liverpool, and, then a few weeks later, her mother went out one night, and she never came home.

But she had seen the man she now knew was her da every day back in Ireland. He tended sheep on the neighbouring farm, hence, that was why she called him her good shepherd, who told her stories of a handsome prince who married a beautiful princess and lived happily ever after, until the ogre declared war and separated the prince from the princess and their little ones. Then, the little prince and princess were sent to the land of milk and honey to be cared for by kindly relatives. And the mighty prince knew he must survive to save them all and be reunited with his beautiful princess.

Lucy would listen to his stories every day and imagine what it must be like to live in a castle by the river.

The thought brought a lump to her throat, and Lucy hurried to the stock cupboard to find methylated spirits to clean dried hair lacquer off the mirrors. It was early afternoon and the sky darkened, growing murkier by the minute. With a flash of lightning, the heavens opened, and Lucy had never seen rain so heavy or intense; you could hardly see the road outside for the rainstorm.

Even for the end of January, the storm was a force to be reckoned with, and the howling gale was making it almost impossible to walk for the few brave souls who had ventured out and got caught up in it all. Watching from the window, Lucy saw stooped pedestrians battling against the elements and she shivered. The busy road, which was normally packed with people, looked desolate for a Saturday afternoon. Obviously busy housewives, who were usually out buying their rations, had more sense than to brave this weather and were staying near their coal fire today.

'Come away from that window and collect the towels ready for the bagwash,' said Madam Barberry as she came into the salon from the staff room next door. 'I doubt we will be busy this afternoon.'

Rachel rolled her eyes. 'Why didn't she say that before we put them all out to dry,' she hissed through perfect, straight white teeth, 'and where's that flaming Saturday girl, this is her job not ours.'

'She went home for her dinner and didn't come back,' answered Lucy.

'I can't say I blame her, neither would I given the chance.' Rachel went into the back room for the laundry basket, and Lucy wondered if they would have to stay here all afternoon on the off chance they might get a client.

'Are you going to enter the Apprentice Finals this year?' asked Lucy when Rachel came back into the salon. 'You've got the flair.'

'I don't know.' Rachel looked despondent. 'You are much better at that kind of thing than me. I'd rather be the model than the stylist.'

'Right then,' said Lucy with determination, as if her mind had finally been made up. 'In that case, I'll ask *Mrs Bouffant* if she will put my name forward and you can be my model.'

'That's the ticket!' Suddenly Rachel cheered up and was much chirpier, but only for a moment. 'I suppose we'll have to lug all the towels to the *baggy*,' she said, dragging the towels off the egg-shaped hairdryer hoods and pushing them into the laundry basket.

'It's not so bad,' Lucy said. 'I would rather put towels into a washing machine than brush and mop the floor.' All she had ever wanted to do was to become a ladies' hairdresser and, one day, run her own salon. But her salon would not be run like an army barracks, like *Mrs Bouffant' s*. 'When I get my own salon, I'll get the laundry collected and the towels will be brought back all clean and neatly folded.' She could see it now. Her salon would be all shiny, with glossy worktops, and open plan like one of those posh ones in town. 'I'll employ a cleaner as well to brush and mop the floors and fill up the shampoo and conditioner containers.'

'I suppose you'll have a waitress to bring Earl Grey tea in delicate porcelain cups, too?'

'Certainly not, I'll have champagne fountains, like Mr Teasy-Weasy.' Lucy closed her eyes and dreamed out loud. 'Raymond – that's Mr Teasy-Weasy to you – has gilt mirrors and crystal chandeliers.' Mr Teasy-Weasy, a famous hairdresser with a salon in Mayfair styled the hair of the biggest celebrities.

'I read that article too, in one of those dog-eared magazines.' Rachel, not to be outdone, added, 'His French accent isn't real, you know.'

'Really?' Lucy giggled. 'Why does he speak like that then?'

'To bring in more clients – sorry, female clientele – but don't let Madam know. She thinks he's the best thing since perm lotion. I'd have to learn the language first, but I would love to learn all about his colouring techniques,' said Rachel, who'd left school with sufficient qualifications to secure her indentures with Madam.

Lucy couldn't help but laugh at her best friend's pragmatic outlook. But what Rachel lacked in ambition she made up for in creative flair, she could match colours with the best of them given the chance.

'One thing I am determined to do is own a salon as good as any of the posh ones in town,' said Lucy. Hairdressing was her vocation, and she gained experience from practising her craft every chance she got. Gleaning ideas from magazines and movie stars. Madam had even given her two regular clients to perfect her creative skills. But Madam was most put out, when one of her own clients, asked for Lucy the following week.

Rachel was still at the stage where she was putting in rollers and handing endpapers and perm curlers to Madam, which would bore Lucy to tears, and she found Madam's style a little staid. She could probably set all her clients' hair in her sleep, whereas Lucy was itching to get her hands on some of the ladies, whose bouffant and French pleats were set in liquid cement, and did not move, from the moment the hair was dressed until the following week when it was brushed out to be shampooed, with dry hair lacquer falling to the floor like snow.

'Do you think, Saint Patrick's church dance will still be on tonight?' Rachel asked, snapping Lucy out of her reverie. They both lived for the weekend dance at the local church hall, where they would almost dance the legs off themselves, to the local band playing the latest songs. Lucy and Rachel had been practising swing dancing in Lucy's front parlour, perfecting the lindy hop, which they were eager to try out tonight.

'I doubt it unless this weather calms down a bit,' said Lucy, who knew an umbrella would not stay up in this wind, 'otherwise we'll get to the dance looking as if we've struggled through a hedge backwards and I dread to think about the hair situation.'

'D'you think she'll let us go early?' Rachel asked, looking over to her boss, who was flicking through a lady's magazine, which had been on the table since the year dot.

Lucy shrugged. 'She'll probably have us up a ladder cleaning the light bulbs,' said Lucy. Then, suddenly, the lights went out, plunging the salon into a dark gloom, and the two girls looked at each other. Then they looked to the ceiling.

'Did you forget to pay the bill, Madam?' Rachel asked, with a mischievous grin, as Lucy collected the rest of the damp towels, wondering how her best friend got away with her cheeky banter.

'Of course, I paid the bill! You impudent girl,' Madam answered. The laundry basket was now full and ready to haul down the road, past the butcher's shop, where the young butcher would stand at the window and wolf-whistle every time she walked past. And even though she loved the compliment, she would toss her head and appear to ignore him. Looking out of the window now, she couldn't see much as the heavy deluge was lashing hard.

'I don't fancy taking this lot to the baggy,' said Lucy, 'we're going to get soaked.'

'I bet she hasn't paid the bill,' Rachel whispered insistently, and Lucy nudged her with her elbow.

'Shush, she heard you!' Lucy said, trying not to laugh. But their mirth was short-lived.

'Don't stand around like pithy on a rock bun,' said Madam, 'go and see if you can find the reason why the electricity is out, see if anybody else has been cut off.'

Lucy grabbed her coat and put it over her head and Rachel did the same, but only moments after their feet touched the pavement, they were soaked right through. Even the awnings outside the adjoining shops were sagging with the weight of water, all shop-keepers along the usually busy road were outside their businesses.

'I've just been talking to the local bobby here ,' said the butcher importantly looking towards the policeman standing nearby. 'He told me all the lights are out this side of the canal. We're on a circuit, see?' he said, as if this was something every-body should know. 'The electric cables have snapped due to this bloody wind and rain, and all the lights have been cut off for the foreseeable.'

'He doesn't look very pleased,' said Lucy, and Rachel nodded.

'Who's gonna pay for my stock? That's what I wanna know.' The butcher pushed his rain-soaked flat cap to the back of his balding head. 'If the lecky' s off and my fridge defrosts, all my meat will go off with it.'

'You could always sell it off cheap, save losing it,' said Lucy in that cheeky but seemingly innocent way she had about her and noticed the glint in the young trainee butcher's eye.

'You mind your own,' said the older butcher, who was one of the most expensive on the block. 'I'm not gonna throw away my profits for the sake of a bit of rain.'

'Even the telephones have been knocked out,' said the beat bobby in his domed helmet and warm cape, 'it's worse than the war.'

'Hardly,' said Lucy, dripping from head to foot.

A short while later, they returned to the salon with the news the power would be off until further notice.

'Well then, there's no use standing around here like one of Lewis's,' said Madam Barberry, surprising and thrilling both girls with the news they were going home early, 'so just take all those towels out of the laundry basket and drape them around the salon – on the chairs, the dryers, anywhere you can, we must have dry towels for Monday – if, by then, the electricity is back on.' Lucy and Rachel wasted no time flinging towels over every surface and brushing the floor of hair.

'Such a shame we didn't get the chance to practise our finger waves and pin curls,' Rachel told Madam, who raised a cynical eyebrow.

'Get going before I change my mind,' said their employer, and both girls did not need telling twice. They were in their wet coats in the blink of an eye.

'Shall we go and see if *Woolies* is still open,' Lucy asked, excited they had finished early, running head down to the large Woolworths shop along the rain-lashed road.

2

'Thank God, you made it home in one piece,' Evie said to her soaked sixteen-year-old sister, who catapulted through the back door on a driving gale, and dripped all over the linoleum floor. 'You look like you've been hit by a tornado.'

'So would you if you went out in that lot, I was blown all the way home,' Lucy gasped.

'I believe half the country has no electricity,' said Evie, hanging up Lucy's coat on the cellar door. She had brought Lucy up since their mother was killed, and their father, Lucy's 'good shepherd', had been incarcerated in an asylum for her murder.

'That's why I'm home early,' Lucy replied. 'The storm knocked out all the lecky in the salon, too, so we couldn't use the dryers.' She untied the knot under her chin and removed the drenched head-scarf, which had done nothing to protect her burnished copper-coloured hair. 'The wind snapped the telegraph wires, so we couldn't take appointments and Mrs Bouffant let us go early.'

'Who'd be daft enough to get their hair done in this weather?' Evie shook her head.

'Some people who have more money than sense,' Lucy said,

wringing rainwater from her plaid, woollen headscarf into the white Belfast sink. 'That's what Mrs Bouffant says, but it doesn't stop her taking their money. Although even she was surprised the shop was so empty after dinner.'

Evie smiled as she poured boiling water into a brown earthen-ware teapot and covered it with a knitted tea cosy. 'You want to be careful calling her Mrs Bouffant; she might hear you and give you the sack.' Evie placed the pot of tea onto the tin tray their mother had borrowed from the Tram Tavern years ago and forgot to take back, while Lucy inhaled the heavenly aroma of a meaty casserole.

'Something smells good, are you baking cakes as well?' Lucy asked, almost breathless as she hung her headscarf on the wooden clothes horse in the corner of the kitchen.

'I'm baking some scones to keep the casserole company in the oven. They should be done by now.' Evie didn't like waste – not even oven space. 'We'll have one with a nice cup of tea while they're still warm.'

'With currants?' Lucy asked expectantly, a look of hope in her eyes.

'You can't get currants at this time of year,' Evie said, knowing the whole country was still experiencing rationing, eight years after the war had ended, 'and for those who *can* afford dried fruit, hoarding makes it scarce.'

'You should have asked Leo Darnel.' Lucy's Celtic lilt, gained from seven years' evacuation in Ireland during the war, held a hint of mischief. 'He'd know where to lay his hands on some.'

'I wouldn't ask that man to throw water on me if I was on fire,' Evie said with a determination Lucy had come to expect, knowing her elder sister, who got along with everybody, despised Leo Darnel with a passion. Evie led the way into the front room. 'If he was the last person on earth, I wouldn't ask him for a push up the kerb.'

Lucy's eyebrows pleated as she followed Evie, who tried her best to dissolve all thoughts of the spiv from her mind. Evie loathed him for the way he made a show of her that Summer in '47, when he burned all the work she had done in night school, the day before her final examination, and then beat her into the gutter while her mother tried to save her. But despite his bullying her mother wasn't persuaded to throw him out.

'Here, come and sit down by the fire, you look perished.' Evie's tone was deliberately bright as she put the tea tray on the table near the window.

Lucy didn't need asking twice and stretched her hands out to the blazing fire while Evie poured the tea. And, turning, Lucy lifted her skirt to warm her legs before sitting down. 'Oh, that's lovely.' She closed her eyes and sighed rapturously when the heat began to seep into her frozen limbs.

'It was good of Madam Barberry to let you go early,' Evie said to her sister.

'Goodness had nothing to do with it,' Lucy scoffed, 'she closed early because the hairdryers don't work without electricity, and all the lights went off. Even the street lights are out, it's like the blackout all over again.' Not that she had seen the blackouts, thought Lucy, she was evacuated to Ireland with her brother, Jack, when they were young.

She sighed, wondering what Jack would be up to now. Drafted into National Service in 1951, he wasn't best pleased that National Service had been extended from eighteen months to two years when the Korean War broke out in 1950. His first posting.

'There's been storm damage from one end of the country to the other,' said Evie breaking into her thoughts, 'the news was on the wireless. I'm glad we've got gas mantles and a gas cooker, at least we've got light, even if it is a bit dimmer than usual and the wireless has a battery.'

'The weather's getting worse by the hour,' Lucy remarked, 'I feel sorry for anybody out in that. I was nearly blown into the canal a few times. Me and Rachel had to hold onto each other in case we fell over. But we did have a laugh.'

'Let's have a scone to tide us over, 'til the casserole is ready. I was first in the queue for the butcher's this morning and managed to get some scrag-ends of mutton, for the casserole. It's been in the oven all afternoon.' Evie handed Lucy a scone slathered in golden butter. Not the sump oil concoction they usually had to eat, pleased to see her sister's eyes widen.

'Where did you come off with the butter?' Lucy asked, enjoying the delicious, if rare, treat.

'Ada Harris brought it up this morning,' Evie answered, acknowledging the look of surprise on her sister's face. Ada, who cleaned the Tram Tavern, was not a regular visitor to the house and never had been, even though she enjoyed the salacious gossip their mother's antics had caused in the past, Ada would prefer not to be caught knocking at their door.

'I suppose she had a visit from Leo Darnel,' Lucy said, 'which would explain where she got the butter from, but why did she share it with us – she never has before?'

'The wedding,' Evie answered crisply, and the two girls nodded in unison. 'I know for a fact, Danny has not invited her yet...' Both girls knew that Ada's husband, Bert, had been blackmailing Henry, who had owned the Cartage business, which he sold to Danny. 'She called on the pretext of having too much butter in her larder, wanting all the details of the wedding. Wanting to know if Meggie had bought her hat yet? And did I know what colour it was. And a June wedding was the best time of the year. And so romantic. And on. And on. And it wouldn't be as big as their Grace's wedding, but it would be lovely all the same. You know how she likes to brag.'

'I do, indeed,' Lucy answered, knowing Ada was as quick as lightning when there was a bit of gossip on the go, and even quicker when she wanted to know what was going on in the area. 'One thing she can't abide is not being in the know. She'll be worried Mim knows more about the wedding than she does.'

'I think she was angling for an invitation, to be honest,' Evie said. Ada had raised Evie's fiancé from a young baby. But the manner in which Danny had discovered the truth about his family had rankled. He was furious he had not been told that Meggie Skinner was his birth mother, who had hit on hard times, and had to give him up to Ada to take care of, so she could work and earn enough to pay for her son's upbringing. Although, in the time she and Danny had been courting, Evie knew he had mellowed towards Ada, realising it was not her fault the way the truth had come out. 'You know what Danny's like, he doesn't hold a grudge – well, not often.' Evie gave a small laugh. 'But he is working so hard trying to keep the business afloat, he probably hasn't given a thought to the wedding guest list.'

'Maybe Ada was trying to get an invite from you?' Lucy said, enjoying her scone.

'I won't step on Danny's toes and invite Ada. The choice must be his. But I think she does deserve to be at the wedding. I'll have a word.'

'He will do what he thinks is right, he usually does.' Lucy, finishing the last of her scone, turned to the window when another downpour of hailstones thundered against the windowpane.

'I certainly wouldn't want to be outside on a night like this,' Evie said, getting up from the table and pulling the curtains across the sash window. Even though it was still only mid-afternoon, the hostile sky made it impossible to see outside, and she wanted to block out the howling wind, rattling the wooden casement. Giving an appreciative sniff, she added, 'A hearty casserole is just the thing when Mother Nature vents her rage.'

'Why did this storm have to wait until Saturday?' Lucy sounded peeved. 'Even the dance in Saint Paddy's church hall will be called off.' She loved her weekly outing to the church hall dance with Rachel.

Evie knew Rachel spent more time here than she did in her own house. And she noticed that now the hot tea had thawed her, Lucy had brightened.

'I'll tell you what, I'll give you a shampoo and set if you like?'

'Shall we leave it until tomorrow,' Evie said, 'then it will have all day to dry.' They, like most in Reckoner's Row – except Ada Harris and the Blackthorns – did not have electricity installed and it would take ages for her hair to dry, and although she wanted to help Lucy by giving her the chance to practise her skills, she didn't fancy going to bed with wet hair on a night like this.

Lucy nodded, she had a natural talent when it came to hairdressing and practised every chance she got.

Evie took a sip of hot tea and her thoughts turned to Danny who was out there in the storm. She prayed that the old wagon didn't give up the ghost in the middle of nowhere. Sure, the battered old wagon would not last much longer, Danny really did have a lot to contend with right now as the horses weren't as young as they used to be either; maybe she wouldn't bother him with thoughts of Ada wanting a wedding invitation.

'I hope Danny is safe and the old wagon doesn't let him down,' she said, voicing her thoughts. 'Even with a lot of luck and hard work,, I doubt the business could afford a second-hand wagon, never mind a new one.'

'Are things really that bad?' Lucy enquired and Evie nodded. 'It doesn't seem fair,' said Lucy, 'Danny working all the hours in the day and Grace Harris married to a millionaire.'

Evie knew what her sister was alluding to. Grace and Danny had been raised as brother and sister although they were no relation. But, even so, Danny would never go cap in hand to Grace's husband, though he liked the chap, nor would he allow anybody else to know the business was in trouble.

* * *

Danny peered out of the cracked windscreen as the wipers fought to keep pace with the lashing rain, but it was impossible and he could see nothing as the wagon rattled and spluttered, struggling to clamber over the dirt road ridges where no proper road had been laid.

As he edged towards the old swing bridge that allowed barges to continue along the river, he could see the water had risen and was bursting its banks, and Danny's hopes of getting home some time tonight seemed dashed when he saw the road ahead was flooded.

He would have to back up and take the long way round, thankful he knew his way round this part of the countryside. The back lanes would make his journey longer, but it was better than the alternative, which was to stay put and sleep in the wagon overnight.

Stretching his aching back, he had been driving all day and the relentless weather made him feel miserable. Not a feeling he was accustomed to, usually. He wanted to get home, devour one of Meggie's stews and crumbles, have a bath, and get ready to go and see Evie where he might get another delicious meal.

His thoughts strayed and immediately his spirits rose, reliving the touch of her velvet skin on his, the feel of her hair running through his fingers, and he was counting down the days when she would be his wife and they could enjoy each other for the rest of their lives. The lingering trace of Evie's floral perfume blended with the leather passenger seat enveloped him, making Danny smile, his spirits lifted – until the engine of the wagon let out an agonised groan and died right outside the high walls of the hospital for the criminally insane.

'Bloody heap of junk!' Danny banged the steering wheel with the palm of his hands, making the cab shake. He could not think of a worse place to break down than here, in the wild, rain-lashed countryside without so much as a flicker of light to guide him. Even the moon had gone into hiding. 'If there's no battery left in my torch, I might as well get my head down here,' he said aloud to nobody.

Reaching into the home-made wooden box, which he kept at the back of the cab and was meant to contain anything useful for a long trip – maps, torches, emergency first-aid kit, spanners, that sort of thing. His fingers rummaged through the junk that was in there and found a five-pack of Woodbines he had forgotten about. Danny took out a crumpled cigarette and put it between his lips and it rose comically at the end. Next, one of Evie's earrings, he smiled. The nylon stocking, which she had sacrificed that time he had been accused of running her over – not deliberately – but never mind, at least it brought them closer than he ever imagined. His dog tags from the army where he had risen to the rank of sergeant and qualified for his heavy-goods licence.

His fingertips shoved bits and pieces to one side. Then he found it, the police torch Angus had given him ages ago. It had come in handy a few times. Danny sighed as he pressed the little black button and shone the torch at the windscreen, giving an almost imperceptible groan when he saw the windscreen wiper had snapped due to the heavy wind and rain. He didn't fancy rummaging around under the bonnet of the truck in this weather, but what choice did he have? It was either that or stay here all night – and staying here was not his preferred option.

Danny pulled down the cold handle and held on tightly in case the wind whipped the door from his grip. The storm hit him in the face and took his breath away.

Jesus wept! The torchlight barely illuminated the flooded fields that surrounded him on one side, and the high granite wall of the asylum on the other. He shone the light up to the top of the wall and caught the glint of barbed wire. The steel spikes reminded him of the day he entered Belson and freed men, women, and children who were little more than skin and bone. The sight would remain with him for the rest of his days, yet there were no words that could adequately describe the horror and revulsion... He shook the thought from his head. He had a job to do.

Lifting the bonnet, he saw the cause of the engine failure immediately.

'Bloody fan belt – again!' Danny went back to the cab to fetch Evie's stocking. 'Nothing lasts forever these days,' he told the nineteen-thirties engine, unsurprised when he got no reply. But what did surprise him – no, shocked him – was the unmistakeable sound of running feet splashing and squelching through the muddy field.

He raised his torch and scanned the area, but he could see nothing. All was silent. 'You're giving yourself the heebie-jeebies. You fool.' Danny gave a shaky half-laugh, knowing the nearby Northbank Mental Institution and surrounding area was now swallowed in total darkness, after the storm had knocked out the electricity. The moon, which would usually cast some sort of illumination, was obscured by black scudding clouds, and Danny's only light was from the torch, which he positioned somewhat shakily, under the bonnet.

He took Evie's stocking out of his pocket.

'Good old Evie, comes to the rescue again.' Ten minutes later, soaked to the skin and frozen to the bone, he cranked the starting handle and was elated to hear the old engine spring into life. Moments later, he was on his way home. Not a minute too soon.

* * *

From the depths of darkness, Frank Kilgaren pulled the tarpaulin sheet over his head and hunkered down for the ride. He had waited a long time for this chance. He had a score to settle. He did not kill his beloved wife. The thought of such a wicked thing and the shock of finding she was dead almost broke him. Leaving him unable to speak.

With Evie's evidence the authorities had put him in the asylum. She said he was responsible. He may have been. But he didn't kill Rene. He couldn't. Not the mother of his children. He went to war to protect his family, and his country, from invasion.

Rene had sent the kids to Ireland, so when he was shipwrecked, sick and disorientated, off the Irish coast, he got work on a nearby farm to where his children were staying. Some might say he was a deserter, but he was no such thing.

For a long time after he was washed up on Irish soil, he had no memory of his family, or where he came from. He worked on the land, and tended sheep, for a small wage, a roof over his head and a hot meal. That was all he needed. Until his memory began to return, and he saw his children, Jack and Lucy, staying with Rene's relatives on the neighbouring farm for the duration of the war.

Frank huddled down under the tarpaulin. All he had wanted to do was to be with his kids, and when the war was over, return to Reckoner's Row and be a happy family again. But it didn't work out like that. Word reached Frank that Rene had installed another man, a 'lodger' who was taking his place, a year after he was pronounced missing, presumed dead. And there was nothing he could do about it. If he went back to Liverpool, the authorities would know he was not dead, and he would be sent straight back to sea. He couldn't face that again.

So, he'd laid low. Worked on the farm. Watched his children

grow up. When the war was over, he intended to stay on at the sheep farm and raise his children in a healthier place than the dockside. .

Or so he thought... He wrote to Rene , telling her that when the war ended, he wanted her to come and live with him, on the farm, in Ireland and she agreed, thrilled he was alive. His intention was to keep the children with him until she arrived. They were his insurance. She promised... But she never came...

He knew now, he was wrong to keep Jack and Lucy in Ireland, hoping she would come back to him. Rene had a stubborn streak three miles wide.

Then, that Christmas in 1946, he brought the children back to Liverpool, to try to persuade Rene to return with him to Ireland. She said she would. But things had changed between them. She was distant. But at least she threw the 'lodger' out when the kids returned. Frank had insisted on that. She said she needed more time. She had been a widow for years and now she wasn't. If only...? If only he had known she was being threatened by the jealous lodger.

Frank closed his mind. The time for 'if only' was over. Having thought about it these past years he was convinced that he knew who was responsible for Rene's murder. And he wanted justice. He must bide his time. Slowly, slowly...

3

Ada Harris woke from a deep sleep and wondered if she had imagined the knocking on the front door. She had been dreaming about the new bedroom suite, delivered only that day. As her eyes became accustomed to the dark, she clicked the bedside lamp, but when it didn't come on she remembered that the electricity had gone off earlier , so she lit the night light which she always kept on the bedside table and strained her ears to listen, but all she could hear was the wind and the lashing rain.

Sitting up, she got the fright of her life when she saw a movement at the bottom of the bed, before realising it was her reflection in the inlaid oval mirror that was the full length of the new wardrobe door.

'Dopey mare!' Ada scolded herself in her Irish lilt promising she was going to put the bed in between the two sash windows overlooking the street tomorrow to save her from frightening the life out of herself. She liked sleeping alone in the big double bed she had purchased second-hand when she and Bert got married all those years ago, and she didn't miss him one little bit. And that wasn't the only thing she was glad of, for sure.

For all that Bert Harris had put her through over the years, he never managed to get his hands on this house and sell it from under her. This house was hers, left to her by a maiden aunt who had owned the one-time lodging house. The biggest house in Reckoner's Row.

Ada listened, but there was no more knocking and as Bobby had not stirred, she realised she must have been dreaming. She squinted her eyes and saw the fluorescent fingers on the clock. Ten fifteen! She had only been in bed half an hour. That Play for Today on the wireless must have set her dreaming.

As her eyes became accustomed to the dim light, she gazed at the matching bedroom suite of walnut wardrobe, dressing table and bedside cabinets. She had never owned anything that matched before, and she couldn't wait to show it off to her best friend, Mim Sharp, one-time landlady of The Tram Tavern, where Ada worked as a cleaner.

She recalled the snooty salesman who got the shock of his life when he asked for the name of her landlord so he could acquire a reference, before allowing her the hire purchase. With a swagger, Ada had informed him that she owned her house and took the deeds out of her handbag to prove it.

He certainly changed his tune after that, she recalled. The snooty accent disappeared, and he spoke in the same way her boys did. He could cut her a deal, he said. Not go through the store, he said. He asked her if she preferred to pay through the new Lenard's Weekly Payments Scheme. A man would call every Friday evening, to collect the money.

Ada had had a short think about it. She was always up for a bit of discount. And she wouldn't have to traipse into town every Saturday morning to make her payments. She'd agreed.

The bugger couldn't sell me enough after that.

She'd preened when she saw the Reckoner's Row curtains

twitch at the arrival of the prestigious Ruby's Emporium delivery van stopping outside her door, immediately feeling absolved from the years of shame her husband had put her through.

Despite the similarity in appearance to her neighbours, who purchased food, clothing, and other domestic necessities in the same shops she did, Ada considered herself a cut above, on account of the rent man never having to knock on her front door.

The salesman told her he had delivered exactly the same bedroom suite to one of those posh houses in Formby only the week before. And Ada, not to be outdone, decided she would have the matching ottoman too. Especially when he assured her, she could pay for all of it on hire purchase, or the *never-never* as it was known locally.

She couldn't sign fast enough, when she discovered the plan was only three and six a week, reckoning that now their Bobby was working in Danny's yard, she could stretch to some new furniture, and had a new gas cooker thrown in for good measure.

Whatever woke Ada unsettled her, especially when she remembered part of her dream, where she opened the brand-new wardrobe door, only to find her estranged husband crouched, naked, inside. *That wasn't a dream, it was a bloody nightmare!*

Ada's thoughts meandered back to earlier that day, before the storm broke, and the furniture was being delivered, knowing she would be the talk of the street.

Nothing unusual in that, she thought, knowing the mothers of Reckoner's Row, liked nothing better than to stand on their step, and have a chinwag, especially when there was a delivery van in the Row.

Well, she thought with a satisfied smile, recalling the lingering looks of her neighbours, at least this time, the gossip was for the right reasons, and would have nothing, whatsoever, to do with her scheming husband. She'd sent him packing three years ago, in an attempt to regain her good name in the community.

Her neighbours might not have much, but they had principles. They put up with a lot of dockside shenanigans, but blackmailing one of their own, as Bert had done to poor Henry Skinner, was not one of them. Next to murder, extortion was what got you on the front page of the Sunday Papers.

Unable to settle since her sleep had been disturbed, Ada wanted a cup of tea, and lying there for a moment, she contemplated ignoring her need and snuggling back down under the warm covers. But she could deny anything, except temptation, and the thought of a nice hot cup of tea would gnaw away at her, until she was powerless to resist.

Braving the winter chill, the rattling of the windowpane and the sound of lashing rain, she pulled back the covers. And she almost jumped off the bed when she heard the hammering on the brass knocker. And it did not sound too friendly.

Swinging her blue-veined legs out of the bed, Ada was sure her sixteen-year-old son, Bobby, went deaf when he slept. Sleeping in the adjoining bedroom, Ada thought the bloody house could fall down round him, and Bobby would be none the wiser.

'Keep your hair on, I heard you!' she yelled, slipping her bunioned feet into tartan ankle-boot slippers. Bending over, Ada grunted, broke wind, pulled up the zips at the front of her slippers, before reaching to the footboard and grabbing her plaid, woollen housecoat, ignoring the pink elastic corset dangling from the end of the bed alongside a matching brassiere, large enough to fit the head of a small child. 'I hate January,' Ada complained to her reflection in the mirror as she went over to the window, pulled back the crisp white net curtain and peered out into the street. It wasn't a pleasant night by any stretch of the imagination, she thought, wiping the condensation from the window with yesterday's drawers, before depositing them into a pillowcase to take downstairs for tomorrow's wash.

Ada could see nobody on the step leading to the front door, and she wasn't going to take a chance on lifting the sash window and allowing this ferocious storm to blow a freezing gale through her bedroom, but from this position, the step looked clear of anything but lashing rain.

Momentarily, Ada wondered if she should wake Bobby, then decided against it. Maybe she *was* imagining things. *Storms can do that to a body.* Now if Danny still lived here, she thought, instead of round at Meggie Skinner's, he would have been down those stairs before the second bang on the knocker.

Ada sighed, she didn't regret throwing Bert out of the house, ending their marriage once and for all, he had never been any good to her, and wasn't the type of man she could depend on. The unbearable situation had been coming for years, although, she stopped short of divorce. She was a good Catholic woman who went to mass regularly, and divorce wasn't allowed by the church.

Ada gave a habitual shrug of her shoulders. She had no intentions of being excommunicated because of Bert Harris. She knew he was a bad lot, only doing as much work as necessary to enable him to gamble on the horses, the dogs, two flies walking up a wall... He would bet on anything. But he wouldn't bet on getting back inside this house.

Looking out onto Reckoner's Row, Ada saw the rain pirouetting on the canal, where Rene Kilgaren had been found murdered in '47, the coldest winter in living memory. The time had gone so quickly, she hardly noticed it had been six years ago.

My life would have been so different if Bert hadn't come back from the war. Ada made the sign of the cross over her ample bosom. As she always did when she had unkind thoughts.

Another rat-a-tat-tat on the front door interrupted her thoughts and she jumped.

'That's a debt-collector's knock if ever I heard one but at this time of night?' Ada's blood began to rise and, turning from the window and taking the light with her, she headed out of the bedroom, along the landing, past Bobby's room and down three stairs before turning right and down another flight of stairs, towards the front door. She opened it just wide enough to check she had not been imagining things, and her heart beat faster when she saw a young man huddled on the doorstep.

'Yish!' Ada hissed, realising she had forgotten to put her false teeth in, giving the adolescent messenger boy cause to retreat down two steps. He was about the same age as her Bobby, she thought, but she didn't recognise him from round here.

'Mrs Harris?' the young man asked, and Ada's head bobbed round the door, making her Dinky curlers rattle as they always did when she was agitated.

'Who wants to know?' She was giving nothing away. 'And what gives you the right to go knocking on people's front doors at this hour of the night?'

'I've a message for you from the landlady of the lodging house in Beamer Street,' the lad said, his black Macintosh dripping wet. 'She says Mr Harris is sick.'

'Oh, that old chestnut,' Ada said, folding her arms. 'I doubt he's half as sick as he makes me.'

'I've got to give you this message, Missus,' he said, holding out a soggy envelope.

Ada took it and the boy asked if there would be a reply.

'Do you mind if I read it first?' she asked, ripping open the envelope and unfolding the single sheet of paper. Her eyes zigzagged the unfamiliar spidery scrawl. Lifting her head, she looked at the boy, and suddenly felt a bit sorry for him. She hadn't meant to be so abrupt. And if anybody had spoken to her Bobby like that when he was doing a good turn, she would not be best pleased and would certainly make her feelings known. Ada's voice softened. 'Tell her I'll call round when I've got some spare time.' She nodded as he tipped the peak of his cap and, turning, he descended the rest of the steps before turning back.

'He's real bad, you know, Missus. Me mam said she doesn't think he'll last the night.'

'I've heard that one before,' she said unsympathetically. 'Tell him I'll call round, if I'm not busy.'

Ada stepped back into the hallway and was forced to put her shoulder to the door to close it against the violent downpour.

So, she thought, Bert was ailing. She didn't believe a word of it, of course. This was another ploy to get her to take him back. Her good-for-nothing husband could make gullible people think he was on his last knockings. He'd had plenty of practice and had been kidding experts for years so he didn't have to go to work, like most decent husbands.

His ailments never kept him out of the alehouse though, did they?

'Why should I go? After what he's put me through,' she said to nobody.

Because he did you the favour of marrying you, the voice in her head replied.

'Aye, and look where that took me.' Her pulse quickened and the muscle in her cheek twitched as it always did when Bert was mentioned. 'And what time's this to be sending messengers round, Bert Harris?' she said aloud. 'Knocking on people's door at this hour of the night. You've got a nerve.'

As she stomped up the hall and into the kitchen the soles of her slippers on the linoleum caused her to bounce like a ball. She slammed the door to the kitchen behind her, making the picture of the Virgin Mary fall off the nail and break the glass.

'Don't you turn against me too,' she said, picking up the holy picture and the slivers of glass. Turning on the battery-driven wireless, she was just in time for the news. And before going into the back kitchen to make a cup of tea, she listened with interest.

'... *Storms lashing the British Isles caused a disaster on the Irish waterfront*,' the announcer's tone was low, respectful, and full of foreboding. '*A ferry, the MV Princess Victoria, sank in a ferocious gale off the coast of County Down*.' Ada's hands flew to her lips... '*Passengers and crew were locked in a terrifying struggle for survival. With a loss of 133 lives, not one woman or child survived the crossing from Scotland...*'

'Jesus, Mary and Joseph!' Ada made the sign of the cross and suddenly her tribulations were nothing compared to those poor souls.

Hurrying out to the back kitchen, she filled the kettle from the cold brass tap and, as she did every time she filled the kettle in this cold kitchen, she felt the urge to go to the lavatory.

She did not light the gas under the kettle but grabbed her coat from the hook behind the kitchen door and put it over her head. Taking the torch from the cabinet drawer, she braved the torrential rain, missing the next news bulleting completely.

'*There is a wide-scale hunt tonight for an inmate who has escaped from Northbank Institution during the storm that knocked out all electricity... People are asked not to approach the man who is said to be extremely dangerous...*'

After she secured the latch on the lavatory door, she turned to the back gate, which was swinging in the gale, banging loudly. She needn't have bothered with the coat, she thought, as the howling wind almost tore it from her hands, and she was soaked to the skin.

With one hand securing the garment that threatened to fly off into the night, Ada gripped the torch with the other hand, picking her way down the yard, careful not to fall on anything that had been blown over. She was sure she had locked the back gate earlier.

It wasn't like her to go to bed without checking everything was locked properly. Anybody could wander in off the docks. She could be murdered in her sleep.

Grow up! You survived everything Hitler's mob threw at you, girl, so what's to fear from a banging gate in a gale!

Putting her shoulder to the gate, securing the bolt to stop it bang, bang, banging against the whitewashed, backyard wall, she turned quickly to head back to the house. She felt a rising sense of unease as she hurried past the domed corrugated roof of the old air-raid shelter, next to the privy. And the scratching noise that came from inside startled her, before she reasoned that the six white hens and ginger-coloured rooster would be just as unsettled by the storm as she was. How could anybody possibly sleep through this?

Slipping the top and bottom bolt on the kitchen door, she sighed, before turning the key in the lock and hanging it on the hook by the cellar door. Although content the house was locked up, on this wild winter's night, a sudden feeling of foreboding washed over her.

* * *

Ada cradled her cup, a while later, staring at the dying embers in the grate, and felt a shiver run down her spine, as a half-remembered dream flitted on the periphery of her mind. Bert was hiding in the wardrobe. Stark naked, he was huddled like somebody terrified. Why would she dream such a thing? Was it a portend? Was he really sick? She felt uneasy now. Maybe she should have gone round to Beamer Street with the lad. She would lie awake worrying, she was confident her dream was some kind of premonition. For sure, hadn't she had the dream before the knock at the door. Surely that was a sign?

Deciding not to dwell too much, she shivered, feeling sympathy for those poor souls who had been lost to the elements. By the time she had finished her hot drink, Ada was convinced she had been forewarned about a tragedy. But what kind of tragedy? There were so many questions swirling round inside her head as she made her way upstairs, all thoughts of Bert and his plight forgotten. Lying awake, she was sure she heard a noise downstairs. But she had no intentions of going back down those stairs again...

* * *

He saw that the house was once more plunged into darkness. Nobody could be expected to survive outside on a night like this. And the air-raid shelter had held little protection for a grown man in need of a drink and a piece of bread. He was as quiet as the grave with the stealth of a hunting cat as he entered the house using a jemmy found in the air raid shelter to prise open a badly secured window. When he had his fill, in the small hours of the night, he groped his way upstairs, entered the empty bedroom at the back of the house, clicked the door shut against the fury of the night and lay down behind it.

4

That afternoon, while they waited for the casserole to finish cooking, Lucy had managed to persuade Evie to let her pin-curl her hair with hairgrips. 'A new hairdo will do you the world of good,' she said.

'I suppose you're right,' Evie said. A little pampering might even take her mind off the worry of Danny having to work all hours, to try to lift the ailing haulage business out of the doldrums, but she doubted it. She looked at the clock on the mantlepiece. It was past ten. Danny said he would call in if he got back early enough. But she doubted he would call in now.

She closed her eyes and imagined the day she would walk down the aisle of Saint Patrick's church to marry her Danny. Enjoying Lucy's soothing fingers working their magic helped her to relax. Even if her hair looked like a bird's nest when her sister finished, Evie didn't care, but she knew it wouldn't, because Lucy could work miracles and could make even the thinnest, stringiest hair look film-star fabulous.

Evie understood that the wedding would be a small affair, just family and a few close friends. Nothing lavish like Danny's sister,

Grace, who wasn't really his sister, as it turned out. Grace had sung on cruise ships after the war, before she met the heir to a shipping magnate and married him.

Evie didn't begrudge Grace her good fortune. She was one of the friendliest, down-to-earth girls she knew. And had never looked down her nose at the Kilgaren family, the way her mother, Ada, had. But none of that mattered to Evie, so long as she was marrying the only man she had ever loved and trusted. Evie believed she was blessed that Danny felt the same way about her, after secretly mooning over him even before he strode confidently up Reckoner's Row in his sergeant's uniform of the King's Hussars.

Their wedding was going to be as special as any, she was sure, and she understood why Danny tried to hide his worries about the business from her, but that was impossible as she was the one who dealt with the accounts, and she was the first to see that the money coming in was not enough to secure the cost of what needed to go out.

The yard meant everything to Danny, and he wanted to make the business a success, not only for himself and Evie, but for Henry and Meggie too. Because they were the two people who had made Skinner & Son the trusted and successful business it had once been.

But since Lenard Haulage opened up along the dock road, with its fleet of brand-new wagons and the men to drive them, Danny's work was on the wane. How could he possibly compete with a business like that?

Even if he did have enough money to buy another wagon and employ a second heavy-goods driver, Evie doubted Danny would secure enough work to compete with the big boys. But what saddened her most of all was knowing Danny's work was good, he was reliable and didn't charge the earth for his services, unlike Lenard's, which could provide a faster service and pay to advertise.

The name and telephone number was plastered over every hoarding, signpost, lamp post and wagon door within a twenty-mile radius. Danny couldn't afford publicity like that. What chance did he have?

Money was so stretched, the business was in danger of snapping. And the downhill slope had been as fast as it was devastating. Evie had no choice but to take on more bookkeeping work to keep the yard ticking over, but she didn't want Danny knowing what she was doing. She didn't like keeping anything from him, knowing they shared everything – their hopes their dreams, their disappointments, everything. Nothing was kept secret – until now. But Evie knew she could not tell him about the extra work. The news might diminish that sparkle in his eyes, and she may never see it again. He would be mortified if he knew she had not taken a proper wage from the business for the last six months. Although, she did ensure that everybody else, including Danny, was paid the going rate. But how much longer could she manage to keep the business going?

'Penny for them?' Lucy asked and Evie pushed her worries to the back of her mind. Lucy didn't want to hear her woes. She was sixteen, had her whole life ahead of her, went dancing and mooned over Eddie Fisher. She longed to have electricity installed in the house so she could save up for a Dansette record player.

Fat chance of that, thought Evie. She couldn't imagine having enough money to live in a house that had electricity. They would make do with what they had and be grateful. At least they had a roof over their heads and did not have to share a house with other families, or cook on a shared stove on someone else's landing, as was the case for many young married couples, after the war had destroyed so many dockside houses.

'I was just thinking how lucky Danny and I will be to live here after we are wed.' Evie was glad her elasticated conscience could still stretch to an off-white fib.

'Well, let's hope you have a better time of it than Mam and Dad did,' Lucy said without hesitation, and Evie wondered if it was bad luck to start her married life in a house with so much tragic history and voiced her concern to Lucy. 'Give over, luck has got nothing to do with it,' Lucy said. 'This house survived the war, so it can't be that bad.'

Lucy was right, thought Evie. She was being daft. And blamed her jitters on the strain of working so hard in the haulage yard office and arranging her forthcoming wedding.

'I wish I had your confidence,' Evie said, knowing her younger sister was sometimes more mature than her years – and then sometimes, she was a downright giddy kipper.

'Of course, you have, look what you did when you put your mind to it, you stopped being a skivvy and used your brains.'

'Da always said I should use them more.' Evie gave a half-hearted laugh.

As Lucy swiftly removed the hairgrips securing Evie's strawberry-blonde pin curls and dropped them into an old tobacco tin that had once belonged to their Da she remembered the letter she received from him yesterday.

Don't think about that now. Lucy's mind swiftly changed focus back to her sister, trying to ignore the niggling questions she longed to ask Evie. She remembered the days when she thought he was the most kind and gentle man in the whole world, her good shepherd, and then to see him on the day Connie got married to Angus. The day they took him away for murdering the mother she barely knew. He wasn't the same man she knew. He was distant. His eyes wild, and when he looked at her, it was as if he had never set eyes on her before.

'Did you lock the back gate when you came in, Lucy?' Evie didn't like the back gate being unlocked when they were both in for the night. 'That wind will have it off its hinges if the bolt's off, and I don't want any old tramps wandering in off the dockside to sleep in our privy.'

'I put the bolt on,' Lucy assured Evie, using her fingertips to loosen the wound Catherine wheels of hair into cascading waves and curls, as she had seen Madam Bouffant do.

Lucy loved the lively conversations, the tittle-tattle, the latest goings-on in the area in Madam Barberry's salon. Listening to local women who spoke to her like an adult, instead of a schoolgirl, was a joy and made her feel very grown-up. The clients gave her tips for washing their hair, too. Or for making them a cup of tea. And she was thrilled when Madam offered her an apprenticeship when she left school, saying she showed promise.

'Shall I do your hair for the wedding, Evie?' Lucy's voice sounded hopeful, and Evie knew her sister was a quick learner, who had come on well under Madam Barberry's instruction. She also knew her sister was a gifted stylist. One day she would run her own salon, of that Evie was sure. There were plenty of local women offering to model the styles Lucy created, confident they would not look like the bride of Frankenstein when she had finished.

'I wouldn't want anybody else to do it,' Evie answered, making her younger sister puff up with pride.

'You'll look like Grace Kelly,' Lucy beamed, 'and I'll look like Marilyn Monroe.'

'You will not!' Evie said, whipping around, before having her head twisted insistently back into place by Lucy's determined hands, and her younger sister's smile convinced her she had been joking.

'Maybe Jane Russell,' said Lucy. 'I've got the same colour hair.'

'I was thinking more like Debbie Reynolds.' Evie had been to the pictures with Danny to see *Singing in The Rain* and had not stopped talking about it since.

'Wouldn't it be lovely,' Lucy said dreamily, 'to have a boy like

Donald O'Connor.' She sighed, knowing how lucky she was to be able to discuss boys with their Evie. Her big sister was *with it,* unlike most girls, whose mothers were very strict, being so close to the docks. Although she could be a bit rigorous, about the time her younger sister came in at night. Lucy was allowed to stay out until nine-thirty, when she went to the local church dance, and no later. She never disobeyed, knowing Evie was only being strict for her own good.

Evie smiled, knowing Lucy's romantic notions were honed from crooned love songs and watching American films at the local picture house.

'I managed to get half a pound of broken biscuits from Woolworths,' Lucy said as Evie glanced in the mirror over the fireplace and gasped, her pleasure obvious, at the transformation to her strawberry-blonde locks, cascading to her shoulders in a halo of curls.

'You've got magic in your fingers, Lucy!' Evie said and gave her sister a hug.

'Give over.' Lucy's face turned a deep pink. 'It's what I'm being trained for.'

'We'll have these for Sunday tea.' Evie cheered up immediately, accepting the bag of broken biscuits Lucy took from her basket put it in the cupboard in the alcove beside the fire, which their mother always called *the Cooeee.* 'Every cloud has a silver lining.'

'It also holds a lot of rain. And sounds like it's getting worse.' Lucy noticed Evie's expression change, her eyebrows furrowing, and her lips gathering in a little screwed-up knot. 'What's the matter?' Lucy asked; she could always tell when their Evie was worried.

'Take no notice of me, I was just wondering if Danny would get back all right, tonight?' she told Lucy.

'He was a sergeant in the King's Hussars during the war *and* a middleweight boxing champion. His muscles are bigger than the rocks on Crosby shore.' Lucy laughed at her sister's unnecessary worry. 'So I don't think a storm is going to bother him. He'll get back home in one piece.'

'I know.' Evie managed an embarrassed smile, she couldn't help worrying about the people she loved. It was as natural as breathing, fostered by years of taking on motherly duties from an early age.

'You don't *have* to carry the full weight of the world's troubles on your shoulders, our Evie.' Lucy's Celtic twang was accentuated, giving Evie cause to smile. She was glad Lucy did not take life too seriously. There would be plenty of time for being serious, later.

Evie brightened, knowing Lucy was a good girl, always ready to have a laugh – something Evie was sorely in need of right now. She didn't like being down in the doldrums and tried to find the positive whenever she could.

'I'm looking forward to a biscuit for my tea on Sunday,' Evie said. Sugar was still on ration, and you had to queue for ages for luxuries like biscuits, which were not easy to come by if you didn't bake.

'There's a few whole ones in there, too, we'll have those first,' Lucy said. '*Woolies* was empty when I finished work because of the bad weather, so I couldn't pass up the chance.'

'That was a bit of good luck,' Evie said. She believed in luck – good and bad – but didn't like to tempt the latter.

5

Danny Harris stepped inside the quiet bar of the Tram Tavern, where the lights were still on the power cut not having affected the building, and saw Angus reading a newspaper. He took off his soaking-wet cap, held it firmly by the peak and shook the rain from it before hanging it onto the hook of the coat stand, along with his heavy donkey jacket, before making his way to the dark-oak bar that stretched the length of the tavern.

'I didn't expect to see you in this weather,' said Angus McCrae, a retired police investigator who became landlord of the tavern when he married his lovely wife Connie six years ago.

'I've just got back from a delivery out Netherford way, and it's getting a bit late to knock at Evie's,' Danny said, glad of the heat the coal fire threw out.

'I don't suppose this weather's much better out in the countryside?' Angus said, folding his newspaper and putting it under the bar.

'I could see this storm rolling in for miles,' Danny answered. Then his words were cut short. And a knot tightened in his stomach, when he clocked Bert Harris sitting in the corner of the bar, hiding behind a broadsheet newspaper.

'The usual?' Angus asked and Danny nodded, resuming his conversation.

'I put my foot down to get home before it got this bad, but the fan belt snapped.'

'It's a good thing we're made of tough stuff round here,' Angus replied, 'a bit of rain does nay hurt anybody.'

Danny looked through the mirrored-glass partition behind the bar as the bar door opened. And he saw Leo Darnel and his latest yard dog, Harry Caraway, entering the bar.

Darnel gave a cursory nod to Angus. And, being his most despised adversary, Danny ignored him completely and knew the spiv had the good sense to keep out of his way – especially after what he did to his Evie. There might be seven years between that far-off summer and now, but Danny had a long memory. He didn't forget or forgive easily.

Darnel was talking in hushed tones to Caraway, who had muscles like boulders, built up when he worked on the docks, handling cargo, big and small, and physically loading or unloading ships. Caraway looked like he was coming up in the world, Danny noted, if the snappy Crombie overcoat and pinstriped suit was anything to go by.

Glancing through the mirror once more, Bert, sitting alone, his eyes taking it all in, looked a bit sorry for himself. Danny recognised the practised expression of dejected injustice that transfixed the weather-beaten face. Danny had even less time for Bert than he did for Darnel. He knew, if the old bugger so much as tried to engage him in conversation, let alone tap him for a few bob, he would have no compunction about putting him on his arse. *So-called father or no so-called father.*

'Another?' Angus asked when Danny quickly downed his pint.

Wiping his mouth with the back of his hand, he smiled. He liked a couple of pints after a long haul, then he would go home to his beloved mam, Meggie, and stepfather, Henry, whom he had thought of as his aunt and uncle, before Bert Harris announced differently to the whole of Reckoner's Row on a charabanc outing three years back. The best day of Danny's life when he discovered that not one drop of Bert Harris's blood ran through his veins. Nor Ada's – the woman who had reared him until he was sixteen years old and so he retreated into the army to do his bit for King and country.

'Have you heard the latest news?' Angus asked, as he slowly raised the pump and placed the pint of bitter onto a new beer mat.

'What news?' Danny asked, deciding to let the last pint settle before he tackled this one.

'The news that was on the wireless just before you came in.' Angus looked sombre and he lowered his voice, 'There's been a breakout at the Northbank Mental Institution.'

'Really?' Danny picked up his pint, but before it reached his lips he asked, 'When did that happen?'

'Late this afternoon, 'Angus answered. Then, as if it had just dawned on him, he said, 'Isn't that where you've just come from?'

'Aye,' said Danny, 'that's where my fan belt broke, right outside the place. There was a power cut because of the storm. It was pitch black, couldn't see my hand in front of my face, it's a good thing you gave me that torch or I would have been stranded in the dark.'

He liked Angus and had done from the moment he came to Reckoner's Row. It was not known among the locals that Angus was once working undercover, investigating theft from dockside warehouses, which were being turned over at a rate of knots.

'It was no picnic being stuck in the back of beyond,' Danny told the landlord. 'The river burst its banks, but I know the back roads like the back of my hand.'

'You didn't see or hear anything untoward?' Angus, always the detective, could not help but ask and Danny shook his head.

'Not many people know that lonely track down by the North-bank,' Danny said, 'but I'd never have got home tonight if I hadn't taken it.' He was trying not to make eye contact with Bert. 'And the night is black as the hobs of hell out in the countryside at the best of times, but usually the asylum is lit up like Church Street at Christmas. Only darkness doesn't bother me.'

'Once a soldier...' Angus chuckled as he placed a polished glass on the shelf over the bar and took down another one.

'Then I remembered Evie's stocking...' Danny stopped abruptly, realising how unseemly the explanation sounded, when he saw Angus's eyebrows shoot to his hairline. 'No! It's nothing like that!' Danny raced to save his fiancée's good name. 'Evie wasn't even with me!' He could feel the heat rise up his neck to his face. 'She wouldn't... couldn't...'

'Give over,' Angus laughed. 'I know Evie's a good girl. I still remember that day you ran her over.'

'*Nearly* ran her over,' Danny said firmly, then he sighed and looked a bit sheepish. 'The stocking has been in my toolbox from that day. I meant to give it her back, but it might have made her feel a bit awkward, so I left it in the toolbox, and forgot all about it. Good job I did.'

'I'm sure you did,' Angus grinned, and Danny shook his head, before taking a huge gulp of his beer. He wasn't one for getting embarrassed, he had been in the army, and worked around men most of his life. But he felt uneasy on Evie's behalf. If she knew he was having this conversation in a public house, she would be morti-fied and would probably throttle him into the bargain.

'I've never known a storm as bad as this,' Angus said, quickly changing the subject, knowing Danny worshipped the ground Evie Kilgaren walked on. 'I'm expecting our lights will go out, too. They've flickered a few times.'

'I can't think of anything else that will shift that old reprobate,' Danny said, glancing through the mirror at the pathetic excuse of human organs that Bert Harris had become. And although Danny would usually keep his harsh opinion to himself, he knew Bert thoroughly deserved the vitriol heaped upon him by the local community when they unceremoniously marched him from Reckoner's Row three years ago. 'What's he after?' Danny asked Angus, recalling Bert, who had been hailed a hero, trying to defend a knocked-off warehouse at point-blank range of a Webley revolver, had blotted his copybook with devious blackmail threats, which took Henry Skinner to the point of ruin, and, so some said, was the reason for Old Man Skinner's weak heart.

Bert Harris was motivated only by money, thought Danny, although he did not have the grey matter to be of much use, or as clever as he thought he was. To the outside, Bert favoured the ease of inertia, with a tendency to do as little as possible for the best possible gain. The man was lazy, had no conscience and put poor Ada through hell before she threw him out. Bert Harris thought the world owed him something just because they breathed the same air. He was resentful of the world and everybody in it. And was especially envious of anybody who appeared to be satisfied with their lot in life.

Eyeing the skin and bone through the mirror, Danny recalled the days when Bert Harris sent shivers of fear through the whole household with his low moods and tyrannical rage – the reason Danny joined the army as soon as he possibly could. He couldn't bear the man, who settled himself into his own little kingdom of oppression. A position that satisfied his need to control the family, Ada being the one most troubled by his domineering. She had put up with an awful lot before she found the courage to finally put the old bastard out of her house. *Her* house. The only one in Reckoner's Row that was privately owned.. The house Bert Harris had never spent a penny on and had never paid towards its upkeep.

Yet, anyone who met him in the pub would think he was a good man, a mild-mannered, good-humoured man, except Danny, who from a young age could see him for what he was, witnessing Bert falling into sulky, rageful moods when Ada had no beer or tobacco money for him. But he crossed the line when he resorted to black-mailing, Danny's stepfather, Henry Skinner.

* * *

Bert Harris sank lower into his seat, his back hard up against the leather. His life hadn't always been like this, he thought. He used to be somebody. People looked up to him, especially when he was a caretaker on the docks, affording him the chance to purloin a bit of this, acquire a bit of that – on the quiet of course. The job offered him plenty of unsupervised control, until Darnel and his yard dogs put paid to his little side-line.

But Bert knew he was in possession of something that made sure Darnel paid the price for what he had done in the past. The past that only Bert knew about. But the scraps of money Darnel threw down to Bert were not enough, and he had risked being turned away from the tavern to come and tell Darnel that.

Bert felt the heat rise inside him, and he tried to draw in a lungful of air. But it was impossible and brought on another of his coughing fits. When it subsided, he gasped and wiped his nose and mouth with a grubby handkerchief. Darnel was still living the high life, while he was left with only dregs. Not enough, he thought. Not nearly enough. And when he regained a bit of strength into his legs he was going to go over there and tell the bloody spiv exactly what he thought of him.

* * *

Danny shook his head. The people of Reckoner's Row did not forget when one of their own turned rogue, like Bert had done.

'He's looking a bit worse for wear,' Angus said in a low voice, nodding to the shrivelled figure huddled in the corner.

'He gave Ada a terrible time,' Danny said in an equally low tone. 'But she was a good wife and mother, there's no doubt about that. And I bet he's sorry now.' Danny was glad the old rogue had nothing to do with him any more.

But taking a closer look, through the mirror once more, Danny could see Bert had not been looking after himself at all well. The weight had dropped from his bones. He was now a shrivelled husk of his former self, and Danny flinched when another lacerating cough ripped from Bert's lips, leaving him gasping.

'Send over a rum to warm the old bugger up,' Danny said, taking a two-bob piece from his pocket and placing it on the bar. 'But don't tell him it's from me. I don't want him thinking he can tap me for a few bob.' Nor did he want his gratitude. The fact that he was no longer bothering Ada was thanks enough for Danny.

The ringing telephone caught Angus's attention as he came back to the bar after giving Bert Harris the rum, which he downed in one gulp before shuffling out of the tavern without so much as a word and looking like death warmed up.

Angus said nothing, leaving Danny drinking his beer to go and answer the telephone in the hallway which led to his private quarters above. When he returned to the bar a few minutes later, his face held a grave yet somewhat thoughtful expression.

'Is everything all right, Angus?' Danny asked, finishing the last of his beer and putting the empty glass back on the bar.

Angus nodded to the glass and Danny nodded back in silent affirmation of a refill.

'That was my old D.I.,' Angus said, slipping a clean glass under the pump and pulling another pint. He lowered his voice, even though the bar was empty except for Darnel and his minder. 'You definitely didn't see anything... untoward on your travels earlier?'

'Like what?' Danny asked. From long years of living with Bert Harris, he had learned never to give a straight answer until he knew the reason for the question.

'Like a hitchhiker, or a lone rambler on a country lane?' He watched Darnel and Caraway leave the bar. Now there was just the two of them.

'Rambling in this weather!' Danny scoffed. 'They'd have to be out of their tiny minds to...' He suddenly stopped talking, remembering the sound of squelching footsteps when he was fixing the fan belt on the truck. 'But now you come to mention it, I did hear something,' Danny said, 'but it was too dark to see anything. The whole area was in complete darkness. Not even a bit of moonlight. If I'd have dropped my torch, I would have had to get down on my hands and knees to find it. Perfect conditions for a breakout.'

'Not just any breakout.' Angus lowered his voice to a whisper and checked there was nobody behind him, 'Frank Kilgaren's done a runner.'

'No!' Danny knew instantly what this meant for Evie. Her father would not be pleased her evidence sent him away under lock and key for life. And he imagined Frank Kilgaren would want his revenge. Danny must do all he could to keep Evie and Lucy safe.

'Will you go and see Evie tonight after all then?' Angus asked, washing the glass that Danny had just emptied.

'Aye,' Danny answered, 'but I won't mention the breakout, I

don't want her lying awake worrying. Thanks for the tip-off, I'll keep my eyes peeled. G'night Angus.'

'Good night, Dan, take it easy.' Angus nodded to Danny's salute and when he left, Angus locked the tavern door behind him, even though it was far off closing time, he doubted anybody in their right mind would brave this ferocious weather for the sake of a pint.

'*I'm singing in the rain,*' Evie sang along with the music on the wireless. And Lucy looked glum.

'You know that wind's so strong, it nearly dragged the skin off my ears on the way home earlier.'

'Go 'way!' Evie laughed, knowing her sister was prone to bouts of exaggeration, but she wasn't overstating the ferocity of this stormy weather, which was causing havoc and keeping everybody indoors. Evie went to get the delicious casserole out of the oven, wishing Lucy wouldn't listen to the news.

'They said on the wireless that the English Channel swelled, and the East Coast is flooded.'

'Oh no, I hope Danny is home soon.' The terrifying storm was sweeping the country, causing catastrophic damage, and even loss of life in England and Scotland.

'They said the force of the storm has washed animals out to sea,' Lucy's eyes were wide with shock, 'and even a ferry has capsized.'

'No!' Evie gasped, she could see that although there was no sign of a howling hurricane here, she had packed all the doors with newspaper to keep out the draught, but even then, the paper had been blown round the kitchen by the strong wind. 'How could anybody survive that?'

Evie was still listening to the news when she ladled the hardy stew from the casserole dish, which she had placed in the middle of the table beside a plate of crusty bread, into two bowls.

'I don't know why anyone'd even consider going out on a night like this,' Evie said, tucking into the casserole that had been slowly cooking in the oven all afternoon, and keeping the kitchen warm. 'I've saved some for Danny. He'll call in if it's not too late.'

'I wonder how our Jack's getting on?' Evie asked, her thoughts turning to her brother. There had been no weekly letter this morning, and Evie missed Jack's lively news. She and Lucy had not seen their brother for almost two years.

'I hope he's all right out there,' Lucy said. 'I wonder what their weather is like?'

'They have monsoons,' Evie said matter-of-factly, 'and paddy fields, where they grow the rice we're having after our dinner, our Jack said the women give birth in the paddy fields and then go straight back to work.'

'Really?' Lucy's eyes were wide.'

'Try not to let it worry you,' Evie said, knowing Lucy had a vivid imagination. 'Play for Today is on the wireless, later.'

'Oh good. It's a thriller.' Lucy's expression brightened immediately, 'I love a good thriller, me. The scarier, the better. Then when I go to bed, I pull the bedclothes right up over my head, and I'm in the land of nod in no time.'

'I'd rather listen to a comedy,' Evie said, knowing her sister had a very vivid imagination, 'or a romance.'

'I love a romance too.' Lucy sighed. 'I wonder what it's like to be kissed by a boy? I had thought of asking Bobby Harris to kiss me, just to see what it was like.' Lucy laughed when she saw Evie's raised eyebrows. 'I decided not to, because of him being one of my best friends, not to mention he's, like, Danny's brother. He might get the wrong idea and think I'd taken a fancy to him. Which I haven't!'

Evie smiled, she loved Lucy's unembarrassed honesty, glad she could talk freely. Something she had never been allowed to do when her mam was alive in case it upset the spiv. Evie never thought of Leo Darnel by his own name, always by the name he had acquired through years of underhand dealing during the war, and much more afterwards.

'You'll have to be patient and wait until you find a nice boy to kiss,' Evie said, not wanting to think about the spiv. If she saw him in the street, she would cross over to the other side, so she didn't have to talk to him. They finished their meal and took the dishes out to the back kitchen.

'I bet you can't wait for the wedding,' Lucy sighed as she dried the bowls Evie had washed, and Evie felt her whole body relax. The thought of walking down the aisle of Saint Patrick's church to become Danny's wife was her most favourite daydream. Not that she was susceptible to such things usually, but she could hardly believe how lucky she was to have such a man. Lucy was right, she couldn't wait to marry Danny, and even though they couldn't afford a honeymoon, it didn't matter.

'Do you think he will change his mind, and invite Ada to the wedding?' Lucy ventured.

'Well, she did bring him up, and we all know she'll be devastated if he doesn't ask her.'

A knock at the front door cut their conversation short.

'I'll get it, shall I?' Evie said, and Lucy smiled, wondering if she should make herself scarce when she heard Danny's voice. But there was nowhere to go on a filthy night like this, so she would have to play gooseberry instead... Not that Danny would mind, he was a peach was Danny, just like his younger brother. Not that she would say such a thing out loud.

* * *

'What are you doing?' Evie asked when she caught Danny staring at her with an expression of deep concentration in his eyes. He had just polished off a bowl of her tasty casserole and the three of them were waiting for the play to start on the wireless.

'I'm looking at you,' Danny said, and the smile that reached his eyes made them twinkle mischievously. 'I like your hair. It's gorgeous, just like you.'

'Really? Why thank you, kind sir.' Evie felt a giggle rise to her throat, and she patted her cascading waves, knowing Danny was the only person who could make her feel giddy. He made her feel safe and protected, since Jack went into the army two years ago.

'I can do that, now we're nearly married,' Danny said, making her smile, and she could feel the heat rise to her cheeks as it always did when he looked at her that special way, 'I don't have to steal a glance any more – I can spend ages just looking at you, imagining our life together.'

'I hope those thoughts are decent,' Evie laughed, knowing their Lucy might look as if she was engrossed in the newspaper, but she missed nothing.

Danny shrugged, looking irresistibly handsome. 'They might not be decent enough to repeat to the priest,' he said in a hushed tone, leaning forward so only Evie could hear, 'but they are clean. Well... maybe a bit off-white.'

'Oh, you are a mucky pup,' Evie whispered and, laughing, she lightly tapped his nose with the tip of her finger. And when Lucy cleared her throat, breaking the intimate moment, they both got up from the table. Danny gave a low chuckle and caught Evie neatly around her shapely waist and pulled her to him, feeling the soft-ness of her lips on his.

'Don't mind me,' Lucy said, folding the paper and taking Danny's dish out of the room. 'I'll make the tea, shall I?'

'No milk in mine,' Danny said, giving Evie a quick kiss on her cheek, and laughed when he saw that lovable deep pink rise to the roots of her strawberry-blonde hair.

'You daft ha'porth,' Evie laughed, giving him a light-hearted push.

'Did we get any letters from our Jack?' Lucy asked, coming back into the kitchen and nodding to the sideboard where the pale blue envelope usually rested against the photograph of her brother in his uniform.

'No, but you have a letter, I forgot to tell you, it's on the side-board, must be off one of your pen-pals, I seem to recognise the handwriting.'

'Jack will be far too busy keeping law and order to worry about writing letters,' said Danny, in mock seriousness; he knew where the dangers lay, out in Korea, and not just from the fighting forces. 'They get monsoons that can tear up trees.'

Lucy picked up the letter from the sideboard and quickly pushed it into her pocket, her cheeks glowing red.

'That's a guilty tinge if ever I saw one,' Danny joked, and Lucy's face grew redder. 'Do we have a secret admirer, Miss Kilgaren?' He was teasing and Lucy knew it, but she was glad Evie wasn't one of those people who opened every letter that came into the house, like Rachel's mam did.

'You're as mad as a mad thing, you Danny,' she said, giggling to try to disguise the quiver in her voice. Danny was a joker and always teased her about something or other. He was as bad as their Jack. But she was glad of the interruption, which stopped Evie asking who the letter was from. She couldn't tell Evie. She would go mad, and Lucy decided to quickly change the subject. 'It's been so long since we've seen our Jack. His National Service must be over soon?' Lucy missed Jack as much as Evie. He had not been home since he joined Commonwealth soldiers who answered the call of the United Nations.

'I hope so,' said Evie, 'and if he's not home for the Coronation of our new Queen, I pray he's home for the wedding, because he is going to walk me down the aisle.'

'Oh.' Lucy closed her eyes and sighed, clutching her hands to her heart. 'Wouldn't that be wonderful... I would be the proudest person there.'

'We all would, Lucy,' Danny said with a fond smile, but he knew that circumstances were way beyond Jack's control. 'In his last letter, he said the weather could dip as low as minus forty-eight – blimey, that's colder than 1947!'

Evie nodded and looked into Danny's loving eyes. 'I remember the day you took off your gloves in the middle of a snowstorm and put them on my hands, because mine were so swollen with the cold.'

Danny's lips parted and his concentrated expression softened. Reaching out, he gently brushed her cheek. 'Fancy you remembering that?' Danny's blue eyes held a hint of surprise that she had not forgotten.

'As if I could forget,' Evie managed a short laugh. 'That was the day Susie Blackthorn looked down her nose because I *was just* the office cleaner at Beamer Electricals. Her whole attitude silently screamed, *how dare she speak to someone as handsome and as magnificent as Danny Harris...*'

They all laughed when Danny put his hands to the side of his head and expanded them to arm's-length. 'Don't remind me,' he said. He had no interest in Susie whatsoever, but she didn't seem to understand that. 'That was also the year the canal froze over for weeks on end and when the thaw came...'

'Your tea is getting cold,' Evie said, her tone subdued, knowing when the canal had eventually thawed, it had revealed the body of her mother who had not run away with her former lover – the spiv – as everybody thought. She had been murdered. Pushed into the water on the night the canal froze over...

7

FEBRUARY

Opening the front-room curtains, Ada could barely believe the storm that had come roaring in like a lion a week ago and had tiptoed out like a new-born kitten, leaving behind a cold, bright, somewhat soggy February. And the raging canal she feared would burst its banks was now as still as a millpond, with not even a hint of a breeze to ripple the water.

The landlady of Bert's lodgings had sent another note to say he was much worse, and Ada decided she should go and see him, even if it was only to see if the old fraudster was pulling a fast one and trying to get a bit of sympathy so she would let him back into the house. But that was not going to happen. Ada had closed that door and was not going to allow him over her threshold again.

She shivered, drawing her woollen housecoat more closely round her plump figure and headed to the back kitchen to cut the bread before putting a light under the frying pan and scraping into it leftover beef dripping from a cracked cup on the shelf above her new gas cooker. Nothing was wasted and fats were still on ration, so everything was poured into the cracked cup and when it cooled it was used again.

Ada placed a piece of thick sliced bread in the pan alongside a couple of rashers of bacon, before filling the kettle from the single brass tap above the sink, her mouth watering when she saw the bread was now turning a lovely golden brown. Even though she could now toast two slices of bread under the low grill, she liked a slice of fried bread with her weekly cooked breakfast.

Removing the golden crisp bread, she cracked two new-laid eggs from her own back-yard chickens, into the pan. The eggs sizzled in the molten beef dripping, next to the back bacon, tomato, and button mushrooms. Even though most of the ingredients were still on ration, Ada could obtain supplies if she had enough money to do so. Black-market goods didn't come cheap, but her Bobby got paid on Friday, so she liked to be first in the queue for her rations on Saturday morning.

Half-listening to the news on the wireless, she heard the announcer giving the latest broadcast about last week's storm tragedy as she ate her fill.

Those poor souls, she thought, rising from the table, and making the sign of the cross, before starting Bobby's breakfast, which was identical to her own, except for toasted bread instead of fried. The kettle whistled on the hob, and Ada wiped her new stove, marvelling at the speed of cooking before piling Bobby's plate with breakfast.

'Bob-beeeee. Break-faaaast!' Ada's voice had enough energy to power a steam engine and taking the sweeping brush from the corner of the kitchen, she banged loudly on the ceiling with enough force to dislodge a piece of ceiling plaster. 'You won't be asleep now, you bugger,' she said, putting the brush back in the corner, and for good measure, she yelled again. 'You will rot in that bed one of these fine days!'

She didn't care that Bobby was up before the crack of dawn every day, working in Danny's haulage yard, mucking out the horses and putting fresh straw down before he fed them their breakfast. If her son decided, he was too old to go to mass with his mother on Sunday morning, the least he could do was eat the delicious breakfast she cooked him.

Satisfied, her voice had carried through the ceiling to Bobby's bedroom, she heard the floorboards creak and movement from above. When he came downstairs, he went straight out to the privy at the bottom of the yard and Ada could have sworn she heard a noise upstairs. That wind must have loosened a roof tile, she thought.

'What were you doing mooching around in the middle of the night?' Bobby asked after he had washed his hands under the tap and sat at the kitchen table.

'The young lad came round again from Beamer Street,' Ada explained, 'and said Bert was still sick.'

'Pity about him,' Bobby answered, unconvincingly. 'Although it must have been serious to come round in the early hours of the morning.'

'It was just after ten, you daft ha'porth,' said Ada when Bobby commented.

'I thought it was much later than that.' Bobby looked confused he was sure he had heard the stairs creak as dawn was breaking.

'Well, you know what you're like, you don't know if it's morning or pancake Tuesday once you've had a sleep.' Ada watched her son devour his cooked breakfast like a starving man, knowing nothing, not even bad news upset her youngest son's appetite 'I suppose I'll have to traipse down Beamer Street after church and before I start work in the tavern, and if that rogue of a father of yours has been playing the old soldier again...' She didn't say what she would do.

'You make it sound like it's my fault he's my father.' Bobby grinned. 'Remember last time? You got all the way there and all he wanted was money for ciggies.'

'He's got more cheek than a porker,' Ada said, replenishing her cup with hot tea.

'You know what you're like, Ma,' said Bobby, wiping the plate with the remainder of his toast and washing it all down with a large mug of tea. 'If he is sick, you'll only whinge about what a terrible wife you are when you know well enough that you have done all you could for him. He's a hopeless case. But the choice is yours.'

'I'll go round there after my cleaning at the tavern, instead,' she said. 'And if he is playing on my good nature, and there's nothing wrong with him, I'll give the deceiving auld bugger something to crow about.'

'That's the spirit, Ma,' Bobby said, pouring himself another cup of tea.

'I'm in no mood for his silly games,' she grumbled.

She knew Bert played the martyr like a pro when he was looking for a bit of sympathy. Well, not today. 'I've got enough on me plate without him looking for a bit of attention.'

'Hardly his fault if he is sick, to be fair, Ma,' Bobby said, and Ada tutted. Opening the sideboard drawer, she took out her headscarf.

'Mind you,' she said, taking her coat off the hook behind the door, 'he's too self-centred to worry about anybody but himself.' Ada almost talked herself out of going to see him again, like she did last week. 'I'll see what Mim thinks.'

'Not that you'll take a blind bit of notice, if you don't like what she says,' Bobby commented. Thankful his mother had made a good breakfast and not the smoked haddock or *finny haddy*, they usually had on a Sunday. He wasn't partial to yellow fish.

'You'll have the pattern off that plate,' Ada said as he wiped the plate with another crust of his toast, which he always saved 'til last and her growing son shrugged. 'You're not like our Danny,' she said. Danny was still thought of as Bobby's older brother and she remembered the times when they were all together, everyone trying to get a word in, chatting over each other, half-listening to every conversations and trying to make sense of them all. 'He'd talk the hind leg off a table.'

Knowing full well she had mixed her maxims, she knew if she had said such a thing to Danny, he would have corrected her immediately. She missed Danny around the place, and the ideas bursting from his overactive mind. The spur-of-the-moment intentions. Positive they were going to make him successful if not rich, but aiming for rich all the same. Ada knew that when his ambitions were pricked like a burst balloon, he never gave up. He just thought of something else to make a success of the yard instead. Never allowing himself to be beaten.

Aye. She missed him all right. And she knew with every fibre of her being, if it hadn't been for Bert Harris making a show of her the way he did, she would be the one helping Danny to arrange his summer wedding – and not Meggie Skinner!

'So as I'm going after work I'll be a bit late back, Bobby,' Ada said to her son, his head down, reading the Sunday newspaper. He nodded, not looking up. 'Depending on how sick – or not - I might be gone a few hours,' she added, 'then again, I might only be ten minutes. D'ya mind?'

'You don't usually ask Mam,' Bobby said, looking up, his eyes, so like his older sister, Grace, they showed the same wisdom, which had developed since Bert and Danny left. Bobby now considered himself the man of the house, and Ada let him. Not only had he matured since he left school, but he had also grown to six feet tall.

'Do you want me to come with you?' Bobby asked and breathed a sigh of relief when Ada shook her head. She had to do this by herself.

'You'll be all right until I get back?' she asked. Nothing fazed the lad, she thought, grateful he rarely asked questions. Ada pulled the plaid woollen headscarf over her Dinky curlers, which were now well hidden, and secured it under her chin with a double knot. 'I'll be back as soon as I can.'

'Ta-ra Ma,' Bobby delivered his answer with mock exaggeration, and took his plate to wash it at the sink, knowing he could now listen to the wireless or read the newspaper in peace. 'Take as long as you like.'

'I will,' Ada's voice hid a smattering of amusement, and she wondered if she was letting him get too big for his wellies, even though she was grateful one of her offspring was still at home with her.

Closing the front door, Ada caught sight of Danny. He was heading towards the Tram Tavern, and he looked like he was in a hurry. She would have a word with him about Bert when she arrived in the tavern. She should have told Danny the truth years ago. But she couldn't. She had made a promise to Meggie. And the last thing she would do was go back on that agreement. And, as if the thought of her made Meggie appear, who had turned the corner and almost bumped right into Ada.

'That was a heck of a storm last week,' Meggie said, and Ada nodded, not wanting to get into conversation, but not wanting to ignore Meggie either. The sight of the woman still brought Ada out in hives of shame, knowing Bert had blackmailed Meggie's husband, Henry, and Danny had subsequently moved in with his birth mother and stepfather. 'You wouldn't credit the weather we get in this country,' said Meggie conversationally, and Ada nodded, eager to get to the Tram Tavern and speak to Danny.

'Well,' said Ada, 'I must be going, I'm off to mass before starting my shift at the Tavern.' She knew Meggie always went to eleven o'clock mass, but Ada chose the eight a.m. as she had to be at the tavern for ten.

'Could you pick up a copy of the *Catholic Pictorial* for me?' Meggie asked. 'They'd all gone last week.'

Ada nodded, keeping one eye on the Tavern, and wondering why Danny was calling there so early.

Ada gave an impatient tut when Meggie said, 'I'll just go and get my purse.'

'No need,' said Ada, 'you can give it to me when I get back.'

As she said this she realised she would be late for church if she didn't hurry and then had the thought that maybe Danny, was taking the wedding invitations to Angus and Connie, with whom he was very friendly. Knowing she still had not received one, she headed towards the church feeling hurt and ashamed.

* * *

Danny opened the door leading into the bar and swallowed the guilt that threatened to envelope him. He didn't want to ignore Ada, but he had no stomach for getting involved in the why and the wherefore of the reasons why he had lived a lie for the past twenty-five years. If it hadn't been for Evie and the business, he didn't know where he would be. Knowing with utter certainty, he would not be still around here.

'Morning, Angus, I brought that paint I promised,' Danny said as he walked towards the bar, nodding a greeting to Connie and Mim, who were having a cup of tea behind it.

Angus made his way to the far corner of the bar where it was quieter, silently motioning for Danny to follow him.

'Is everything okay, Angus?' Danny looked and sounded concerned. Angus was well-respected around the dock road, and nobody tried to pull the wool over his eyes.

'I heard a whisper,' Angus said in that deep Scottish brogue, giving his usual impression of brooking no fools.

'Go on,' Danny said with caution, knowing Angus did not throw information about lightly.

'Frank Kilgaren is still at large.' Angus watched the colour drain from Danny's face, and he pushed the small brandy he had already poured across the bar in Danny's direction. Swallowing it down in one, Danny took a deep breath.

'Jesus wept,' he breathed, 'what should I tell Evie?'

'Nothing,' Angus said succinctly. 'You mustn't tell her anything.'

'D'you, think he saw the announcement of our engagement in the newspaper? Poor Evie,' Danny mumbled, 'this will tear her apart if she finds out, but I suppose she will find out soon enough. You can't keep something like this quiet around here.'

* * *

'You look like you've lost a pound and found a tanner,' Mim Sharp said when Ada entered the Tram Tavern to do her cleaning later that morning before the tavern opened for trade.

Ada sighed and eyed her long-time friend, the former landlady, who retired from serving when her daughter Connie came home from nursing during the war. Mim did as little work as possible but was reluctant to let go of the tavern reins altogether.

Ada was already undoing her coat buttons as she rolled her eyes. She didn't want to tell Mim about Bert and the note, as she knew it would only set her off.

Mim and Bert had never seen eye to eye and neither of them hid the fact, prompting many a slanging match – especially after last orders had been called. Bert would never disrupt his drinking time arguing with a woman, but when it came to closing time, he quite looked forward to a war of words with the experienced landlady, who had dealt with many a rowdy customer and feared nobody – much like her daughter, Connie. But Ada could not keep anything from her best friend and so she told Mim the whole sorry story.

'I don't know if I should go and see Bert at all?' Ada said, opening the door under the stairs where the mop and buckets were kept.

'He's never been a good husband,' said Mim in her straightforward way. He hadn't even been an average one. 'He'd been bloody awful if the truth be told, with his gambling and underhanded skulduggery. Always on the cadge for money, except for when he had extorted money with menace from your poor cousin, Henry.'

'Don't hold back, Mim,' Ada said, fastening her pinny round her ample waist, covering the wraparound apron she always wore over her clothes. 'After all, we can't all have saints for husbands, can we?' Ada's eyes rolled to the ceiling, knowing Mim liked nothing better than to slate Bert every chance she got. 'I dreamt he was in my new wardrobe last week, naked as the day he was born.'

'You and your dreams,' Mim said with a hint of sarcasm to her oldest friend, 'I don't know why you don't get a booth on Southport promenade.'

'I wouldn't think of such a thing,' Ada preened. Being thick-skinned, she was rarely offended about anything her friend had to say, but Mim seemed to be in one of her cantankerous moods this morning. 'I was upstairs when there was this great rat-tat on the door...' Ada said, pouring a thick glug of Aunt Sally disinfectant into the mop bucket, and continued with her story.

'Well,' Mim huffed, 'the cheeky bugger! I take it you're not going to see him?'

'What can I do,' Ada was disconsolate, 'he *is* my husband.' She picked up the bucket of hot water and brought it through to the bar.

'An anchor round your neck more like,' Mim grumbled as she washed last night's glasses. The bar had been busy, and there was a fair bit to do this morning.

'Did you hear the news?' Connie said, wide-eyed, coming into the bar carrying her daughter Angela, but people called Annie, named after the royal princess, because she was born on the very same day three years ago. Mim's airs and graces knew no bounds when the local paper called Annie *Liverpool's Royal Baby*. 'You know that asylum out Netherford way?' Connie asked, and her mother's ice-blonde marcel waves didn't budge when she shook her head, but when she nodded Ada's steel curlers gave a good rattle beneath her headscarf which was now tied as a turban. 'Well, they're saying there was a breakout during that storm last week!'

'A breakout?' Ada repeated the words to make sure she had heard properly.

'They kept it very hush-hush, so as not to panic people,' Connie nodded. Although she didn't repeat the news Angus told her, that the fugitive was Frank Kilgaren, knowing her mother and Ada Harris would have a fit of conniptions if they thought Frank Kilgaren was on the loose. 'They're saying you must not approach him, as he is very dangerous,' Connie said, and all three women nodded. News like this was meat and drink to the mothers of Reckoner's Row who liked nothing better than a scandal or, as they called it, a bit of jangle.

'Did they give a description? In case we bump into him and accidentally put ourselves in danger, like?' asked Ada.

'Rust-coloured hair, clean-shaven – well, he was when he escaped – and gaunt,' Connie said.

'That could be anyone,' Mim remarked, her voice full of disappointment. She had been hoping he had a distinctive feature, like a limp or just one hand or something similar.

'I think I will go and see Bert.' Ada took courage from the understanding that Mim would have something more important to focus on than her marriage – or lack of.

'I suppose it's the wifely thing to do,' Mim said. She struggled to find a kindly word, and plumped for a typically unsympathetic retort: 'Let us know if we need to get our black coats out of storage.'

'Take no notice, Ada,' Connie said, giving her mother a

cautionary nudge with her elbow 'you know what she's like – all heart – aren't you, Mim?'

'I speak as I find,' said Mim, knowing if Ada decided to take that two-faced snake back, she would have no more to do with her, 'we both do, don't we, Ada? We understand each other?'

'Oh aye.' All the while they had been talking, Ada was doing her morning chores and when she finished, she put on her coat, her usual forthright Irish cadence wilting under the weight of her melancholy mood. She could do without acting the Florence Nightingale today. She had to deliver Meggie's *Catholic Pictorial*, but that could be done later. And she still had to get that leg of mutton in the oven. But she had a duty as a wife, even if Bert had been the worst husband that ever walked down Reckoner's Row. 'I'll call in on me way back and let you know how he is.'

'Only if it's no trouble,' Mim said, ignoring the icy glare from Connie.

* * *

'Lucy, will you get that door for me, while I put these potatoes in the oven,' Evie called from the back kitchen.

Lucy took a deep breath, reluctant to move from the cosy heat of the dancing flames, folded the Sunday Post newspaper and got up off the sofa.

The front door was closed to the cold February weather, and she expected to see Danny standing on the step. However, when she opened the door, Lucy was surprised when she saw two official-looking men standing there, dressed in dark overcoats and trilby hats. The only other man she had seen dressed like this was the insurance man who came on a Friday night, never on a Sunday.

'Hello, my dear,' the older of the men said, lifting his hat slightly, 'are you Evie Kilgaren?'

Lucy could feel the hairs on the back of her neck stand on end. What did these men want with their Evie?

'No, I'm Lucy, Evie is my older sister.' Lucy was about to call Evie when the taller of the two men stepped inside, followed by the younger man. And before she could shout for Evie, the kitchen door opened and Evie came into the hall, wiping her hands on a tea towel.

'Can I help you?' Evie's voice was cold but civil, she didn't like the idea of strange men walking into her house unbidden. She gave a slight jerk of her head to let Lucy know to shut the front door.

'I'm sorry to bother you, Miss Kilgaren,' said the older man, 'but may we have a word... in private?'

Evie wanted to tell him that anything he had to say could be said in front of Lucy, but something told her that what he needed to say was not for Lucy's ears.

'Can you go and get me a packet of gravy salt please, Lucy, there's a love?' Evie said, reaching into her apron pocket for some loose change and, without question, Lucy agreed, but her eyes told Evie she was concerned.

'I'm Inspector Davison and this is Dr Johnson from the North-bank Institution.' 'Come through,' Evie said, leading the two men into the warm, cosy kitchen, as her mind conjured up many questions.

'That's a good blaze you've got going there, Miss,' said Dr Johnson, the younger of the men and Evie nodded. She wished they would get on with whatever they had come to say.

'Can I get you a cup of tea?' Evie asked politely, 'or would you like to tell me what this is all about?' There was no mistaking the inference in her tone.

'We will come straight to the point,' said the older man, Inspector Davison, as all three stood in the middle of the room. Evie did not invite them to sit down, suspecting the news they were about to give her was not going to be good. 'Last week there was a breakout at the Northbank Institution.' He paused, watching Evie closely, her face devoid of expression, as if waiting for him to continue. Then he saw her eyelids widen.

'A breakout?' Evie's muscles stiffened and she suddenly had no clue what to do with her hands, gripping them tightly to try to stop them from shaking. Her father was in Northbank.

'Yes,' said Davison. 'Your father escaped during the power cut, caused by the storm. Have you seen anything of him?' His tone was grave when she did not answer. 'It would be in your best interest to tell us the truth, Miss Kilgaren.' Evie could feel her hackles rise.

'I can assure you, if there is so much as a sniff of my father, I will be calling the police myself!' Evie tried to take a deep breath but couldn't, her heart was hammering against her ribs, and she was staring without seeing.

Her father had spent the last six years in the asylum for the murder of her mother. He pled guilty of the charge and had not spoken another word since. Not even in the witness box. He said nothing that would give any indication of why he had cut her mother's life short, nor did he say anything that might exonerate him. Not one word.

'From the time of his arrest, through his trial, and in the six years he has been incarcerated, he has not spoken one word of the terrible crime,' said Dr Johnson. 'If he came back here, to this house, we fear he will do you or your sister some harm.'

'He would never hurt Lucy,' Evie said. However, she wasn't so sure he felt the same way about her. It was her evidence that had locked him up in a mental hospital. And although his incarceration saved him from the rope, he was never going to forgive her for what she did.

'Make sure your doors and windows are locked at all times,' said Inspector Davison as they made their way towards the front door, and Evie nodded in agreement. She didn't want her Da doing to her what he had done to her mother.

'If he does get into this house, I will fight him with everything I can lay my hands on after what he did to our mother.' She must. For Lucy's sake.

Davison handed her a piece of paper, which she stuffed into her apron pocket when she saw Lucy coming down the street with the packet of gravy salt she did not need. 'If you see or hear anything suspicious, ring that number immediately.'

'Of course,' she said, her mind scrambling to make sense of what he was telling her as images of her father flashed through her mind.

'Jolly good,' said Davison and the together the two men raised their hats once more, 'We'll bid you good day.'

'Yes,' Evie, dazed, felt as if she had been hit with a house brick, but she had to remain calm for Lucy's sake. Turning, she went back inside and left the front door open for her sister, not waiting to see the black saloon car disappear down Reckoner's Row. Knowing what a fevered imagination Lucy had, Evie didn't want her younger sister to know their father had escaped and was on the run.

'Look at this,' Lucy's voice was high, her eyes wide as she thrust the *News of the World* into Evie's hands. 'He's out! Da's escaped. It says so on the front page!'

'I know, Lucy,' Evie flinched, trying to calm her sister. 'But don't worry, we will just have to make sure all the doors and windows are fastened tight. Keep them locked at all times. We don't want him getting in here.' *God knows what he might do.* Nevertheless, Evie kept that thought to herself.

Lucy knew their Evie had not had an easy time of things since their mam *died.* She refused to entertain the word '*murdered*' in relation to her mother, considering her own father – *her good shepherd –*

had been tried and found guilty of the shocking crime and was now – or was – serving a life sentence in an asylum for the killing.

He declined to speak of the heinous crime, even in the witness box when he went on trial at Saint George's Hall, Evie told her only last year when she left school, supposedly old enough to understand. But, to this day, Lucy did not understand. Why would their father not say why he had killed the woman he had loved so deeply? Not one word. He would not answer questions. Nor give a single reason why he did it. Not even in his own defence. Nothing. And that had been his downfall. He never uttered another word after pleading guilty.

Lucy's brow creased into a thoughtful frown. She couldn't understand it. He was the kindest, most softly-spoken man she had ever met. When she and Jack were evacuated to family over in Ireland during the war, he was one of the first people she met outside of the family she lived with. She didn't know then that he was her father, a war hero who had survived his ship being sunk by torpedoes in the south coast waters of his homeland. He had made it to the mainland and was rescued by farmers who kept him out of harm's way during the war, at least that's what they called it – *desertion* was never a word that was uttered – while his wife and children believed he was dead. He taught her how to herd sheep and how to whistle Shep, the black and white sheepdog who rounded up the sheep. A child back then, Lucy was easily taken in by a kind word.

'Oh Evie,' Lucy's lip trembled, 'I'm scared...'

'Don't worry, Lucy. I'll keep you safe.' Evie's stomach tightened, and she prayed Lucy would be reassured by the tone in her voice. After all, Lucy was not the one who gave evidence against the man who killed her mother and revealed to the jury what a terrible husband he had been. No, Evie knew for certain, Lucy wasn't the one her father was seeking.

8

Holding her head high, Ada walked down Reckoner's Row, her back poker straight. Looking neither right nor left, but ahead, towards the steps up to the small bridge at the bottom end of the Row, which led to Beamer Street and the house in which Bert had been lodging for the past three years.

On the other side of the bridge, Beamer Street was much longer than Reckoner's Row and went right down to the docks. These houses were the usual, three-up, three-down, with an outside lavatory and no bathroom or hot running water, but most of them were well-kept, despite the perseverance of the Luftwaffe's intent during the May Blitz to blast them off the face of the earth. Built during the last century in the days of the old Queen, Victoria, Ada could not help but marvel at the soot-covered red-brick houses still standing now they had a new Queen, Elizabeth, whose coronation was eagerly awaited by the whole country. There were going to be lots of celebrations – even though rationing was still in force – and Connie had already started collecting money from each house in the row every Friday night. The money would go towards a street party, and other things like bunting, and there was going to be a mock Coronation for the youngsters.

Ada had been squirreling away some of her rations: sugar, flour, dried fruit – that kind of thing. She was going to show the others in Reckoner's Row that she was not of the same ilk as her snake-in-the-grass husband.

Determined not to dwell on the underhanded things Bert Harris had done to her over the years, Ada had done everything she could to get back in her neighbours' good books. Knowing at the age of eighteen, she had been in love with one man, but had to marry another, Ada recalled what Bert Harris never let her forget – he was the one who took her on. At first, she was grateful to him, then she was beholden to him. Then she despised him.

Bert never was a man to exert himself, especially after he came back from the trenches with a toe missing. She had heard rumours that he had shot himself to get back home. And as the years went by, she came to believe it, especially when he had no compunction about cluttering up her house and blaming his war wound on the fact he could not get work. Even though she had seen many others with much more serious injuries who worked and provided for their families. But not Bert.

Bert would sleep on the sofa when he wasn't in the pub or gambling her hard-earned money. Without a conscience, he would dip into her purse and spend her housekeeping money. And when she lost her temper and another row ensued, he would walk out of the door and not come back for a few days. Then, for the sake of appearances, he would pretend he was sorry, adopt a little-boy-lost expression and tell her how rotten he felt, how he was such a terrible husband, and he didn't deserve a wife as good as she was. She doubted the heart-lurching panic she felt when the cupboards were bare ever worried Bert, as long he had his beer money – that's all he was concerned about.

The canal veered off at the other side of the bridge and further down Beamer Street, there were a few warehouses and factories on the left, unlike Reckoner's Row where there was nothing but the canal to see, which suited Ada, who had no wish to look out onto nearby industries going about their business even on a Sunday.

The smell of the hides and dyes grew stronger as she neared the tannery and her nose wrinkled, knowing that when the wind changed, the stench blew all the way over to Reckoner's Row. Passing the wood yard, timber mixed with various other smells wafted on the wind and she could hear the buzz of the lumber saw behind the huge gates, before almost being knocked sideways by a runaway tractor tyre.

'Sorry, Missus,' a few young lads chorused, rolling the huge tyre along the cobbles.

'You will be,' Ada said tetchily, breathing heavily as she reached the end house in the street, causing her nostrils to flare and her lips to turn down at the corners as her eyes travelled the length of the three-storey property, almost identical to her own house, except this one was nowhere near as clean or well looked after. This one was unmistakeably a dosshouse, with grey, sagging nets at the windows and chipped, bottle green paint at the war-torn front door, which was closed to the street and looked ominously foreboding.

But such things didn't trouble Ada. She wasn't here to buy the place, she thought, and wouldn't if she could afford to. No, she was here because she was summoned, and didn't want to appear heartless to Bert Harris's plight. That was the only reason. There was no love lost between him and her, and there hadn't been for donkey's years.

Giving a loud rat-tat on the dirty brass door knocker, Ada's pale green eyes surveyed the dust-covered skylight above the door while she waited impatiently for someone to answer. A moment later, she heard footsteps and the door opened a crack.

'Well?' asked the wizened old woman in a shapeless cardigan that had seen better days, while on her feet she wore a pair of baggy, navy-blue ankle socks and men's carpet slippers that were much too big, her tone and her attitude confrontational.

'You sent a note, a week or so ago and again last night. With the boy.' Ada's tone was equally unfriendly.

'Mrs Harris?' said the husk of a woman. 'You took your time.'

'It's none of your business,' Ada said in a no-nonsense tone.

The woman opened the door just enough for her to squeeze through into the dimly lit lobby. Ada's nose wrinkled in disgust when the powerful smell of cat pee, and stale ale hit her. This place was only fit for back-entry-diddlers and no-marks, she thought scathingly, not in the least surprised this was where Bert Harris had ended up.

'You owe me two shillings and sixpence.'

'Two and six! What for?' Ada said. She owed nobody. Not any more.

'The doctor,' said the old crone with her hand out and Ada studied her with a raised suspicious eyebrow.

'Do you think I've just come over?' Ada asked. 'The doctor's fee, you say.' Ada threw her head back and laughed. 'They stopped charging back in 1948 – I'm sure you must have heard of the National Health Service, free for all at the point of service.'

'I... He... He's up there,' the landlady nodded to the top of the murky stairs, 'first on the left.'

'Bugs,' Ada said, 'I can smell them. They lurk in dark corners and behind the wallpaper. You need to get this place fumigated, and if I take any home with me, you will get them back in an envelope.' She made her way up the groaning staircase, taking no chances on the rickety banister that looked none too safe. 'And the place is riddled with damp.'

'I suppose you can smell that, too,' the landlady said before slamming her own door and shutting off what little light there had been, clearly disgruntled.

When she reached the landing, Ada turned and knocked on the shabby door of the dosshouse that accommodated the down-and-outs, drop-outs, winos, doxies and outcasts, down by the River Mersey. So, this was what Bert had sunk to. She knew he would. She felt it in her bones. But she took no pleasure in knowing.

When there was no answer, Ada was about to turn and go, when she heard a feeble voice on the other side of the door urging her to come in.

Opening the creaking door, she did not expect to see a room on a par with the Adelphi Hotel, but she didn't expect this either. The sight that met her turned her stomach. A broken window allowed the sulphurous stench of the gasworks to meander into the austere room, where Bert lay hunched in a foetal position, still in his black Crombie overcoat on a stained mattress. The narrow iron bed sagging in the middle looked like it was swallowing him whole. A thin mantlepiece was littered with beer bottles, a small ash-lined bowl overflowing with browning cigarette stumps, an open box of Swan matches, a dry shaving brush, a thin stick of shaving soap pointed like a sharpened pencil, a near-empty bottle of liquid paraffin that Bert always used to slick back his thinning grey hair, a soap clogged razor and a comb with most of the teeth missing. A frothy yellow pool of bile covered the faded lino at the side of his bed, and the stench of destitution filled the sour air.

The freezing draught from the broken window made the room icy cold, and Ada took the Sunday paper from her bag and begrudgingly filled the hole with a scrunched-up ball of Meggie Skinner's *Catholic Pictorial*. The window looked out onto the busy docks and warehouses, active and alive even on a Sunday, every worker wanting double-time pay for Sabbath-day labour. Ada's eyes narrowed at the back-yard clutter below, spying a tin bath hanging on a six-inch nail, and she wondered momentarily if it was ever used.

'I heard you're not well,' Ada said, having blocked the draught, determined not to go anywhere near the bed. If this was a cry to come back home, Bert Harris was sadly mistaken, she thought. He had pulled the wool over her eyes one time too many. She was quite happy on her own and glad not to be at the beck and call of a man who thought of nobody except himself.

'I'm dying, Ada,' Bert's rasping voice was barely audible, 'I haven't got long left.'

'Don't tell me you're going to pop your clogs when the pubs are open, Bert.' Ada's tone was unsympathetic, she no longer believed a word that came out of his mouth. But, when she looked closer, she could see his pallor was grey, like uncooked pastry that had been left standing too long, and Ada knew he was in a bad way. 'How long have you been like this?' she asked, and he gave a half-hearted shrug, not answering. 'Well, you can't stay here. You'll be dead when you wake up.' She doubted the landlady had a telephone. This place didn't even have a mantle on the gas pipe sticking out of the wall, let alone a vital means of communication. 'I'm going down to the phone box to call an ambulance.' And, for the first time, she saw Bert move his head from the depths of his chest.

'No.' His words were the rasp of cinders under a door, but they also held a note of panic. 'There's no need for any of that. I have to tell you something... and I don't want strangers putting their sticky beaks... into my private business.'

What kind of private business? Ada said nothing.

With every ounce of strength, he could muster, Bert pointed a shaking finger to the alcove at the side of an unlit grate before his arm slumped onto the mattress.

Ada looked to a makeshift door where, she presumed, Bert kept all his worldly goods, because there was no sign of any clothes in the room. There was no food on the bare shelf in the alcove at the other side of the fireplace, where she would have expected a crust of bread and a packet of margarine at least. This place was little more than a hovel and she would die of shame if anybody she knew saw that her husband was living here.

'Look,' she said, 'even though you were not a good husband to me, I cannot have it on my conscience to let you die in this hovel, although I doubt anybody would blame me.'

'You're a good woman, Ada, I don't know what I'd do without you.'

I do. Ada looked round the stark, unadorned room with its slanted ceiling and peeling wallpaper. Bert Harris was not in his cups, no matter what the empty beer bottles suggested, he was sober as a judge. But if he was about to tell her how much he loved her, or how sorry he was for the pain and heartache he had brought her over the years, trying to persuade her to take him back and getting him well enough to torment her all over again, he was sadly mistaken. Nevertheless, she could never have been prepared or foreseen what Bert Harris was about to tell her...

'I know who really killed Rene Kilgaren...'

* * *

'Open the door,' Bert gasped, 'go on, open it.' He stretched his neck, gasping for every snatched amount of air, and Ada stared straight ahead, her eyes fixed on this shell of a man who once had the power to make her insides sink with fear and dread.

I don't want to know... But thinking and doing were two different things as far as she was concerned.

Ada reached out her hand and gripped the handle of the door, pulling it with all the strength she could muster, but the door of the makeshift cupboard built into the alcove would not budge, as if it had not been opened for years, and her thoughts were confirmed when she saw the thick layer of dust laying undisturbed on the thin rim on the frame.

'Frank Kilgaren...' Bert's words were slow, laboured, 'did not kill his wife...'

A weight of her husband's admission pressed heavily on Ada's chest, robbing her of breath as the blood drained from her face, her heart thudding against her ribs.

Please don't tell me it was you... She could not bear the disgrace of another of Bert's humiliations as, once more, she tugged at the makeshift cupboard door. Managing with much force to open it caused her to stumble backwards. Steadying herself, questions fought for space in Ada's head as she peered inside the closet. She could not bear the shame of her husband being responsible for the death of Evie's mother. She would have to leave Reckoner's Row. Danny would despise her.

I will never get an invitation to their wedding if this comes out.

Bert Harris had brought her nothing but trouble and heartache. He was a wastrel who spent every penny in the pub. And the money he didn't hand over the bar went into the bookie's pockets, never hers. The reason she had to go skivvying, to feed her children.

'There's nothing in here,' Ada said, turning her head towards her hunched spouse lying on the coverless bed. In days long gone she would have wished for moments like this. To see him powerless and vulnerable. However, she could not summon the energy she needed to scorn this man who had caused her so much misery. She couldn't summon the energy to feel anything at all.

'Knock on the panel at the back...' Bert's words faded as they came to the end, and Ada peered into the darkened cupboard, her eyes searching the back and she did as Bert told her to do, tapping the back panel of the built-in cubbyhole. It sounded hollow, and she knocked again. 'Push it...' Bert gasped, and Ada used all her considerable force, built up from years of scrubbing and cleaning other people's houses, offices and pubs, and immediately a loud crack echoed in the cupboard as the panel scraped the ceiling and gave way, causing her to fall into it.

Trust Bert to have a false panel in the bloody cupboard!

A wooden box, larger than a shoebox but smaller than an orange box, lay in the space behind the plywood divider, and she stared at it for a moment before dragging it towards her. It was not heavy but jagged, covered in splinters and closed tight with nails. The box was coated in a thick layer of grey dust that told Ada it had not been disturbed for some time.

'There's nothing here except this tatty old box,' she said, waiting for instructions. When none came, she popped her head round the makeshift door and she froze momentarily, her eyes blinking rapidly as she tried to process the image of Bert's unseeing eyes staring up at the cracked ceiling. Ada's mouth fell open and she covered it with that palm of her hand. She couldn't get enough oxygen into her lungs and needed to sit down, but there was nowhere to sit except the bed, and she had no intentions of sitting there. Leaning against the cupboard door, she was aware of the sound of children playing outside, their youthful voices filling the frosty air.

She didn't need to be a doctor to see Bert was dead. Lightly stroking her throat, she waited for the inevitable tears, but none came. Instead, she had an uncontrollable urge to laugh, and she had to press her fist to her mouth to stop herself from an outburst. What would it look like if she was heard laughing and her husband lying dead?

9

'He's been sick for a while, now,' said the shrivelled landlady, putting in her two pennorth of information when she opened the front door to let in Doctor Soames, who had turned up to formally pronounce Bert extinct. 'And he can't be left in here, I have other boarders to consider.' She followed the doctor up the stairs. 'I did send for the wife last week, but she didn't see fit to attend.'

Looking out of the window on the landing, Ada saw a group of children gathering round the doctor's saloon car.

'I sent the lad round in that terrible storm, but her ladyship saw fit to stay indoors. The lad was soaked right through when he got back. I'm surprised Mister Harris has lasted as long as he did.'

Rolling her shoulders, Ada turned her head, her eyes narrowing, intending to wipe that smug expression from her face. 'I'm sure the broken window, and lack of bedclothes did much to speed up the race to meet his maker.' Ada's voice, so sharp it could have sliced leather, momentarily startled the landlady.

'I am so sorry for your loss, Mrs Harris,' the doctor said. Ada had known him from days gone by when she cleaned his house and medical surgery.

When the doctor went into the room, he closed the door behind him, stopping the landlady from entering the room and leaving both women on the dark landing.

* * *

Bert was pronounced dead, and the doctor spoke in hushed tones when he told Ada.

'The body will remain in situ until the undertaker comes to collect. You may take any personal effects with you.' The doctor's voice was gentle. He knew Bert Harris of old. And he also knew Ada had not had an easy marriage.

'Why has he got to stay in here?' The landlady's eyes widened.

'We'll sit him in a chair by the front door, if you've got another lodger lined up?' Ada could see this old hag would want this room vacated as soon as possible.

'I saw Mister Harris last week ,' the doctor informed Ada, 'and he was most adamant he did not want to go into hospital.

'As I've already said,' the landlady piped up, telling the doctor, 'I did send for the wife, but she saw fit not to come until today.' She glared at Ada.

'There was a catastrophic storm last week,' he replied, knowing man and wife were estranged. He had heard the rumours, and was not surprised, given the many beer bottles littering the place and cigarette stumps stubbed out on the narrow fireplace. He felt sorry for Ada, who looked most uncomfortable, which was hardly surprising. She was such a clean, houseproud woman, whose husband had stooped to his lowest, almost dragging her good reputation along with him. Doctor Soames would not have been the least surprised if Ada had refused to come here at all.

'I didn't think he was this bad.' Ada averted her gaze from the bed upon which her dead husband lay.

'Even if he had gone into hospital, I doubt we could have saved him. You have nothing to reproach yourself for, Mrs Harris.' His kind eyes looked to Ada. 'And may I offer my sincere condolences.' Then looking to the landlady who was hovering in the background he said more sternly, 'I will have an undertaker take the body to the mortuary this afternoon.'

'Thank you, Doctor,' Ada's usually powerful voice was now barely a whisper, and she swayed a little, still unable to meet his gaze, no matter how kindly his words, and she felt herself shrink, her arms hanging redundantly at her side. She wanted to run as fast as she could down those stairs and out of the front door.

'Can you stay with the body until the undertaker arrives?' the doctor asked, and Ada nodded.

'I will show you to the door, Doctor,' the landlady said as she hurried to lead the way down the stairs.

* * *

'This won't get into the paper, will it?' the landlady asked when the undertaker arrived and entered the sparse room, 'I don't want my tenants disturbed by all of this...' Her voice withered to a whisper as the undertaker looked round pointedly.

'We will do what needs to be done, Madam.' The undertaker gave a sneering glance and Ada felt vindicated. She had been a good wife to Bert, and he would still be alive if he lived in the comfort of Reckoner's Row.

Ada was given the coroner's phone number, to ring after they'd carried out a post-mortem and they would tell her when the body may be released for burial. She nodded, trying to take in everything she was being told, but Ada couldn't hold on to any of it, except that Bert was now *the body* and no longer a living, thriving human being.

'I'll only take the box from the cupboard,' Ada said, knowing whatever was in it would tell her who or what had killed Rene Kilgaren, and that kind of information was for nobody else's knowledge except hers.

'You're quick off the mark, considering.' The landlady gave a loud tut, folded her arms and shrugged her shoulders.

'Considering?' Ada's eyes were like daggers, and she leaned forward, giving the other woman cause to step back.

'I was only saying... He didn't have nothing worth keeping.'

'I'll be the judge of that,' said Ada, ending the conversation. 'I will send my son round to pick up the rest of his things. Do you have a spare key?' Ada asked and the other woman nodded. 'And when is his rent paid up to?'

'Tomorrow.' The landlady's glare was defiant, as if daring Ada to question her, but Ada only nodded and looked, for all the world, like a woman in full control, but her insides were turning, and she swallowed several times as the tingling sensation told her she was in danger of throwing up her breakfast.

'Right then, I'll take the box now,' she said, stepping back as the undertaker's men removed Bert's body from the room. 'You can give me the spare key and Bert's key. I don't want anybody prowling around in this room until my son comes to collect his effects.'

'You're welcome to them, love. I can't see there's anything worth...' In response to Ada's cold stare, the words died on the landlady's lips.

* * *

'Hello, Mrs Harris.' Evie's eyebrows puckered when Ada didn't answer. The older woman looked deep in thought as she descended the steps of the little bridge known as *the brew*, carrying a rough, wooden box. 'Is everything all right?'

Ada seemed a little confused when she looked to Evie, on her way from the haulage yard after picking up some papers to work on at home. Evie needed to keep her mind occupied, so she didn't dwell on the fact her father was at large.

'Oh, hello Evie, I got a bit of bad news.'

Evie stopped, waiting for the older woman to reach the last stone step.

'I'm sorry to hear that, is there anything I can do for you?' She and Ada Harris had not always seen eye to eye over the years, but Evie would never ignore anybody in distress. Like a lot of mothers, Ada had a lot to put up with, but she had grit and determination, which was evident when she threw that scheming husband out three years ago and refused to take him back or have anything else to do with him.

'Bert's *diseased*,' Ada said in a low voice, not meeting Evie's concerned gaze, who was trying to make sense of the news.

'Diseased?' asked Evie, askance. There was only one disease that was talked about in hushed tones round here and it usually came in with the ships and sailors. 'I'm sorry to hear that, Ada,' said Evie.

'I'll have to arrange the funeral. There's nobody else to bury the old rogue.' Ada's eyes widened and she scratched her forehead as if trying to get her thoughts in order as Evie realised, she meant deceased, not diseased and she gave a huge sigh. Poor Ada.

'Surely you won't be the one who has to bury him?' Evie asked, collecting her own thoughts, not sure if Ada and Bert were legally separated or even divorced – although she doubted that, given that Ada was a church-going Catholic, and divorce was against the church's teachings. Women round here, in the mainly Irish/Catholic dockside community, put up with a hell of a lot from their husbands and would never dream of divorcing them, it was unheard of.

'Well, he wasn't flush with family – or friends come to that.'

Ada's nostrils flared. 'And I can't leave the old bugger to rot, no matter how much I'd like to. He'd be a bloody health hazard.'

Evie clenched her lips between her teeth. Even in grief, stoic dockside women like Ada revealed the dark sense of humour that got them through many of life's hardships. A small clearing of her throat restored Evie's equilibrium and she put a sympathetic hand on Ada's arm. The older woman silently nodded; the unspoken gesture was a hopeful sign.

'Shall I tell Danny,' Evie asked, 'or would you rather, do it?' Even through the weak, watery sunshine the air was bitterly cold, and Ada shivered.

'I'm not one to shirk my duties,' Ada said stiffly, 'it's only right I tell him.' She lowered her eyes to hide the fact that she thought the information might also elicit enough sympathy to get an invitation to their wedding.

'If there's anything you need, Ada,' said Evie, 'you only have to ask.'

'Thank you.' Ada wondered if Evie would be so sympathetic if she knew Bert had information regarding her mother's death. 'I must get on; our Bobby will be wondering where I am.'

'Ta-ra, Ada.' One thing was for sure, thought Evie, Ada would have no more worries about Bert knocking on her door for handouts.

She wondered how Danny would take the news. Would he go and see Ada?

She watched the older woman trudge up the steps towards her door and put the key in the brass yale lock. Evie had never seen her look so downcast. But why wouldn't she? He was her husband after all. And, although he would never be the husband her Danny would be, Evie knew it must have come as a shock to Ada to find out he was dead.

* * *

'The tavern stayed open during the Blitz, but its doors were bolted tight and all for a spot of wind and rain!' The one and only disgruntled customer who had braved the storm when his own lights went out had found the doors of the tavern locked and he was letting everybody know. 'Shocked I was, shocked! And all for a spot o' rain.' Connie was barely listening, knowing this particular customer only came into the tavern at the weekend.

'Tell it to the landlord,' Connie said, feeling tetchy because her three-year-old daughter, Angela, whom everyone called Annie, had been up most of the night with a nasty bout of croup. Connie's nursing skills had quickly come to the fore, and she had been boiling kettles throughout the night, so the vapour could open little Annie's airways, helping her breathe and ease the seal-like bark. Nevertheless, when her darling child settled, Connie was unable to get back to sleep for worrying about her. 'Angus is the one who makes the rules round here,' Connie added, placing the pint of bitter on the bar towel between them. She took the customer's money, rang it up and slammed the money into the till. Angus had not stirred once during the night. Nor had Mim. Connie had a good mind to make her mother work the late shift with Angus.

'Looks like you're in the doghouse, Angus,' said the cheeky stevedore who had just finished a Sunday morning's work on the docks, 'she's got a right old flea in her...'

'And quite right too,' said Angus, who would not allow anything detrimental to be said about his wonderful Connie, the love of his life, a better wife any red-blooded man could not wish for, who had not so much as said good morning to him, let alone held a conversation. 'My wonderful wife has been up all night with young Annie and when we close this afternoon, I am going to cook her a gourmet roast.'

'My husband gets his soft soap by the bucketload, did you know?' Connie said, raising a finely pencilled eyebrow, trying not to smile as she reached for a glass above her husband's head, allowing him to inhale the new scent he had bought her. Angus was the only man who had the power to dissolve her rotten mood with a warm smile on a cold day. He could charm the birds from the trees, she thought, and could also clear the bar in five minutes flat.

* * *

Evie turned and headed back towards the haulage yard in Summer Settle, and the house in which Danny had lived with Meggie and Henry for the last three years. For the first time, Evie hoped that Danny was not home, because it was Meggie she wanted to talk to.

'Come in, love, you look perished,' Henry exclaimed in his usual friendly way when Evie knocked on the side door of the house, situated at the far end of the yard. 'Meggie's just made a fresh pot of tea so that'll warm you up.'

'Thanks, Pop,' said Evie, using the name the family called Henry by. 'Is Danny in?'

'No, lass,' said Henry, 'he's gone down to the dock to collect the horse food.' He stood to one side to let her in and the delicious smell of beef roasting in the oven filled the air.

'That's good,' said Evie, 'because it's you and Meggie I've come to see.'

'Sounds ominous,' said Henry as he led the way into the sitting room, where Meggie was just bringing in a tray of tea things. Meggie put down the tray and greeted her future daughter-in-law with a kiss and a hug.

'Hello, love, it's lovely to see you. I'll just go and fetch another cup.'

As they sat and drank their tea, Evie told them that she had just encountered Ada, and she gave them the news about Bert.

Meggie shook her head and looked grim. 'Well, you wouldn't wish such a thing on anybody,' she said in a low voice, 'but he were neither use nor ornament to poor Ada.'

Henry nodded in agreement.

'Ada said she would tell Danny herself,' said Evie, 'so I thought it was best to come and tell him that Ada wants to see him. In case he found out by accident from a stranger or kids in the street. You know what they can be like.'

'I've just seen Ada,' Danny said, coming into the sitting room. He had overheard every word and immediately went over to Evie and gave her a kiss on the cheek, not in the least bashful about showing his true feelings in front of his parents, who had taught him that not all marriages were battlegrounds. Many couples did love each other and thought nothing of treating each other with the love and respect they deserved.

'I'm sorry, lad,' said Henry, 'it must be a shock?'

'I won't speak ill of the dead,' said Danny, 'but I will say this. At least Ada will get a widow's pension. Small compensation for the aggravation she has suffered over the years.'

'Did you see Bobby?' asked Meggie and Danny nodded, sitting down at the table while Meggie poured him a cup of tea.

'He's gone round to Beamer Street to collect his old man's paltry effects,' Danny answered. 'I did offer to take him in the wagon, but he said there wouldn't be that much to collect.'

'I suppose he was upset,' Evie said, recalling how she felt when she got the news about her mother. She had been knocked sideways, as if she was outside her own body looking at the scene from across the room.

'He seemed fine,' said Danny. 'Obviously he would be disappointed for his ma, but on the whole, I think Bert burned his bridges when he brought shame to the family.'

'Aye, lad,' said Henry, 'but Ada can't be held responsible for what her husband did, can she?'

'I don't expect she can,' said Danny, who began to feel guilty he hadn't asked Ada to attend his and Evie's wedding. But there was going to be plenty of time for all that. There was a funeral to organise before then.

'I'll go over and see her,' said Meggie, knowing all the women pulled together at a time like this.

* * *

Ada had pushed the unopened box into the gas metre cupboard and closed the door. She had stared at the cupboard for hours, not knowing what to do. For as much as she would like to open the box to see what secrets lay hidden inside, she knew without doubt, she could not withstand two shocks in one day.

'What if Bert was the man who killed Evie's mother?' she whispered, quivering at the thought. She could not live with the knowledge she had been married to a murderer.

No, she decided, it would be better to let sleeping dogs lie and keep the cat in the bag. What the eye didn't see the heart couldn't grieve over. This was a secret she would have to carry to her grave, and for the first time in her life, Ada knew she could not share it with anybody – not even Mim.

10

Susie Blackthorn peered in the mirror over the sink, touching up her dark roots to match the rest of her platinum blonde hair. She would have asked Lucy Kilgaren to colour her hair, but she didn't want Evie, that stuck-up sister of hers, to know the reason she wanted to look her very best.

She soon got a job at Lenard's Haulage Company after Evie Kilgaren so ruthlessly dispensed with her exemplary services, which just goes to show how competent she really was when Harry Caraway, General Manager of Lenard's, took her on as a filing clerk. Although when she told him how she hungered to become office manager - in charge of finances like Evie, and let it slip that she was in possession of the Skinner files, his eyes lit up. Harry had all but promised her the job of office manager and she was going to find out tomorrow. Maybe then Danny Harris would see she was more than just a wiggle and a pout.

When Evie had fired her from Skinner's office, she took copies of Danny's files with her. And now she would use them to ruin the man who had destroyed her hopes and dreams.

Tomorrow she was going to take Harry the files, which she had copied from Skinner's private client list. Names. Contacts. Pricings. Everything he would need to secure the coveted Skinner's Haulage Yard, situated on prime dock land. Worth a fortune in the right hands.

Harry had promised her that, if she was to acquire the information he needed, he could put Danny out of business and get Skinner's yard for a steal. Something that would enhance both their careers. Because Harry had hinted, Mr Lenard, whom Susie had never yet set eyes on, was desperate to get hold of the land on which the yard was situated. And that was a good enough reason for Susie to hand over Skinner's files – and get a huge promotion in the process. Wouldn't that put Evie Kilgaren's nose out of joint – and show Danny Harris that Susie Blackthorn was more than just a pretty face.

Susie blew a kiss to her reflection in the mirror. She wanted to look her best when she lit the blue touch paper that would blast Danny Harris's dreams of becoming one of the biggest haulage contractors in the North-West.

Would Danny still think Evie was Skinner's saviour, or would he see she was totally incompetent and realise he had his eye on the wrong girl. Susie smiled at her reflection; she was going places. She was going to be Someone. She was the one who was gong to be hiring and firing. She was going to be the one in control of company finances. Harry had said as much when she told him she was in receipt of Skinner's files. In fact, he had been so excited he invited her out for a meal in that big Hotel in town.

She had been sacked from every job she ever had. But the office managers had all been women and she knew how jealous they could be when they were faced with a glamorous woman. They all saw her as a threat. She realised that now. When she got this job – and she always knew she would – because the then office manager was a man – she did it with every intention of ruining Danny Harris. Nobody got the better of Susie Blackthorn and got away with it. Not Evie Kilgaren, and especially not Danny Harris.

'Hell, hath no fury like a woman scorned,' she said to her reflection. Giving her best Marilyn Monroe pout in the rust-flecked mirror, Susie knew she could charm any man without even trying. Except one. But there was still time. Danny Harris wasn't married yet.

'Never say never,' Susie told her reflection.

Tomorrow was a day that would change her life.

* * *

She had been hired ten minutes after entering the building and started work immediately with the promise of those lunches with the boss. Susie had been pleasantly surprised when she saw Harry, an old flame, sitting behind a large desk that first day.

To ensure she got his full attention, she had slipped the red swagger coat from her shoulders and put it over her arm, taking small steps in a black, pencil-slim skirt. Her tiny waist accentuated with a waspy belt over a tight-fitting red sweater, and Susie felt a sliver of satisfaction when she got his immediate attention.

Loosening her grip on the coordinating red box bag that perfectly matched her stiletto heeled shoes, she saw Harry's eyes widen appreciatively and she knew then she had got the job. He had always been a sucker for a pretty face.

'You didn't tell me you worked in the office here.' Susie had purred. 'You naughty boy.' Her eyes took in the whole office with a single sweep of her heavily mascaraed eyes, knowing this was a whole ladder up from Beamers Electricals, the place where she had been a clerk when Evie Kilgaren was a mere cleaner.

But Lenard Haulage was a palace compared to the little wooden hut she had been forced to share with Miss Snooty in Skinner's Yard where she worked next. Evie flaming Kilgaren had gone out of her way to steal the only man Susie ever loved and having become qualified in finance was now in charge of the books there.

'I run the place, lock, stock and wagons.' Harry's eyes had roamed the length of Susie's shapely figure, making her want to squeal with joy. She had this job in the bag – what man could resist... 'Come in, try this chair for size,' he'd said with a wolfish grin and Susie did her best eyelash flutter.

For me? she'd mouthed, as he got up to let her sit behind the desk.

'Do you think you will like working here?' Harry had asked and she'd simpered.

'Of course, especially now I know you work here, too.'

She had given Harry Caraway a deceptively coy smile, vowing this job would bring her just rewards. Being well in with the boss had done her future no harm. No harm at all...

* * *

'Good morning, Lenard Haulage, how may I help you?' Susie Blackthorn asked after fixing the seam of her black stockings and had answered the ringing telephone. This job was everything she had dreamed of. She was in charge of three clerks in a spacious, carpeted office overlooking the pier head. Very posh, she thought. There was plenty to look at from the large windows that let in a good deal of light, and she was treated to long lunches by Harry Caraway, leaving the other clerks to do her work.

Danny Harris's problems were only just beginning she thought. She would not be satisfied until she had ruined him completely, knowing she given Harry an exact copy of Skinner's contacts, accounts details, the lot.

All it would take to ruin Danny's business, initially, would be for Lenard's to undercut Danny's prices. When his business failed, as it most certainly would, she would be there to pick up the pieces. Because the ambitious Evie Kilgaren would have run for the hills by then.

11

Frank Kilgaren had been hiding out at Ada's house in Reckoner's Row since escaping from the institution on the night of the storm. He laid low in the bedroom only creeping out when he was sure no one was in the house or they were in bed asleep.

On this day, Frank opened the door of the bedroom and peered into the darkness of the landing, listening. And only when he was certain Ada, or young Bobby, were not lurking in the shadows, would he make his move. He had something to prove, but he could not do it behind locked doors and high walls.

He did not kill Rene, and he was going to prove it. But only if he remained free. If he was captured, he would never be able to prove his innocence. His only hope was with the help of his daughter, Lucy. The only one of his offspring who gave him the time of day, and who had been writing to him regularly over the last twelve months.

Pulling up the collar of an old jacket he had found in the wardrobe, he knew it would offer little protection from the pre-dawn squall. The sleeves showed his wrists and came only halfway down his back, and he knew that if the jacket had belonged to the big fella, Danny, it would have fitted right enough. But beggars couldn't be choosers. He had certainly learned that much.

The house was silent, save for the gentle snoring of Ada Harris along the landing at the front of the house. The middle door to Bobby's room was closed tight shut, and Frank began to creep down the stairs. Careful not to make a sound. The back bedroom of Ada's house had been his lone sanctuary for the last week or so, but he couldn't stay there forever, so grabbing a slice of dry bread and a cup of cold water, he crept out of the house. It was time to get to the truth. Bring the real killer to justice.

The frosty night air had a biting chill, although what did he expect? Frank Kilgaren thought as he sneaked out of the gate. The sun had sunk below the horizon long ago, and in a short while it would rise again. But he wasn't here to contemplate the weather. He had a job to do, and he had to be quick about it.

Most people were still warmly tucked up in their beds, but not for long, he suspected. Very soon, the streets and alleyways would thunder to the sound of hobnailed boots, belonging to men looking for a day's work on the docks, and would clatter on the cobbles as they headed down to the river with more hope than expectation.

* * *

Pushing the back door of the hairdressing salon just a crack, it was enough to ease the jemmy into the space, and in no time at all the door was open! Closing it quickly behind him, he luxuriated in the peace and quiet of the strange chemical-scented room.

All was still, the only sound being the tick... tick... tick... of the clock on the wall and creeping closer to the stairs, he stopped and listened. All was silent, which gave him cause to let out a long, heart-thumping sigh as the illumination from the waning moon gave him just enough light to check out his surroundings.

To his left was a door with a notice saying 'staffroom, no admission to the public.' At the end of the narrow corridor was a small flight of three wooden steps, which he descended and he could make out the four cubicles, closed off with pink net curtains. A large window, also covered in the same material, was in front of him and to his side was a couple of washbasins and a tall cupboard, which was locked.

'Please forgive me, Lucy,' he whispered, 'but this has to be done...' He prised open the cupboard door before lighting a match, inside was an array of bottles and containers. Powder bleach, hair colourants, hydrogen peroxide, ammonia. What the hell did you do with all these? he wondered. He didn't have a clue. All he wanted was a bottle of dye to put on his dark auburn hair, beard and moustache. Obviously, some knowledge and skill was called for. and he did not have one iota of either. A thought struck him. Should he ask Lucy? Could he...?

* * *

Lucy had received a note, brought by a young lad to the salon. She was shocked when she saw it was from her father, saying he wanted to see her. As she knew that Evie and Danny were going out this evening, Lucy replied on the back of the note telling him to call round about seven, when they would most likely have left the house.

'Are you and Danny still going out tonight,' Lucy asked Evie, trying to keep her voice as normal as possible.

'Yes,' Evie said, not paying much attention, as she was reading an article in the Sunday newspaper about the arrangements for the Royal Coronation in June. 'Doesn't our new queen look fabulous. You wouldn't think she was the mother of two children and will be the most powerful woman in the world.'

'I wonder if she gets her hair permed?' Lucy asked, trying to keep her tone light.

Evie lifted her head from the newspaper and, shaking her head she said, 'I can't imagine our new queen sitting under a hairdryer with a head full of curlers. Do you think she'll reign as long as Queen Victoria?' Lucy didn't answer, obviously daydreaming about some boy or other she met at last night's dance. 'We're going to the pictures,' Evie said, turning the page of the broadsheet newspaper, half listening to 'Family Favourites' on the wireless while the potatoes were roasting in the oven.

'When are you leaving?' asked Lucy, her voice, although casual, raised Evie's suspicions. Lucy wasn't curious about her evenings with Danny usually.

'Why? Do you want to come with us?' Evie said and a wry smile lifted the corner of her lips when another thought struck her. 'Or have you got a visitor coming?'

'No! Of course not,' Lucy answered quickly, her freckled face turning bright red, and Evie raised an eyebrow, her jocular tone was light.

'It's fine, I don't mind if you've got a boy calling, maybe I could meet him.'

'He's very shy.' Lucy sounded annoyed, and hurried to the kitchen, ripping dark green leaves from a savoy cabbage. When she realised her remark would only invite more curious questions from Evie, she called through to the other room, 'I don't even like him that much.'

Evie gave a thoughtful nod. Lucy had a boyfriend. She was growing up fast.

On the other side of the door, Lucy was taking huge gasps of air. She had nearly blurted out everything. She didn't like keeping secrets from Evie, but she knew this one was explosive. She must stay quiet. For all their sakes.

* * *

As soon as Danny and Evie left the house, Lucy bolted the front door, knowing she must be quick. Evie and Danny would be back home by ten o'clock, and she wasn't as experienced as she liked to think she was. With trembling hands, she unlocked the back door and opened it, allowing the father she had not seen for the past six years into the house he once shared with his wife and family.

'You look ill,' Lucy said, sounding much more grown-up than she felt. 'The police are out searching for you. They could even be watching the house.'

'Don't fret, me darlin', I only ever go through the back jiggers,' he answered, looking like a shadow of the person she once knew. Lucy's heart lurched for the man who had only ever shown her love and kindness. 'Please, darlin', help me just this once, and I will be on my way. Nobody will be any the wiser.' There were tears in his eyes and Lucy threw her arms around her father's neck. He couldn't have done the things everybody said he did. 'I took a chance on writing you the note because I was desperate,' Frank said. 'But I have to right the wrongs. I am an innocent man, Lucy, you've got to believe that. I didn't kill your mother. I couldn't...'

'I don't believe you did,' said Lucy. 'I don't think you could do such a thing to the mother of your children.' She put the kettle onto the stove and cut thick slices of bread, thickly slathering it with the butter Ada had brought. 'I don't like keeping things from our Evie,' Lucy said, 'she's been good to me and Jack.'

'I understand that, darlin',' Frank answered, 'and believe me, I don't like it either, but I must prove I didn't kill your mother. The killer is still walking free.'

'She said we were going to go back to Ireland, on the last night we saw her, she said we were all going to live on a farm.' Lucy caught a glimpse of the man her father once was in the gentle radiance of his eyes.

'She said that?' he asked, and Lucy nodded. 'It does my heart good to know she said that,' said her father. 'It took me years to save for the tickets, I didn't earn much and had to pay rent.'

'But why didn't you come back here after your ship had sunk?' Lucy asked and her father slumped into a chair, weak from lack of food and sick with worry.

'I had no memory of what happened to me at first,' he said, looking down at his hands, 'I was rescued by an old farmer, whose wife nursed me back to health.' He drank the scalding tea in one gulp, and she poured another. 'I was a deserter, plain and simple,' he said. 'The authorities would have sent me back to sea. I reckoned that God had saved me for a reason, so I could see my children grow.'

'But how did you know where we were?' Lucy asked and her father shook his head.

'I didn't know to begin with,' he answered, 'but when I discovered you were both on a neighbouring farm, I decided the man up there,' he raised his thumb in the direction of the ceiling, 'had better things lined up for me and mine. The authorities would have stopped me from seeing my children. My wife.' He spoke as if talking to a stranger. 'And when the war was over, I discovered Rene had a lodger,' Frank gave a mirthless laugh. 'A lodger, is that what they call them these days?' He looked up to Lucy, his eyes were now full of despair, and she knew that wasn't the expression of a guilty man. 'My only hope of bringing my family back together was keeping you and Jack in Ireland.'

'So that was why we never went home when all the other children did?'

'I wrote to her, and she answered.' Frank took a deep breath. 'Told me the lodger didn't live in the house any more. I booked a long-distance call to the Tram Tavern the week before, so I could speak to her, and we talked for the first time in years.' Tears shimmered in his eyes. 'We decided, if we were ever to make another go of our marriage, it couldn't possibly be in Reckoner's Row.'

'She didn't say a word to either Jack or me in her letters, all she said was that she had a surprise, and we would like it.' Lucy sat down opposite her father.

'The night she disappeared will stay with me forever,' said Frank, 'because it was all my fault, you see.' He stopped talking and his eyes lost their sparkle. He was in another place, inside his mind, where nobody else was allowed to go.

* * *

Lucy mixed the tint and the peroxide, while he sat in silence. And when she put a towel round his thin shoulders, he gave a start, as if being woken from a dream.

'If I hadn't had Ada's old air-raid shelter to sleep in, I would have been dead long ago,' he said. However, he kept the news that he was now staying in her back bedroom to himself. There was no point in causing his youngest any more problems than necessary.

'Here, have this,' Lucy said, cutting another thick slice of bread when she had finished applying the tint to his hair, and made him some more tea. 'It's not much, but it might keep you going.'

'Good girl,' Frank said, tucking into the bread and tea.

Her father didn't say a word as he devoured the food, obviously starving, 'I'll make you some more, once I've washed off the tint.' She had been taught not to call it hair dye as tint sounded more refined.

She had also been taught to be honest, never tell lies. Yet, she was disguising a man who had escaped from a secure asylum for the criminally insane, for the murder of her own mother. In any other situation like this, Lucy would have been terrified. But she had never felt safer. He was her father. She wanted to fight his corner. When he was arrested six years ago, he did not deny murdering her mother. In fact, he had told the authorities it was all his fault. Not one word in his own defence. Why didn't he speak out?

'You remember when we were all in Ireland together,' Frank said and Lucy nodded. 'I was working hard to earn enough money to bring us all home, collect your mother, and go back to the farm where I was working and living. I then brought you both home. And, thinking I would be arrested for desertion, I laid low.' He paused for a moment, gathering his thoughts. 'But I was told, coming from Cashalree, I wouldn't be arrested.'

'Was Cashalree not in the "Emergency", Da?' Lucy asked her father, knowing the people from the Republic never called the invasion of Europe a 'war'.

Frank shook his head. 'No, we were neutral. Although many of my countrymen did go to war and many died.'

'I feel so sorry for everybody who lost someone,' Lucy said, checking that the tint was working. She had learned so much more about her father in the last few minutes than she had in all the years she had known him, realising that desperation would make a man vulnerable.

'I went to the tavern to see your mother,' Frank told Lucy. 'Evie had no idea I was still alive, like you did.'

'I thought you were my guardian angel,' Lucy answered, and Frank threw back his head and laughed for the first time in six years.

'Did you never look in the mirror?' he asked. 'That beautiful titian hair, those marine-coloured eyes – you didn't get those from your mama.'

'I did have her sense of fun, though,' Lucy said. Her Da was one of the kindest men she knew, when she was growing up. He told her stories from books, which she retold to Jack. 'D'you remember taking me to the wonders of Middle-Earth with those treasured adventures of Bilbo Baggins in *The Hobbit*?'

'I never was one for girl stories,' he told her, thinking back.

'Well, you might have been a couple of times,' Lucy answered, 'because I recall you introducing me to Enid Blyton and *The Magic Faraway Tree*, then one Christmas you gave me a copy of the freckled, mischievous Pippi Longstocking, which I still have on the shelf in my bedroom.'

'I was talking to Rene by the bar...' His voice, almost a groan, continued as if there had been no interruption. '...We were leaving for Ireland on the night boat and I let her out of my sight for just a few minutes.' His face crumpled, as if in pain.

'Where did she go?' Lucy forgot about the books and the adventures, realising now how much she had never known.

'She didn't go anywhere,' Frank answered, 'I did... I went to the gents' before we were due to leave...' He shook his head as if trying to rid himself of an intolerable thought. 'When I came back, she was gone!'

'Did you not go after her?' Lucy asked, surely her mother's abandonment had not been so simple.

'Of course I went after her, but she was nowhere to be found. The streets were deserted. Hailstones pelting the pavement.' He stopped talking and was silent for a moment. 'Little did I know, she was already as good as dead. I should have been there to protect her...'

'So that was why you pleaded guilty?' Lucy said and her father nodded.

12

The following day, Danny was heading to the stable with a new bale of hay on his shoulder and looked up when one of the two large gates opened and he saw a shabby-looking man in a too-small jacket, a flat cap covering his dark brown hair and a woollen muffler pushed up over his bushy black beard and moustache, covering his mouth against the biting cold weather.

'All right, mate?' said Danny cheerfully. 'Can I help you?' He stopped and waited for the man to get nearer. By the look of him a big bowl of Evie's scouse would stick to his ribs and do him the world of good.

'I was wondering if you had any jobs going spare,' the man spoke in a broad Irish accent, but that was nothing unusual around here, there were many men and women who came from Ireland originally and had settled in Liverpool. 'It doesn't have to be much, just a bit of tidying here and there, or making the tea, like?'

Danny thought for a moment, wondering if there was any way he could offer this poor soul a crumb of hope, but he knew if he was to take on any more labour it would ruin his business. And, as his wise and wonderful stepfather, Henry, was wont to say, *there's no sentiment in business.*

'I can see you need something sooner rather than later, mate,' said Danny, wishing things could be different, 'but the truth is, business hasn't been as brisk as I would like and there's only enough work for the lads I've already got.'

'To be sure,' said the man, touching the rim of his flat cap as he shuffled towards the gate, 'thank you kindly anyway.'

'I'll tell you what, though,' Danny called, trying to soften the old fella's obvious disappointment, 'I have heard that Lenard Haulage are looking for men.' *Owing to the fact they've pinched most of my business.* But Danny didn't say as much, and the old man looked a bit confused.

'Lenard Haulage...?' He took off his cap and scratched his head, his auburn eyebrows sloping to the middle of his creased forehead, and Danny thought he looked a little odd close up, and not as old as he first appeared. But no matter.

'It's at the other end of the dock road, you can't miss it. Because it's signposted every few yards.'

The man put his cap back on and once more saluted Danny.

'Many thanks to yer,' he said over his shoulder, 'and may you reach the pearly gates before the divil knows you're dead.'

Danny watched him amble out of the gate, familiar with the Irish platitude, knowing Ada said it all the time. Now he came to think about it, Danny was sure he had seen the old man before, but for the life of him he couldn't think where?

* * *

Frank Kilgaren walked, head down, hands in pockets, ignoring the dock road, busy with working horses moving back and forth between ships and warehouses, flatback wagons vying for road space, the noise from cranes hauling huge bulky merchandise from ship to shore, the sound of men calling to crane drivers, waving them on. Shore-gang riggers bringing ships in and sending them back out again, winching the derricks, opening ship's hatches for the dockers who were preparing loads for transportation on road or sea. The world's trade going back and forth, day in, day out.

He would try his luck at Lenard Haulage, knowing he had just looked his future son-in-law in the eye. Danny Harris didn't even recognise him after Lucy had changed the colour of his hair, beard and moustache from dark auburn to gypsy black. She didn't take much persuasion when, for the first time in six years, he actually spoke. Because from the moment he was arrested and pleaded guilty, he never uttered another word. Not even at his trial.

He still considered he was guilty his wife was dead. The woman he had loved from the moment he set eyes on her as a sweet colleen back in their beloved Emerald Isle was no longer here because of him. And he would never forgive himself for that. He told Lucy he blamed himself. But he wasn't the man who had killed Rene. All he had to do was remain free long enough to get the evidence he needed. And that was the tricky bit…

* * *

'Can I help you?' Susie asked, wondering if this deadbeat tramp shuffling through the door should be thrown out on his ear, but she knew she had to be polite.

'I was wondering if you have any jobs going?' The dishevelled man standing before her gave Susie cause to wrinkle her tip-tilted nose and she was about to tell him to clear off when Harry came back into the office.

'Can I help you, old man?' he asked in a friendly, I-know-I'm-better-than-you, tone.

'He has come to see if we have any jobs going spare?' Susie said wide-eyed, giving Harry a smile of condescending amusement, as if the mere thought of giving this old tinker a moment's work was as far removed as the country he came from.

'The wagon yard could do with a tidy-up,' Harry ignored her, taking pity on this poor man. *There but for the grace of God and all that*... 'Go and see the foreman, tell him Harry sent you. He'll find you something to do, we will talk about wages later, but you won't be disappointed.' Harry knew it was men like this, who had nothing, their pride diminished, who were worth their weight in church roof lead, because they were the desperate and, by the looks of it, destitute. This one had nothing but his ebbing self-respect, which could only be restored by being useful.

Frank Kilgaren didn't realise it would be so easy to get a job. No identification needed. No particulars taken. If he had known, he would have done it sooner.

Lucy had promised to say nothing, knowing he was on a quest to find her mother's killer. In the meantime, Frank knew he had to get out of Ada's back bedroom before he was discovered.

'I know you are going to think me so hard-faced,' he said a few days later, 'but, well you see... Well, it's like this, Sur...' He stepped from one foot to the other and Harry Caraway didn't need to look too deeply to realise that the man had been through a rough time. His ill-fitting clothes were nowhere near robust enough for this weather.

'You need a sub on your wages?' he asked and Frank, feeling a surge of hope, overcome his natural pride, nodded. The other man reached to his inside pocket and took out a wad of pound notes, as thick as his thumb. He peeled off a couple of pounds and handed them to Frank.

'Thank you, kindly, Sur,' Frank touched the peak of his cap, 'I'll work this off in no time at all.'

'I know you will,' said Harry, slowly nodding his head, 'and, seeing as you work here, the sooner you pay it off, the less interest you'll owe.'

Frank hadn't expected to pay interest, but he realised that a firm the size of this one didn't get here by giving money away buckshee. He was so desperate to get some money in his pocket, he would agree to anything. He had been given the address of a lodging house in Beamer Street. And he went to see it after work. This would suit him just fine.

* * *

News of Bert Harris's funeral spread like wildfire.

'Bert's funeral's this coming Friday,' Connie informed all her customers, if by any chance, they had not read the obituary in the *Echo*, 'half past twelve in Saint Patrick's.'

Now that he was dead, forgiving souls who knew him spoke kindly. Others, like Leo Darnel did not show any interest one way or another.

'I'm working tomorrow, queen,' said the stevedore, 'but I'll pop in after work and raise a glass.'

Connie knew many had no interest in Bert, given the life he gave his wife, but Ada would need the support, she was sure.

'What did Danny say about Bert's death when he came in?' Connie asked Angus when they were washing glasses behind the bar.

Angus shook his head. 'You know Danny, he doesn't wear his heart on his sleeve, he likes to keep his own counsel.' Angus lifted the wooden flap of the bar and went to collect more empty glasses. He was sure Connie knew, as far as Danny was concerned, Bert Harris had died years ago. But Danny did say he had gone to see Ada, and gave her a shoulder to lean on. Having put off the duty too long already, he also invited her to the wedding.

* * *

'Hiya, Danny,' Ada had said, 'come in.'

'I wanted to talk to you... Get something off my chest...'

'Well?' Ada said, pouring him a cup of freshly made tea, and Danny raised his eyebrows in surprise, knowing she never made fresh if there was still some in the pot, no matter how stewed it was.

'I should have come round before now, but...' he wasn't going to be a hypocrite and tell her he had been too busy, 'I didn't know if I would still be welcome.'

'And why wouldn't you be?' Ada's Irish inflection was reed thin. 'I've never stopped you coming home.'

'But it's not my home, Ma, and it never was.' He looked at her now and recognised that look of disappointment in her eyes. The look of hopelessness she used to get when she discovered Bert had spent her last coppers. 'You tried to make it good for all of us, and you did. It couldn't have been easy.'

'You're right,' Ada said. He could have come round before now. He could have given her a shoulder to cry on. He could have done her one last good turn and offer to carry Bert's coffin...

* * *

Meggie made her way across the flat piece of land that ran between her house and Ada Harris's. Neither grass nor flowers grew on the ground where two houses once stood during the war, before the Luftwaffe paid a visit and razed the buildings to the ground. The only adornment these days was the rare sparkle of weak February sun hitting the broken glass.

Meggie gripped the mass card. She had obtained it from the local priest at Saint Patrick's church with a donation to the parish fund. Stepping onto the cracked paving stones in Reckoner's Row, she surveyed the tall, three-storey house, so like her own, at the end of the block of smaller terraced houses and realised, for the first time, it had been years since she last visited. How quickly the time had passed. Danny had been living with her and Henry for the last three years and it seemed like only yesterday he left this house. So much had happened.

When Danny was younger, she would come to Ada's house regularly, for that was how she thought of this place: Ada's house, not Bert's. Those were the days when Danny called her 'Aunty Meg' and ran to her with open arms. Most likely for the sweets she brought every Friday night, as that was the night she brought Ada the money for looking after her son.

Opening the black-painted gate at the bottom of the short tiled path that led to the steps, she sighed as a ray of weak sunshine caught the gold band on the third finger of her left hand and, for all her days, she would thank the good Lord above for guiding her to Henry Skinner's door and making an honest woman of her. Even if she was not allowed to keep her darling boy, she knew he was being well cared for by Henry's cousin, Ada, who often said she loved Danny like one of her own. Meggie paid for the privilege, and was glad to do so, it meant she was not so far away and could watch him grow every day into the strong, handsome man he was today.

Reaching the top step, Meggie knocked with a confidence she did not feel, knowing Ada could be quite formidable when she had a mind, and when she heard the distinctive footsteps on the linoleum covered floor on the other side of the door, her heartbeat quickened.

Ada pulled open the front door and the difference between the two women was stark as Ada's hair was covered in the usual turbaned headscarf, while Meggie salt-and-pepper-coloured waves were testament to her weekly visit to the hairdressers on Stanley Road.

'Hello, Meg,' Ada said in those hushed tones used by some who had been recently bereaved, her full-length flowered apron giving a little colour to the black skirt and cardigan underneath, while Meg's warm woollen coat covered a neat pale blue twin set and grey kick-pleat skirt.

'Hello, Ada, I hope you don't mind me calling, I've brought a card.' Meggie stood on the step and held out the mass card. 'I just wanted to let you know me and Henry are thinking about you, and if there is anything you need, you only have to say.'

'Well, don't just stand there like pithy on a rock bun, come in,' Ada said in that forthright way, so recognisable around the dock-side, and she stood to one side. She hadn't expected to see Meggie but was glad the other woman had come. 'I've just put the kettle on,' Ada said over her shoulder as she led the way down the passage towards the kitchen.

'I don't want to intrude, if you're busy,' said Meggie, knowing Ada had a wide circle of friends, but her main friend was Mim Sharp, whom Meggie only knew in passing, as she didn't drink in public houses. 'You've got this place lovely,' remarked Meggie, as the smell of lavender furniture polish wafted through the house. The furniture was old but well cared for and highly polished. The same furniture Meggie remembered from the days when she used to come to see Danny and pay his 'keep' – as Ada called the weekly allowance Meggie gave her to look after her much-loved son.

The two women sat drinking tea and sharing their thoughts about Danny and the wedding before the subject of Bert Harris was aired. Ada wasn't sure what to say to Meggie, who knew more about this family than anybody.

'Do you want me to come over and do the walls?' Meggie asked, knowing when the deceased was brought home, the body was usually laid out in the parlour with the walls covered in white pleated sheets, while a black silk ribbon cross adorned the head of the open coffin with church candles in brass candlesticks beside it. Although Meggie was not surprised when Ada shook her head, knowing she probably had somebody else to make the place fit for Bert's last resting place.

'I'm not bringing him back here.' Ada's voice held a defiant edge and Meggie gently nodded her head. It was an unusual occurrence, given that most families round here would have the body laid out for people to pay their last respects. But, as far as many of the occupants of Reckoner's Row were concerned, Bert Harris did not deserve any respects.

'I've ordered a hearse and one car to take me and Bobby to the church, Danny said he will make his own way with Evie...' Ada's voice trailed, and Meggie felt so sorry for her.

'What about Grace and Bruce?' asked Meggie knowing Ada's daughter had not been home since she married her millionaire businessman.

'She is out of the country, but she's hoping to be back in time for the funeral – or just after.' Meggie leaned forward and patted her hand and Ada gave a wan smile. She was not one for pity and didn't feel she deserved any, especially now, knowing Frank Kilgaren had not killed Rene and her husband, Bert, could have been the killer.

Her eyes trailed to the gas metre cupboard. If people knew what lay inside, would they be so sympathetic?

Ada did not have the courage to look inside the box that held the secret of who killed Rene in case that person was Bert, and if he had not killed Rene, then he certainly knew who did. Even in death he was leading her a merry dance, causing her problems. She owed it to Rene's memory to set things right for Evie. And that was not the only thing that worried her. If Bert knew Frank Kilgaren had not been involved, then the wrong man had spent the last six years locked up for a murder he did not commit. Ada could not stomach the thought of her husband lying in her front room for days before the funeral. The thought gave her icy shivers, and she was having no part of it.

'He haunted me in life,' said Ada, who was adamant, 'and I'll be buggered if he does so in death.'

* * *

'I really don't want to go to Bert's funeral tomorrow,' Evie told Meggie when she called in after work. Meggie who was in the kitchen making a steak and kidney pie for tea lifted her head. 'I'd feel such a hypocrite because I couldn't stand the man.'

'I know, love,' Meggie answered as she crimped the edge of the pie with her finger and thumb. 'I thought he was an idle, greedy man, and Ada didn't deserve a husband like that. She's a grafter, is Ada, and she would have seen more clean plates than full ones if she had to depend on Bert Harris.' She brushed the pale uncooked pastry with a little milk and sighed.

'Danny isn't keen to go either, but he understands he will be there to support the mourners. Ada, most of all. I do know he will help Ada now she's a widow, and I expect he will want your assistance too.'

'You're right,' said Evie, helping Meggie tidy the table, 'I didn't think of it like that. I just assumed Bert would have a pauper's funeral with the least amount of mourners present.'

'Ada would never stand for that,' said Meggie, and Henry who was sat at the table nodded, agreeing with every word. 'She might never have had much, but she would never let on.' Meggie put the pie in the oven and closed the door, wiping floury hands on her apron. 'She's got her pride and wouldn't have it said she didn't give him a proper send-off. After all, he was the father of Grace and Bobby.'

'I will go, for their sake,' said Evie, fixing the tablecloth into position, 'and for Ada.'

'That business with Bert extorting money from Henry upset her more than she ever let on, because every week there was an envelope pushed through our letterbox. No name no signature, just a few pounds a week for months.'

'How did you know it was Ada?' Evie asked, pouring tea into plain cups for the three of them. Knowing Lucy wouldn't be home from work for another hour or so, Evie knew she had time for a cuppa and a catch-up.

'Henry saw her putting the envelope through the letterbox and scurrying back across the debris to her own house every Saturday morning.'

'I begged her to stop,' said Henry, lifting the cup to his lips, 'the debt was not hers, and she should not have to go without, to pay it.' Meggie nodded in agreement.

'We didn't need the money by then, you see,' Meggie continued, 'and that's why we will be there to support Ada.'

'We certainly won't be going to the funeral to pay our respects to a man who didn't deserve any,' said Henry, and Evie was a little surprised to hear that from a man who never said a bad word against anybody. 'We are going to support Ada who paid her dues over the years.'

'More than paid them, I'd say,' Meggie answered. 'She deserved a man like my Henry, or Danny, someone who would do you a good turn whether you needed it or not.'

Evie agreed immediately. She knew Danny would never humiliate Ada, by abandoning the funeral. 'Danny has said he will go but he will not carry the coffin,' she said..

'I carried him long enough.' Danny told them as he came into the kitchen having heard Evie's remark.

'It's not the dead who need you Danny,' Meggie told her son, 'it's the living. And as a family, we have a lot to be grateful to Ada for.'

'She might not be my true mother,' Danny answered, 'but she did her best for me.'

'And if truth be told,' Meggie said with a twinkle in her eye, 'she loved you like one of her own.'

'I'll do my bit,' Danny promised, his deep blue troubled eyes gazing into the eyes of his true mam, the woman who was never allowed to keep him, but always supported him financially and emotionally and helped to make him the man he was today.

Evie smiled, knowing Danny would never have the heart to refuse either mothers' wishes.

13

Ada sat solemnly in the front pew of Saint Patrick's parish church, her son Bobby sitting by her right-hand side, dressed in the good black suit, white shirt and new black shoes she had bought in Henderson's prestigious store in Church Street. She thought Bobby looked smart and very grown-up with his thick dark hair tamed with Brilliantine hair oil. She held her chin high and kept her shoulders back, knowing everything was paid for in full.

Grace had sent the money to pay for the whole funeral, the clothes she and Bobby were wearing and also for the reception after Bert's *terminus* at Ford Cemetery. The reception was being held in the Tram Tavern as Ada could not face a large crowd of people cluttering up her parlour, and she would rather someone else did the cleaning for once. Danny had been at the house from early morning, and when mourners came later, he did the honours by giving them all a warming glass of whisky, as was traditional on these occasions.

Danny and Evie crept up the aisle towards Ada and Bobby, who were kneeling in the front row, their heads bent to meet their joined hands. Danny noticed Susie sitting directly behind Ada, but it wasn't Susie who drew his attention, it was the man she was with. Harry Caraway, dressed in a black suit with thickly padded shoulders, was a very close associate of Leo Darnel, who, Danny observed, was conspicuous by his absence.

Ada's eyes were closed when she sensed a small disruption near her. When she opened her eyes, Ada could hardly contain her joy as Grace, accompanied by her millionaire tycoon husband, Bruce D'Angelo, joined them in the front pew. Followed by Danny and Evie. However, Ada's moment of pride and joy at the reunion of her family was fleeting. What if the man they were now burying, she wondered, was the same man who had killed Evie's mother? The thought turned Ada's blood to ice.

Ada hadn't been sure if anybody would turn up to say goodbye to the old bugger, and her jaw dropped when the pews on the right-hand side of the church began to fill.

'There's a few long-lost acquaintances, an' all,' Ada whispered. 'Those who probably haven't heard of Bert's little blackmailing schemes.'

Danny didn't say anything, aware that even on the day of his funeral, Ada could not forgive Bert for the shame he had brought upon her family over the years.

Turning her head, she saw people shuffling to the end of the pews behind them. Even at a time like this, Ada was unable to ignore the goings-on around her. She nodded to Susie Blackthorn, who had brought her not-so-young man and was glad the girl had seen sense and was courting someone, instead of mooning over Danny.

* * *

Susie Blackthorn knew she looked every inch a grieving mourner, dressed from head to toe in black. She sat immediately behind Ada and Bobby Harris and when Grace, her one-time friend arrived with her millionaire husband, she realised she could not outdo her. Peering through the dark lace mantilla, Susie sat upright, her shoulders straight and back as Ada and Grace were doing, and she pursed her lips, knowing a real mink coat when she saw one.

Grace had completely forgotten herself, thought Susie, knowing her so-called friend had not stepped foot in Reckoner's Row since her wedding to Bruce D'Angelo three years ago. Honeymooning all over the world, Grace mixed with the rich, famous and elite. Whilst she, having been her best friend for donkey's years, had not received so much as a postcard.

Barely able to drag her eyes from the fabulous coat and matching hat Grace was wearing, Susie noticed that Ada looked every inch the stoic matriarch of her family. *Ada will be loving this*, thought Susie. Having her family around her, reunited for the first time since Grace's luxurious wedding at the Cheshire country estate, which had been passed down to Grace's husband when his father died.

Susie's eyes rested on Evie. Smug little Evie, who leeched Danny's strength and was nothing without him. She recalled that Grace had told her about the day she had watched from her bedroom window and witnessed Evie, that stuck-up madam, being flung into the gutter by her mother's fancy man and rescued by Danny. Evie had no friends at that time, and Susie suspected the girl from the gutter would be invisible if it wasn't for Danny's film-star looks and captivating charm. *Whereas I would be Delilah to his Samson.* Susie preened. *Hedy Lamarr to his Victor Mature...*

A strong hand squeezed her arm and, as if brushing the sleeve of her coat, she pushed the hand away, not giving Harry Caraway, the general manager of Lenard Haulage, a second glance. He was here for one reason, and one reason only, and that was to show Danny she wasn't in need of the rare scraps of attention he threw her way. She could have any man she wanted. She was in charge of her own office and the company secrets, while Danny was scraping around for work. Because *she* was the one in charge. The one who held the ledgers that told the true story of Lenard Haulage, who could undercut Danny's haulage prices. She was the one who was in a position to break Danny, who so publicly ditched her three years ago.

She knew Evie was ringing round every business in Liverpool, beseeching warehouse managers and ship's companies to put work Danny's way. But Susie knew Skinner & Son could never match the low prices Lenard Haulage charged. If truth be told, she knew Lenard's did not need the work. The firm was a cover for other nefarious practices, which only she –the office manager– and the goon beside her, knew about.

Danny's fortunes could all have been so different, she mused, if only he had picked her instead of that piece of work, Evie Kilgaren. And, for as much as she should give Danny a wide berth for the way he had so publicly denounced her, she couldn't. He was *her* Danny, from the moment she set eyes on him when she moved into Reckoner's Row as a young girl. He was playing football with other nondescript lads from neighbouring streets. Quick, lithe and athletic, he didn't even look up when her father helped her down from the back of the removal wagon, like all the other boys did. He was a challenge even as a boy and in no time, she had made friends with his sister, Grace.

What Susie wanted Susie got. All except Danny Harris – or Danny Skinner as he was now known – she thought, clenching her teeth together.

* * *

Ada's eyes widened a little when she caught sight of Henry and Meggie Skinner, who had also come to pay their respects. They were the last people Ada had expected to see after the way Bert had relieved Henry of a lot of his money when he blackmailed him to keep quiet about Meggie being Danny's real mother.

But everybody found out at the Netherford Fete, and nobody thought any less of Danny or Meggie – but they all turned against Bert, and for a short while even herself.

Many of the mourners were tavern customers, and Ada suspected Mim and Connie had played a part in making sure she had some decent support after what *he* had put her through.

Ada had asked the new priest to deliver the eulogy, sure in the knowledge that there weren't many in the congregation who would have a good word to say about Bert Harris. Father O'Shea had taken down the few particulars, which Ada had given him. Details like the year she and Bert married, where he had worked, what he had done during the Great War, explaining why he walked with a limp after some of his toes were shot off saving his unit in the trenches. Although that was a matter for debate, thought Ada, knowing he would do anything to get out of war service – even sustaining a self-inflicted Blighty wound.

However, she had never let the secret slip to anybody. Nor the fact that when he was held up at gunpoint, supposedly protecting the dock warehouses, he wasn't defending them, he was helping himself. He never worked again after that, and nor did he snitch on the gang who robbed the warehouse. All she knew about the this episode was that Bert was never without the price of a pint or a packet of cigs again after the dockside heist.

'...Albert Sidney Harris worked hard at his chosen career...' said Father O'Shea, and Ada felt every muscle in her body tense. The new priest was more empathetic than the older priests, probably because he hadn't known the old rogue. The young priest hadn't been at Saint Patrick's when her husband had been so publicly run out of Reckoner's Row.

Staring straight ahead, Ada was deep in thought, but her ears were cocked for low whispers, or any kind of interruption that would contradict the priest's declaration: 'a man who was liked by everybody and loved by his family' – because nothing could be further from the truth. She was waiting for a wagging tongue to inform the new priest that Bert's chosen career had been blackmail and obtaining money with menace and fraternising with racketeers. His eminence may not have been so complimentary about a man who, behind closed doors, was a bully who was given to violent outbursts, and content only when he was drinking beer, smoking baccy, or betting on anything that moved.

But, of course, nobody did. This area of dockside community was full of tough, hard-working Irish Catholics who would never defy or disrupt the parish priest when he was speaking.

'Since the 1840s, the population of Liverpool swelled with Irish immigrants after the failure of the potato crop,' said the priest. 'The great starvation drove many from their homes in search of survival. So, some might say, it was inevitable Albert would follow in the footsteps of his countrymen...'

She gave a contemptuous snort, which echoed in the silent church, and Ada quickly masked the sound with a clearing of her throat. Her husband wasn't one of those men who came over, looking for work and providing for his family, which was her role when he came back from the trenches. Some days, Ada recalled, she had to squeeze a penny so tight, she was sure she could hear it scream.

After the eulogy, Father O'Shea asked the congregation to say a silent prayer for the repose of Albert Sidney Harris's soul and Ada's knees protested something shocking as she lowered herself to the burgundy leather kneeler studded with shiny brass tacks.

Closing her eyes, she lowered her forehead onto tightly balled fists, for all the world looking like a woman deep in prayer. And she would blush scarlet if anybody in this church could see the terrible thoughts running amok inside her head. She was relieved he was gone, suspecting that every other member of the congregation felt the same. This was his last journey, and she really shouldn't think ill of the dead, but Ada was sure she knew exactly where Bert Harris was heading, and it would take more than the prayers of this congregation to save his heathen soul.

There had been many sleepless nights for Ada since Bert's shock admission that he *knew* Frank Kilgaren was not Rene's killer. And in that moment when he confessed to knowing this to be the absolute truth, Ada wondered if she could trust one word that the snake with the forked tongue ever uttered.

She had not dared to open the wooden box, brought back to the house along with a few other measly belongings. Ada hoped, when Bert received the last sacrament, and was laid to rest, he would be able to look his Maker in the eye. But she doubted that very much. She shuddered in the cold church, but it wasn't the draught creeping round her ankles that froze her to the bone. It was knowing the contents of that dark cupboard in her front parlour may hold the evidence that could change or end somebody's life.

14

Meggie slipped from the church to go and help Connie and Mim, who had been busy getting everything ready for the funeral party. Cups and saucers were laid out next to a huge urn where the mourners could get a hot cup of tea after the church service and the long trip to the freezing cemetery.

'Let's clear away the cups now,' said Mim when she was sure everybody had had a cup of steaming hot tea. 'There's some here who won't put their hand in their pocket if they can get free tea all day and will never buy a drink from behind the bar.'

'Trust you to think of the profits, Mim.' Connie looked to Meggie, who gave a gentle laugh.

As the day wore on, more people joined the funeral throng in the Tram Tavern, men who had finished work came in to pay their respects, more for the family's benefit than for Bert's. Also, to fill their empty bellies with sandwiches, pork pies and homemade sausage rolls donated by the mothers of Reckoner's Row, the table replenished many times.

'This'll keep the cold out and stick to your ribs,' Mim said as she and Meggie filled bowls with hot scouse from a huge cauldron used specially for such an occasion. Large plates of crusty bread and rolls of butter were placed on the table for everyone to help themselves. And the bar was filled to bursting with people who knew that even though the country was still suffering food rationing, they were sure to get a good feed from Ada.

Eyes bulged when they saw silver salvers of ox tongue and boiled ham on the long tables which were draped in immaculate white tablecloths, curtesy of the D'Angelo shipping line.

Ada knew if she had acquired half as much food from Leo Darnel, she would have been paying through the nose for his black-market meat for a long time to come. But thankfully, she thought, sitting near the long table, her daughter and beloved son-in-law had spared no expense and the tables groaned under the weight of food.

'Nobody can say Ada Harris did not put on a good spread,' she said to Meggie and Mim a short while later when they were having a well-earned mothers' natter.

'Of course not, Ada,' Meggie interjected when she saw Mim, who, she was sure, was going to pop Ada's inflated pride with a sarky comment.

'Has anybody seen our Bruce and Grace?' Ada asked after a couple of fortifying sherries.

'I'm sure I saw them earlier,' said Mim, collecting empty plates from her seated position. She looked at Meggie and whispered, 'It's *our* Bruce now, is it?' As mother-in-law of the tavern's landlord, one time police inspector, Angus McCrae, Mim could not say she was mother-in-law to a millionaire, but she certainly wouldn't want anybody else for her Connie

Mim and Ada had been friends since before the Great War, when Ada came over from Ireland to work in her aunt's lodging house – the one that was now the Harris family home. The two women were in constant competition with each other, one was always trying to outdo the other, and although they rarely saw eye-to-eye, they were still the best of friends and the first one either of them turned to in a time of crisis.

'Me and Grace had a lovely natter earlier,' Mim said to Ada, noting that, dressed in a good black coat and hat, she looked every inch the grieving widow even though she had not seen her estranged husband for the last three years.

'She's good like that,' Ada said, patting her velvet hat, 'very *hopsitable*, my Grace, she'll talk to anybody.' She was peeved her only daughter talked to Mim before she passed the time of day with her own loving mother.

'You'll have nobody to worry you now, Ada,' Mim said. 'Nobody can say you didn't give Bert a good send-off.'

Ada, cocking her head to one side like a little bird listening for a cat, narrowed her eyes. 'Be careful of the words you say, Mim. Keep them soft and sweet, because you never know from day to day which one's you'll have to eat.'

'I don't know what you mean,' Mim's eyes widened as she stroked a row of pearls at her throat. 'I didn't mean any offence.' Mim, irritated at her friend's high-handed attitude, directed her remark to Meggie, who said nothing, giving only a sympathetic smile.

'Take no notice of me,' Ada said. 'My words came out stronger than intended.' She took off her black hat and looked striking in her black two-piece and high-necked white blouse. 'I'm just having a bit of an off day.' But her thoughts were scathing, knowing the tavern was making a small fortune at the moment.

'Oh, here she is now,' Mim smiled as the door opened, and there was a gentle hush that descended over the room.

Ada stood to see who had just come into the smoke-filled bar. Usually, the only time the bar went so quiet was when Leo Darnel or one of his cohorts came in looking for trouble, which Connie and Angus were well able to deal with. But Ada was not expecting, or in any way ready for, what she saw.

Standing on the other side of the room was Bruce with his arm round Grace's shoulders and in Grace's arms was a well-wrapped bundle of cherubic contentment. Her jaw dropped in astonishment and Ada's eyes were as round and wide as saucers.

'It can't be?'

The people in the bar parted to make a clear pathway for Ada, who had never been lost for words, walking towards her daughter who was holding the baby with the love and pride of a new mother.

'When? Where? How?' Ada could not voice the thoughts scrambling round inside her head as a huge smile stretched her glowing face. 'I mean... You didn't say... You never told me... What is it? What does it weigh?'

'Bloody hell, Ma, let her shoehorn a word in,' Bobby said with a grin, and Grace stepped forward, proudly placing the bundle into Ada's eager arms.

'Ma,' said Grace, whose huge smile showed off expensive, perfectly straight, white teeth. 'Meet Niamh. Your granddaughter.' Grace watched as her mother's jaw dropped and her eyes were as wide as side-plates.

Ada gazed in awe at the most perfect, peachy, paragon of angelic innocence. Her eyes and her heart melting. 'Hello, Niamh,' she said softly, so proud she could burst with happiness on what should have been the saddest day of her life. 'I am your grandma, and I am so very, very pleased to meet you.' Ada could not take her eyes from the precious bundle and her voice dropped to a whisper. 'Shall I let you in to a secret...? You have the very same name as *my* mammy.' Tears of joy welled in her eyes and for Ada there was nobody else in the room as she continued to talk in hushed tones to the sleeping baby. 'Your mammy and daddy have picked the perfect name for you, because do you know something, there was another little girl called Niamh, just like you. Her daddy was called Manannan, and he was the god of the sea.' Ada looked up and gave her daughter and son-in-law, Bruce, a smile that told them they had done a good thing, a special thing. 'Niamh with the golden hair, she rode her white horse and married Oisin, and they lived together in Tir-na-nOg. Yes, they did...'

The baby's mouth formed a perfect O as if she understood every word and Ada's eyes took on an expression Grace had never seen before. They were full of wonder and delight. Warmth radiated from her, and Ada was oblivious to anything or anyone except this miraculous creation.

'I would have brought her to the house,' Grace tried to make her words light-hearted, knowing she was about to say something that would not go down well with her mother. 'The little madam didn't want to settle for Nanny.'

'Nanny?' Ada's brows creased.

'Nanny Jane, she has been with us since we found out we were expecting.' Grace looked to Bruce, her eyes pleading for assistance.

'We are so lucky to have her,' Bruce said quickly his arm back round his wife's shoulders, 'she has been a nanny to the children of some very famous people...'

However, as Grace suspected, Ada did not take the news well, obvious by her interruption.

'The children of Reckoner's Row do have nannies,' said Ada in a pithy, no-nonsense tone, 'their grandmothers!' The soft lilt had turned to steel, giving her daughter cause to shrink a little, knowing her mother was the only person in the world who could make her feel this way.

'She'll come round,' Bruce whispered to the wife he adored. 'The sherry seems to have loosened her tongue.'

'Not that she needs any help in the loose tongue department,' Grace smiled, grateful she had Bruce to lean on. His words, like balm on troubled waters, gave her strength, and she knew she had done the right thing by moving as far away from the dockside as possible. If only she could persuade her mother to do the same. But Grace knew Ada would never leave here, where her family and friends lived cheek by jowl.

'And they certainly don't employ strangers to raise their children, while they go out to work.' Ada nodded to Mim, resisting the opportunity to keep her feelings to herself.

Grace forced a smile. Why did her mother have to bring everything back to the dockside? 'I must go and chat to Meggie.' There was no mistaking the inference, Ada had been paid to raise Danny so Meggie could work and keep a roof over both their heads. While Grace would never have to work again. Not unless she wanted to.

Grace sighed when she thought about where she would be now if she had not married Bruce. She would have had to sing for her supper, like her mother and Meggie had to work to keep body and soul together. Mersey mothers who had never taken the easy way out, knowing it would have been a blessing to be given the option.

Today was not the time for nit-picking about who was rearing whose children, Ada realised, her family were all back together again. This delightful gathering of family and friends was the only decent thing Bert Harris had left her with, she thought, reluctantly handing back her granddaughter.

'Would you like a drink, Ada?' her cousin, Henry, asked, getting up from his seat, and Ada lifted her hand, shaking her head.

'I think I've drunk enough sherries to sink a battleship, but do you know what I would like most of all?' Ada was feeling the effect of the alcohol and realised she had not eaten a thing all day. 'I would love a cup of tea.'

'A cup of tea coming right up,' said Henry, who knew his cousin was not accustomed to alcohol, and realised the community would be very open-handed at a gathering such as this. Ada had mingled, thanking people for coming to pay their respects, accepting a drink from most of them. It was the thing to do on occasions like this.

'No thank you, Henry,' said Ada. 'I'm going home now to have a nice cup of tea and a bit of supper, then I am off to my bed.'

Feelings were running high as the drink flowed, she could see, and some people who had not forgotten the past things Bert Harris had done were beginning to voice their recollections as the beer loosened their tongues.

* * *

Although Danny did not wish to defend a selfish man who gave Ada nothing but heartache and misery, he was not going to have her day ruined by people who had initially accepted her hospitality.

'Ada's life will be much better now that she is free from the worry of him turning up out of the blue,' Danny whispered to Evie.

'She's going home by the look of it,' Evie said and could see the small muscle in Danny's jaw twitch. 'Maybe we should go too?' She wanted to get him away before there was any trouble.

'I'm off, too, now, Ma,' Danny said, finding it strange after three years to call the woman who reared him, but who was not his real mother, by the name of 'Ma.' But it would have been stranger still to call her Mrs Harris – or even Ada!

'Thank you for coming, Danny, it was very good of you.' Ada's tone was formal as she tilted her cheek to accept a kiss, something Danny remembered of old. His insides tightened. For, as strange as it had been not to call her 'Ma', it was equally peculiar to be thanked for attending an occasion that would be deemed essential in any other circumstances.

'Are you going now, Danny?' Susie said, elbowing her way through the throng. Her companion, Harry Caraway, had long since left the funeral gathering and Susie had chosen to stay on, not wanting to miss anything. 'I do worry about going past the jigger when it's dark, Danny. You never know who's lurking down a dark entry.'

'I'm sure nobody will bother you, Susie,' Danny said drily, 'and there are plenty of people around if you shout loud enough.' He knew that if there was one thing Susie could do, it was make a bloody noise.

'Thank you for coming, Susie,' Ada said, giving the trouble-maker a hard, direct stare, knowing the girl did her best to come between Danny and Evie every chance she could.

'Don't mention it,' Susie smiled, letting Ada's warning glare sail right over her head, batting Ada's words away like swatting a fly. 'I wouldn't have missed it for the world.'

'I can believe that.' Ada knew Susie was never away from her door when Danny lived there, but since the summer fete in Nether-ford, three years ago, when Danny went to live with his real mother, Meggie and his stepfather, Susie had never visited once.

'I'll call in and see you tomorrow, Grace,' Susie said. 'We have a lot to catch up on.'

'Sure, we have,' Grace said with a wry smile. In her regular letters her mother had given her every detail of the people of Reck-oner's Row and, by the look of it, Susie was still as self-centred and selfish as ever. Thinking only of herself, with no thought for anybody else.

'I think I've had one too many, and need somebody to lean on,' Susie's words were suddenly slurred. 'You might have to walk me to my door, Danny.' Susie knew Danny was too much of a gentleman to let a tipsy girl walk home on her own, even if it was only a few doors down the row.

'Dan, I just need to ask your opinion?' Bobby was stone-cold sober and had heard every word. 'Can I speak to you for a minute?' He immediately saw what Susie was up to. The girl was obviously trying to come between Danny and Evie and that was not on, he wouldn't stand by and let her do her best to ruin his brother's happiness. Bobby gave Evie the nod, as much to say *watch her,* knowing how conniving Susie could be, especially when she hooked her arm through Danny's. Evie nodded. She knew Susie of old and knew what she was up to, trying to get her talons into Danny. But she also knew that Danny had eyes for nobody but her and that made Evie feel like the luckiest woman in the world.

'I'll see you back at *ours* when you're ready, Danny,' Evie matched Susie Blackthorn's unrelenting glare. She noticed the other girl's hands curling round Danny's arm as she swayed from side to side, unsteady on her stilettos. Her peroxide blonde hair, which earlier had been Veronica-Lake-peek-a-boo perfect, was now a bedraggled mess. She was saying her goodbyes like a seasoned performer addressing her audience when Evie unfurled her from Danny and guided her towards the door. 'Come on, Susie, I'll walk with you as far as your gate, we don't want you falling over in the street.'

15

'You look a bit out of place,' Danny said in the dockside café, when he brought back scalding tea in thick white mugs on sturdy saucers.

'I don't feel out of place,' Grace, dressed in an expensive beaver lamb coat that cost more than a docker's yearly wage, accepted the tea. For all her knowledge of the high life, she understood the dock road like the back of her hand, and the canteens and cafés. She had even worked in one as a Saturday girl when she was younger and felt very much at home sitting here opposite her older brother. Grace refused to acknowledge the fact that Danny, this good-natured, handsome man she had known all her life who had grown into the kind of man any girl would be proud to call her brother, did not have the same blood running through his veins as she did. He had been there for her when she was growing up, encouraged her to follow her dreams.

'How's Ma?'

'She's in good spirits, considering,' Grace answered, lighting an American cigarette, much longer than their English equivalent. 'She's devastated that you haven't asked her to the wedding, though.' Grace did not pull her punches where Danny was concerned, and why should she? He would be the same with her, she was sure. Danny was one of the only people whose opinion she trusted. Being surrounded by 'yes' men and sycophants got tiresome very quickly, and she couldn't trust a word any of them said, knowing they were trying to curry favour with her husband.

'I could've sworn I asked her before the funeral,' said Danny, 'but she had a lot to think about with people coming and going – the furthest thing from her mind would be a wedding. I'll go and remedy that today,' Danny said. 'You know what I'm like, always thinking about work – I leave the wedding stuff to Evie.' He paused for a moment, thinking. 'It was only when I left the tavern, the night of the funeral, which got me thinking...'

'About what?' Grace asked, blowing a long stream of smoke so elegantly she was causing quite a stir among the carters who stopped off for a mid-morning bacon and egg butty .

'As I was leaving the funeral,' Danny looked out of the steamed-up window, seeing nothing, 'Ma thanked me for coming.'

'What's wrong with that?' asked Grace, lifting the cup to her lips.

'It's not what she said,' Danny explained, 'it's the way that she said it... ever-so-politely, like I was a neighbour or a long-lost acquaintance of the deceased.' Danny could have bitten his tongue off. He had not intended to voice his discontent, especially to Grace, who had not been home for the past three years, but he could not stop himself. His dissatisfaction poured out like water through a weir. 'I felt like I had been verbally slapped in the face, to be honest. And thinking about it now, she must be feeling the same way about the wedding.'

'I always thought you were quicker on the uptake than that, Dan,' Grace said as Danny wiped the window and looked out onto the dock road, unable to look Grace in the eye. 'Let's face the fact, it wasn't her fault Bert was such a bad old dog. He wouldn't have known if you were carrying his coffin, but she would.'

Danny sighed, feeling ashamed of his ignorant behaviour towards the woman who had brought him up. 'The misery and hardship Bert Harris put her through, and she kept most of it hidden.'

'The best thing she did was to throw him out.' Grace ground the half-smoked cigarette into a tin ashtray advertising Cain's Bitter. 'She's only known peace of mind in the last three years. She told me so when she wrote.'

'Does she write often?' Danny asked. He missed catching up with the family news. Bobby didn't say much about his mother, unlike Grace, who told him everything, and made him see that, for as much as he loved his birth mother, Meggie, and Henry with all his heart, Ada had been the one who had to borrow from Leo Darnel or Mim Sharp to pay off her husband's gambling debts or put food on the table. And he realised, no matter whose blood runs through your veins, the thing that makes your heart beat a little stronger is the people you call family.

'Every week, without fail,' Grace said with a wry smile, 'she writes and tells me anything and everything. Births, marriages and deaths, or as she calls it – hatches, matches and dispatches.' They both laughed. 'She saw the phrase in some newspaper, and thought it sounded very clever and sophisticated.'

'Aye,' said Danny, 'if there's one thing Ma likes more than anything else it's a man who is clever with words.' He looked over the Senior Service cigarette he was about to light.

'Or woman!' Grace shifted in her seat, looking most put out at the insinuation, while Danny shook his head, making her frown.

'No,' he explained, 'a woman who is good with words is a threat because Ma's always getting hers mixed up.'

Grace smiled. It felt so good to be back in her old stomping ground, and although she would have no wish to live among the warehouses and wharves permanently, she needed to get back to her roots every so often. The waters of the River Mersey ran through her veins and every now and then she needed to replenish it. 'I love it when she gets her words mixed up.' Grace beamed over her teacup. 'And she won't be corrected. Do you remember the glares she used to give us when we tried?'

'Don't I just?' Danny laughed, he missed talking over old times. 'They were fierce those glares. I used to hide under the table.'

'Give over! You never did,' Grace laughed. 'You were the one who got away with murder. I remember asking you to speak to her if our pocket money was late or we wanted more. She loved it when you used to come over all shop steward and say: *Now listen Ma, I think we need to go into arbitration for a pocket-money rise.*'

Danny threw his head back and let out a burst of unrestrained laughter, and it did Grace's heart the world of good to hear that familiar sound. 'I remember,' he said, shaking his head and wiping away a happy tear with the pad of his hand. 'I wonder where I got the courage to speak to her like that.'

Their conversation went on over another cup of tea, then another, until finally they had exhausted every topic, and Danny was convinced his wedding would not be the same without the only family he had known for most of his life.

'I'll call around after tea,' he said to Grace, and she nodded.

'Ma is going to be ecstatic,' Grace said. *Unbearable – but ecstatic.*

* * *

Susie was looking out of the window of her plush office, which still smelled of paint and linoleum. The dock road beyond the busy haulage yard was bustling with activity and she dreamed of what her life would be like if only she could get away from here.

Look at Grace, Susie thought, all her friend had to do was sing a few songs on an ocean liner, catch the eye of the millionaire owner and then, boof, she was set for life and forgot who her real friends were. *While I'm stuck in this godforsaken place.*

Turning from the window, she sighed, she would have a word with Grace, see if she could get her a spot on an ocean-going liner. Because she had no intentions of sticking round here forever. When she put Danny Harris out of business once and for all, she would be off, and she was never coming back. 'And let's see if lady muck Kilgaren sticks around then, or will she do what her mother did, and go hunting for the next rich man who wants to spoil her rotten?'

16

MARCH

As March winds blew in off the Mersey, Grace watched her husband put the last of the suitcases into the boot of the gleaming Bentley. For the past week she and her beautiful baby daughter spent their time in Reckoner's Row with her mother, giving Nanny Jane the time off, seeing as Bruce was away on business. She had loved coming home to see her mother, who had spoiled her granddaughter rotten, picking her up the moment she so much as sighed. However, Grace did draw the line at allowing her mam to ply her granddaughter with chocolate, which had come off ration in February.

Closing the boot, Bruce went over to Ada, gave her an affectionate kiss on the cheek and took his beloved daughter from Ada's loving, if sometimes overbearing, arms and handed Niamh to the nanny sitting in the back of the car.

'Don't go on, Ma,' Grace told Ada when she saw her mother's expression darken at the sight of another woman raising her precious granddaughter. 'Bruce said it will do little Niamh the world of good if her mother is rested, and to be honest, I don't mind letting someone else take the strain now and again.'

'Take the strain?' Ada's eyes were like saucers. She had never heard the like. 'In my day, that was called child-rearing and I was always very proud to raise my own children thank you very much.' She shrugged her well-padded shoulders and pursed her lips.

'And other people's too,' Grace added. 'Do you think Meggie would have let another woman raise her child if she didn't have to?'

'That's my point,' said Ada, 'you have the money and the time to raise your own child.'

'I don't, though, Ma,' Grace said. 'For as much as it goes against everything I believe in, I must be at my husband's side. He has a lot of meetings and events to attend in the name of the D'Angelo Shipping Line. I have to be by his side.'

As Grace climbed in the car beside her husband who was driving, Grace felt that sinking feeling that always followed a meeting with her mother, who never failed to remind her she was a girl from the backstreets of Liverpool and not to get above herself.

'I'll see you at the end of June,' Grace told her mother. 'It's not that far off.' She wished that Danny and Evie had accepted her invitation to have their wedding in the little village church in Cheshire and the reception at Grace Hall, the name Bruce had given their palatial home after their own marriage. But they wanted all the neighbours and friends to attend, so the Tram Tavern it would be.

'If you're sure you can spare the time,' Ada said, mentally kicking herself for the icy atmosphere she caused, after she had been so thrilled to have them all here. But Grace's departure always left her with that tug of confusion. Glad Grace had done so well for herself, but sad that she had to live so far away.

* * *

'I've just had the strangest telephone call,' Evie said on the Monday morning after Grace and her family had left to go back to Cheshire.

Danny's forehead creased when he came into the office and Evie asked him, 'Since when did you decide you are selling the yard to Lenard Haulage?'

Danny shrugged, looking equally bewildered, as he crossed the office and planted a kiss on her cheek. 'I'm as baffled as you are,' he answered, perching on the edge of the desk. He loved having Evie so close, even though he worked in the yard, or was on the road, knowing she was doing a sterling job keeping everything running smoothly – a far cry from the days when Susie Blackthorn ran the office. 'What exactly did he say?'

'*She*,' Evie answered, 'she asked when would be the most convenient time to arrange a meeting for Mr Caraway to discuss the takeover of Skinner & Son?'

'What woman?' asked Danny. 'I haven't spoken to any woman about the yard, or anything else for that matter.' And he certainly had no intentions of selling up either.

'She said her name was Miss Peabody, but I'm sure I recognised the voice.'

Danny shook his head. Skinner & Son, the name he kept when he bought the haulage yard from Henry Skinner for just one pound, was in a prime position close to the north-end docks and huge warehouses. He and the men he employed were well respected for being honest, fair, and did not let the client down. For how long, though? Danny wondered, but he was not going to voice his worries. Evie was excited about their forthcoming wedding, and he was not going to let anything spoil her enjoyment. 'If she rings again, you can tell Miss Peabody from me, this place is not for sale.'

'Thank goodness for that,' Evie answered on a sigh, visibly relieved to hear that their business was not going to be sold off. Lenard's might be top dog on the dock road, she thought, knowing the new firm had plenty of wagons and men, but Skinner's had loyal clients who had been with the company for years. 'I know we haven't got a fleet of wagons as big as Lenard's, but we are still a viable concern.' *But only just,* Evie thought. Nevertheless, she did not want to worry Danny about business affairs when he must surely be worrying about Ada.

'Business will pick up when the weather warms up a bit,' said Danny, knowing they still had a good stable of horses who didn't break down or cost a fortune in fuel. 'Everything looks bleak at this time of year.'

'I believe you,' Evie said nodding. *But many wouldn't.* However, she did not voice the fact, but wished Danny's positive outlook would rub off on her. But she was far too practical. Her job was to second-guess the future and minimise the risk. And if business carried on going downhill, in the same way it had been going, she doubted they would still be in business by the time of the wedding – *if they could afford to get married.* 'I have every faith in you my love,' Evie said as she stood up to put the folder she had been working on in the filing cabinet, and a low and pleasant hum warmed her blood when Danny caught her round her slim waist and kissed away her worries with a passion they were both finding increasingly difficult to resist.

Evie felt she was melting, and imagined she was sliding to the floor in a puddle of hormones and liquid lust. Every skin cell tingling, every nerve fired by the touch of his lips upon hers gave her heart a jumpstart, causing it to slam against her ribcage.

He stopped abruptly, looking to the floor, before letting his gaze drift up to her face, his eyes glazed as he brushed his hand across that familiar scarlet heat burning her cheeks. Danny promised he would respect her wishes to wait until they got married before they consummated their love for each other, and at times like this, in the heat of his ever-growing passion, Evie wished he would break his promise, but she was far too shy to say so.

Danny turned away, his long strides devouring the floor. As he reached the door, the telephone startled Evie out of the deep contemplation Danny's kisses evoked and he lightened the charged atmosphere by saying: 'If that's Miss Busybody, tell her I'm out and you don't know when I'll be back.' Danny began to whistle as he withdrew from the office and closed the door behind him. If she had the strength, Evie would have laughed, knowing he had deliberately got the caller's name wrong.

'Good afternoon, Skinner & Son.' Evie took a deep breath to steady her racing heart, and she was surprised to hear the same voice she'd heard earlier this morning. 'No, I am sorry, Miss Peabody,' Evie said, 'Mr Skinner is not available to take your call, he is out on business, and I do not know when he will be back,' Evie gave herself a mental pat on the back for being professional enough not to call the woman by the wrong name. 'However, I shall tell him you called, *again*.' The emphasis on the last word did not go amiss, she could tell by Miss Peabody's tone.

'Please do,' Miss Peabody said stiffly, 'it is in his own best interest. Goodbye.' The telephone clicked and the purr of the dialling tone left Evie staring at the black Bakelite receiver, bemused. Why would anybody want to buy a small firm like Skinner's when there were plenty of other premises that could be purchased at a much cheaper price than Lenard's were offering?

'It's in his own best interest,' Evie repeated the statement in the same hoity-toity voice of Miss Peabody and her head wobbled from side to side. Placing the receiver in its cradle, she sniffed. 'Well, we will soon see about that,' she said aloud, knowing there must be something she could do to drum up business. Although being a hauliers and not a branch of Woolworths, they could not have a winter sale to keep the wolf from the door. She sighed and ran her fingers through her soft, honey-coloured curls. What could they possibly do? She didn't want to tell Danny they would have to lay a man off – the workforce had been here longer than both of them.

* * *

'Trust Evie Kilgaren to sound so upbeat and positive when their business is sinking faster than a stone in water,' Susie Blackthorn said as she replaced the receiver. She had hoped Danny would still be in the yard and she could speak to him, but it was not to be. Susie would have enjoyed telling him Lenard intended to run him out of business, her only disappointment, not being able to see the look of shock on Danny's face. But even that had been snatched from her by that cow Evie Kilgaren.

Susie knew, with her help and knowledge of Skinner's business acquaintances, Lenard had been able to undercut Danny's haulage prices to the bone, to entice his most lucrative business contacts, and she surmised that any time in the next few months Danny would be begging Lenard to take his ailing haulage yard off his hands at a knock-down price.

'We'll soon see who the big cheese is then, Danny boy.'

17

Ada was walking down the steps of the bridge leading to Reckoner's Row, Grace had taken her beautiful granddaughter back to Cheshire, , and she missed them both so much. She had been deep in thought when she noticed Leo Darnel standing on her doorstep. He had his back to her, but she recognised the slight stoop in his posture, which she surmised was caused by many years of keeping his head down. *What does he want?* she wondered, hurrying down the row.

'All right, Ada?' Darnel said as she approached her gate, and he descended the steps to help her with the meagre bag of groceries she had queued for. Her life revolved around food shortages, rationing, points, food substitutes, shopping, cleaning, and queuing and had done so for more years than she cared to remember.

She didn't mind queuing usually, that was where she caught up with most of the local gossip, but this morning, housewives were huddled under umbrellas to shelter from the fine rain that drizzled down soaking everyone and everything in its path.

'Hello, Mr Darnel,' she said, nobody called him Leo to his face, 'long time no see.' She recalled that the spiv had been conspicuous by his absence at Bert's funeral, and she had seen neither hide nor hair since. 'I thought you'd left the country.' Ada, unlike other people she could mention, had no fear of this man, even though he had a fierce reputation. She had always found him to be a bit of a charmer who never intimidated her like he did others.

'I know, Ada, it's been a while, but I've had a lot on, business-wise, but I'm here now to pay my respects to Bert's memory.'

I doubt that's all, thought Ada, slipping her key into the polished brass lock. Most front doors stayed open from morning 'til night in the area, even when the house was empty, on account of having nothing worthwhile pinching, and there was always a nosy neighbour or two who would keep an eye on the place until you got back. But Ada never left her house unsecured. It wasn't in her nature, and she wasn't going to have any Tom, Dick or Leo snooping round her house when she wasn't in it.

'Come in, I'll put the kettle on,' she said, leading the way up the narrow passage.

Closing the half-stained-glass vestibule door behind him, Darnel followed her to an identical door at the end of the narrow passageway, which led to a large back kitchen.

'Sit down,' Ada said as she put the kettle under the tap, before taking off her coat. 'We don't stand on ceremony in this house.'

'This is a lovely house, Ada, and you keep it immaculate,' Darnel said, looking around at the pale green painted walls and the neat shelves covered in paper upon which Ada displayed her shiny dishes and pots.

'Well, there's nobody else to do it,' she said pragmatically, 'and I can't abide an untidy home, can you?'

'No, Ada,' Leo Darnel said, assuming that if any passing dust landed on Ada's furniture it would be quickly dealt with and removed. 'This house would pass muster every time.'

What would you know about mustering? she thought. *You've never served your country a day in your life.* 'I like to do my bit,' she said, pouring the freshly made tea into a gold-rimmed porcelain cup, handing it to him and noticing when he took the dainty cup in his huge left hand it made the cup look very small indeed. 'There's milk in the jug and sugar in the bowl, help yourself,' Ada said with the wave of her hand, pouring neither into her own cup. Over the years, she had got used to sacrificing her own taste for the benefit of others.

'Is your daughter and her husband still with you?' Darnel asked as he stirred his over-sugared tea, and Ada's eyebrow raised just a fraction. He wasn't one for small talk, she knew, and wondered what he had really come here for.

She shook her head and said with a tinge of sadness, 'Our Grace went back to Cheshire a week or so after Bert's funeral.' She got up from her seat and took down the framed photograph from the shelf. 'Grace had this specially commissioned after the baby was born.' She handed it to him and could not resist saying, 'Bruce has offices in London, New York and of course here in Liverpool.' Ada loved nothing more than to crow about her rich son-in-law. 'They come home as often as they can, but I must say I do miss them.'

'I'm sure you do, Ada,' Darnel said, aiming to flatter. 'A staunch matriarch like yourself thrives on having her family around her.' He noticed Ada stand a little straighter, her shoulders pushed back, and a look of pride made her all-seeing eyes glow.

'I've still got Bobby at home,' Ada relaxed a little, 'he works with our Danny in the yard and has done since he left the Co-op as a delivery boy.

'I hear Danny's doing well in his business,' said Darnel, 'a good thing too after so much heartache when Bert...' He paused.

'Danny's got his head screwed on,' said Ada proudly, 'he and Evie run that place like clockwork.'

'I heard he's been getting offers for the yard,' Darnel said, 'any idea who wants his business?

'Not a clue,' Ada said, her mouth set in a stiff straight line and her double chin quivering under the weight of her pride. 'But I'll tell you this much, that yard has been a little goldmine – sitting on prime dockland.' She leaned closer and said in a low voice, 'And it will be again.' She tapped the side of her nose and Darnel raised his chin.

'I was wondering,' Darnel said after he drank half of the scalding tea in one gulp, 'did Bert mention a package he was minding for me, before he died?'

Immediately, the hair on her head tingled, and Ada was aware she must be very careful what she said here. 'A package?' she asked, her elbow resting on the wine-coloured chenille tablecloth, and she tapped her chin. Her eyes, moving from side to side, in deep concentration. 'What sort of package?'

He didn't answer immediately, which gave Ada a chance to gather her thoughts. The only thing Bert had left was the box now secreted in the gas cupboard in the parlour, and whatever was in that was not going to be shared with the spiv. She hadn't even looked in it yet.

'It doesn't matter,' said Darnel, 'it was nothing special, a birthday present for my wife, that's all.'

He couldn't think much of his so-called wife if he was unperturbed about her birthday present, thought Ada. And since when did Darnel have a wife? As far as Ada was aware the only woman, he had shown any interest in was Rene Kilgaren.

'When they brought me his things, there were no packages. In fact, all he left was a bit of tat that was only fit for the bin, which was where I threw it. Says a lot, doesn't it?'

'He never was one for keepsakes and the like,' said Darnel, knowing Bert would have sold his own mother if he could have got a decent price. But Darnel was certain of two things. The first was that Ada would make a great poker player. The second was, if Bert had given her the box to bring home, she would have opened it and there would be police crawling all over the place by now.

* * *

Huskisson Dock saw the import and export of over a million tons of foodstuffs: flour, grain, peas, beans, and thousands of tons of meat, fruit, raw materials, scrap metal, wood, iron, steel that moved in and out of the port every day. A veritable inventory of goods, which was still a scarcity for Joe Public nearly eight years after the end of the war.

The dock road hummed to the sound of cranes, machinery, shouting voices and ships' horns, up and down the River Mersey. The bustle of this busy port could be his shop window during the day. But now the sun had sunk, and the only sound was that of the incoming tide and the gentle lapping of dark, murky water against the enormous dock wall. The blackness would only be broken by the light which glowed from the small window of his office at the far end of the dock, out of sight not only to passers-by but from the large warehouses that had gone up after the war, which was not ideal.

Leo Darnel paced the wooden floorboards. He did not like to be kept waiting. And Caraway was late. Commanding total respect from his men, Darnel paid handsomely to those who looked out for him. When the old lags came out of clink, he made sure they had a few bob in their pocket, a decent suit on their back and a job in haulage. And his generosity encouraged loyalty. However, he had heard along the way that the man he had come to trust the most was not pulling his weight. He was getting sloppy. Letting his love life cloud his judgement. Giving that brainless blonde a job and a promotion when she didn't have the sense she was born with. Maybe it was time he had a word.

* * *

Harry Caraway was making a telephone call before he left the plush office of Lenard Haulage to partake of a sumptuous meal in town with the lovely Susie. But he was late, very late. He had to see Darnel. But before then he had to make the telephone call. Tapping his fountain pen against the dark mahogany desk, he waited for the telephone to be answered. He looked at the clock. Four thirty. He should have been at Darnel's office an hour ago. The telephone stopped ringing.

'Harry, darling, I thought you were never going to ring.'

'I'm so sorry, Penelope,' he said in a low voice, knowing Susie had only gone to collect her coat and handbag from the staffroom. 'Something has come up. I can't make it home tonight.'

'But, Harry, the boys are so excited.'

'I know, my darling,' Harry said in hushed tones. 'There has been a huge accident with two of our lorries and I have to sort it out' he lied.

'But you promised the boys you would come home when you telephoned last week.'

'I know I did, my love, but as I am in charge, I have the responsibility.' He took his handkerchief from his top pocket and mopped his brow. 'But don't worry, we'll soon be able to buy that little place you've always dreamed of.'

'It's still vacant, the boys and I go past it every day on the way to school.'

'And it will be ours, just as soon as I finish up here.' His pockets had been well-lined with the money he needed to enable him to buy his family a fancy home in the suburbs. Only small change to the likes of Darnel.

He rose from the desk and locked the filing cabinet situated behind him. He heard a slight creek in the corridor outside and listened for a moment. But everything was silent.

'When shall I tell the boys you will be home.' His wife's voice broke the silence.

'Tuesday, my darling, I promise.' His heart began to race. He would have all the money he wanted by then.

'I'll count the hours,' said Penelope, and Harry sighed. This time next week, he would be out of here and Darnel would not have a clue where he was.

'Me too, Penny, darling.' He imagined his hands caressing the contours of Susie's voluptuous curves and wanted to cut the call short before she came back into the office.

'Oh, and Harry...'

'Hmm?'

'I've got something to tell you when you get home. Or do you want me to tell you now?'

'Tell me later, darling,' he said, impatient to put the receiver down. 'When we are alone.'

'Hurry home as soon as is humanly possible, my darling,' she said and he rolled his eyes. Susie would be back any moment and he didn't want her to come in on the tail-end of his call.

'I'll see you on Tuesday.'

'Kisses,' Penelope said and Harry looked towards the office door. This had become a nightly ritual since he had been away from home, and he could hear her making the kissing sound on the other end of the line.

'Goodbye, my darling,' he said, not wanting to indulge her tonight.

'Harry? Kisses,' and he made the kissing sound that would reassure her he was missing her as much as she missed him. He waited until he heard the click at the other end of the line before he replaced the receiver in its cradle. And his head shot up when he heard the office door open.

'Touching.' Harry Caraway nearly jumped out of his skin when Leo Darnel walked into the office and pushed back his trilby to reveal a face any fox would be proud of. 'You're late.' Darnel's voice was a low growl that terrified those who crossed him. 'You said three-thirty and I waited for the ledger.'

Harry Caraway wasn't intimidated by Darnel's threatening manner. In a few days, he wouldn't even be here. And he wasn't going to leave a forwarding address.

'It's in a safe place,' he lied. 'I can get it to you by, let's say, Wednesday.'

'Let's not.' Darnel had been standing outside the office door and had heard every word. 'Let's say Tuesday.' There was a lot at stake in those ledgers. Stuff that could get him put behind bars for a very long time. The haulage business did a sterling job cleaning the money he would never be able to explain otherwise. But the 'proper' ledgers, the ones that showed the true picture of his business, had the power to ruin him financially and also destroy his reputation as one of Liverpool's most notorious underworld bosses.

'Fine,' said Caraway in equally cool tones, 'seven thirty in The Tram Tavern on the corner of Reckoner's Row.'

'No chance,' Darnel said, aware this punk was getting above himself. Caraway should know he was not a man to be double-crossed. 'You have until five-thirty. If you haven't got them by then...' He picked up the remains of Harry Caraway's brandy and swigged it down in one, then he drew a line very slowly across his throat with the tip of his forefinger.

'I'll be there,' Caraway said in a mock friendly, I-don't-know-what-you-mean attitude, 'it's all good.'

'It'd better be,' Darnel said with a cynical glare, not sure if he should pop a bit of lead into this wise guy now – but then, he would never know where Carraway had hidden the original files.

When Darnel left the office, Harry Caraway opened the filing cabinet and took out the half-filled bottle of brandy and, without pouring it into the glass, took a huge slug straight from the bottle. Leo Darnel could go and throw himself into the canal for all he cared. After all, he mused, that's where Rene Kilgaren had ended her days at Darnel's hand... Caraway knew it was this knowledge that had kept him in Darnel's favour – up to now.

'Come on, Susie,' he said, tapping the desk with his fingertips, looking at the expensive watch that had found its way from one of the warehouses and onto his wrist. He was relieved that she was so vain and had spent ages making sure her make-up was on straight.

It was also a good thing that he was a quick thinker and had an answer for all the questions she asked when she saw Leo Darnel leaving the office. There was only one way he could think of, to take her mind off things that didn't concern her. His hands began to wander over her voluptuous curves and, as usual, she pushed his hand away.

'You wouldn't do that if I asked you to marry me, would you?' Harry said, gazing into her eyes, his loins on fire.

Susie's jaw dropped and her eyes were like spider-legged saucers. 'Marry you?' Her words were a barely audible whisper. 'Of course I'll marry you!' Her mind was working fast. He would surely expect her to give up her job when they married, and she would have the life she dreamed of, being wed to the general manager of Lenard Haulage. Susie was far too busy planning her future to fully engage when Harry pushed her against the desk and lifted her skirt...

Harry wondered if he had made a bit of a balls-up when he stood back to fasten his trousers. Mentioning marriage to a girl like

Susie was risky, but in the heat of the moment he felt it was a risk worth taking, to take her mind off things that didn't concern her. And how else was he to obtain the creature comforts his body craved, without a promise, for the carnal pleasure of her, across the office desk.

Later, when she went to tidy herself up, Harry took his cashmere overcoat from the stand near the door and fished in his pocket for the keys to the safe. He opened the safe and took out a long brown package, stuffed to bursting with two thousand pounds worth of crisp white five-pound notes, which fitted neatly in his jacket pocket.

* * *

'You're quiet tonight, Harry,' Susie said dreamily, seductively curling a tendril of hair round her finger in the candlelight of an exclusive restaurant. Now she had given herself to him, he was sure to want to marry her as soon as possible. She could see it in her mind's eye: she sailing down the aisle of Saint Patrick's church, with Harry standing at the altar rails watching her glide towards him, dressed from head to toe in virginal white, her mother dabbing her eyes with a lace handkerchief while her father, so proud, walked her towards her future husband...

'I'm just contemplating the moment you agreed to marry me,' said Harry, wondering if he had been a bit hasty mentioning marriage, Susie, would dig her claws in and hang on for dear life. He had heard the rumours of the years she had pursued poor Danny Harris. Yet, now his stomach had been satiated, and they had quaffed expensive cognac, his thoughts, once more, turned to activities of a more lascivious nature. Susie had told him earlier she had her place to herself, as her parents had gone out and would not be back until late. The night could be finished off perfectly.

* * *

'Oh Harry,' Susie gasped, loving the things he was doing to her body. If she had known lovemaking could be so exquisitely, all-consumingly satisfying, she would have done it years ago with Danny. Her breathing quickened, as hungry for more loving as he was.

'Why don't we stay here by the fire, where it's warm,' he coaxed, feeling her body relax, allowing him to explore the smooth flesh above her stocking top.

Later, as they lay in the glow of passion spent, her hands rested on the bulge in his jacket pocket. 'It's money for our new house,' he said, certain she would now do whatever he asked.

18

Evie picked up the receiver of the office telephone and her finger trembled slightly as she dialled the number of The River Warehouse Company, one of the biggest warehouse operators in the whole country She knew a contract with this company could change the fortune of Skinner & Son forever.

Evie had been beyond excited when she opened the envelope and saw the headed notepaper containing all the details. This was just the kind of business Skinner's needed right now. R.W.C, as the company was known, wanted a consignment moved from one of their huge dockside warehouses and transported to London. Thence, said the letter, if Skinner & Son could accommodate in a professional and timely manner, there would be many more lucrative orders to warehouses all over the country.

Evie knew this was the lifeline she could only ever have dreamed of. A huge order like this would set Danny back on his feet and restore his usual zest for life, because even though he did an excellent job of hiding his worry about the business in front of the carters, she knew any hint of a decaying business could send some scurrying for other work. And who could blame them? Men needed to feed their families, keep a roof over their heads and be able to buy the odd pint in the tavern.

Evie wanted to let R.W.C. know Skinner's would guarantee all work that would be undertaken. It did not do any harm at this stage of the proceedings to offer their usual friendly, personal service.

'Hello, this is Evie Kilgaren from Skinner & Son,' she said when the telephone on the other end was answered. 'We have received your instructions in this morning's post, and I wanted to let you know immediately we will be able to transport any consignment, no matter how large or small. Obviously, we will send written confirmation in the post, and I also wanted to let you know, one of our drivers is on his way to collect your—'

'Who did you say you were?' asked a rather condescending voice on the other end, interrupting Evie's well-rehearsed introduction.

'I am Evie Kilgaren, from Skinner & Son, cartage and haulage contractors,' she answered politely.

'I don't know anything about any haulage contractor,' the female voice was now filled with disdain. 'This is Henderson Funeral Directors, and we certainly do not transport our clients on flat-backed lorries. I think you may have the wrong telephone number. Good day.'

Evie heard the click on the other end of the telephone, and she stared at the receiver for a long time. Evie wasn't beaten yet. Picking up the heavy telephone directory, she quickly thumbed through the tissue-thin pages until she came to the section under 'R'. Evie's fingertip scrolled down the page. 'Ah, here we are.' She checked the telephone number against the one on the docket she had received through the post that morning and they didn't match.

Tapping her short, well-shaped fingernails on the desk, her mind was running free, and her thoughts took an obvious turn. The business was ailing, but it wasn't dead yet and was far from needing an undertakers. The letter was obviously a prank, which could only have been sent by someone who knew Skinner's business was on a slippery slope. But who could know? All the information was kept locked away...

Who could be so spiteful to do such a thing? she wondered. Who would know that business had been declining of late?

'You've been listening to too many crime stories on the wireless, Evie.' She told herself, picking up the business directory once again, and opened the page she was looking for. Checking the number on the letter against the name in the directory, Evie was not in the least surprised when she saw the number for Lenard Haulage and the number on the letter were both identical.

She had been hoodwinked. The long-distance job had been a hoax. Evie put her face in her hands as a loud groan emanated from her downturned lips.

Looking through the order book, Evie saw they had nothing that would keep the wolves at bay for much longer. Their regular clients were being tempted away by Lenard Haulage's more rewarding conditions, and lower rates was only one of them. If only she could think of a way of getting enough money to buy more wagons. Because that was where the future of haulage lay, not in the plodding horse and cart companies.

'Maybe it's not so far-fetched as it sounds,' she said, telephoning the *Evening Echo* and putting an advertisement in the following evening's edition. She was going to advertise for more accountancy work. There were plenty of companies in the dockside in need of an independent auditor. Although, to save any embarrassment to Danny, Evie put the forwarding address as her post office box.

Reaching for her handbag, she took out the keys and locked the office door. She needed to get to the post office and put another advert in the window before it closed. The sooner the work rolled in, the better.

* * *

After replacing the receiver, Susie Blackthorn had laughed out loud. Evie Kilgaren's voice had a definite air of desperation in the faint tremor. Susie was determined to bring Skinner & Son to its knees.

'Danny Harris will be so jealous when he finds out I am going to marry his biggest rival,' she said, staring malevolently at the telephone. Susie went to the filing cabinet and unlocked the top drawer marked 'private'. In this drawer were kept the records of every transaction, every job that had been done over the past week and the money those jobs had earned. These were the files that went unseen by the auditors and, more importantly, the tax man.

The other file was the one she had filched from Skinner & Son when she was fired by Evie Kilgaren, and Evie was going to rue the day she ever crossed Susie Blackthorn.

* * *

When Danny came back to the office later that day, he took off his cap and threw it across the room, expertly landing it on the hook behind the door. His usually cheery, handsome face was troubled.

'I take it you went to the R.W.C?' Evie asked, feeling the anxiety he tried so hard to hide. Danny nodded and went into the staffroom to put the kettle on.

'Did I tell you there's going to be an auction of World War Two army wagons?' Danny asked, changing the subject and Evie nodded. She knew when Danny had something on his mind. And if he didn't want to talk to her about it, then the matter was more serious than even she predicted.

'Will you be bidding for any of them?' Evie asked and she saw Danny's wide shoulders give the merest shrug and his back stiffened. Evie knew he was trying to save her from worrying, but she was the one who dealt with the day-to-day business, the orders and the money. So, she knew the business inside out. Evie also knew they were in no position to bid for a new tyre, let alone a whole wagon. But she had an idea.

'Never mind,' said Evie, getting up from behind her desk and taking her cup into the staffroom, 'little acorns grow into mighty oak trees.'

'I wish I had your positivity,' said Danny, putting his arms round her slim waist and pulling her close, inhaling the clean fragrance of lemon shampoo, and the floral *Arpege* perfume, which he bought for her birthday after the George Henry Lee assistant told him it was one of the most romantic, popular perfumes they sold.

'You can do anything you set your mind to,' Evie said, gazing into his mesmerising blue eyes, burrowing into his soul, filling him with the belief he so desperately needed at the moment. 'Don't be downhearted, as long as we are together, that's all that matters.' Evie was determined to get to the bottom of the prank orders.

'What would I do without you?' Danny asked, loving everything about her. He always had.

'Don't even think those words let alone say them,' said Evie, 'you are going to have to put up with me forever.'

'Thank goodness for that,' Danny smiled, drinking in the beauty of her marine-coloured eyes that, at times, could be so soft and gentle and loving, while at others were determined and confident, like they were now, giving him the added layer of optimism, he so needed right now. 'We are going to conquer the world,' Danny said.

'That's the spirit,' Evie answered, knowing that with Danny by her side they were indestructible. But first she had something she needed to do. She needed to find out how Lenard Haulage knew so much about Danny's business dealings, his contacts and his deliveries. Because Lenard's knew what Danny was doing, even before she did.

19

Since Harry Caraway's proposal he had seemed distant somehow and then a day later Susie had heard him making his usual daily telephone call to his mother, as was his habit, before leaving the office. She had been going to the ladies to refresh her lipstick when she remembered she had left it on her desk.

Not one to pry, she listened outside the office door – in case Harry was still talking to his mother – but she had never heard a man declare his undying love in such a graphic manner. He was telling her how much he longed to feel her sexy body next to his. As soon as he could, he would be on the next train home to her and the boys. The boys?

'Of course, I miss them,' Harry had said, 'what father wouldn't, they are growing so fast my darling and soon we will move into our new house – the money has already gone through...'

Susie had stopped breathing. Unable to believe what she had just heard. A ship's horn bellowed in the background, bringing her to her senses, and her limbs trembled. Harry spoke as if talking to a lover - a wife! '...I will be home on Tuesday, with you and our boys, my love...'

So, he had been stringing her along, too. Just like Danny had for all those years. She heard him replace the telephone receiver, and she drew in a long, shuddering breath to steady her nerves. Why did men do this to her?

When the office door opened and Harry had stepped out, she showed no signs of having her world ripped to pieces, and when he bent to kiss her, she knew what she had to do.

Harry had not been in the office since and Susie realised that she didn't need him to help her ruin Danny, she had her own plan.

The recently hired handyman, who lumbered around the building doing odd jobs every day, had been easy to coerce for the right price. He didn't ask questions. Just took the money and got on with the job. She had given him the address to take the files to, and all she had to do was sit back and wait for the fury to erupt. Harry Caraway would soon realise she wasn't the dumb blonde he thought she was...

The front door of Lenard Haulage was unlocked, and Frank Kilgaren managed to enter easily. Tiptoeing past the desk of the gently snoring security guard, he sloped into the shadows. Taking the stairs two at a time, he quickly reached the second-floor corridor, knowing Lenard's offices were at the other end. He had worked here long enough to know where everything was kept and hoped that the empty-headed girl with the halo of peroxide candy-floss hair had done what she said she would do – and left the door and filing cabinet unlocked

His long, rapid strides consumed the maroon-coloured floor,

and he was soon gripping the shiny brass doorknob of the door leading into the office. It turned easily, as he guessed it would, having already oiled the creaking door hinges in readiness this morning.

The information he needed was within his grasp when he heard the tread of heavy boots marching along the corridor. Thankfully, Frank had the good sense to secure the doorknob with the back of a straight-backed chair and secreted himself on the other side of the filing cabinet, when the doorknob rattled a couple of times. Frank held his breath, hoping the chair would hold, knowing if he was caught lurking in the office, it would mean instant dismissal and likely the police would be brought in. He could well do without that right now, he thought. First of all, he needed to find out if his suspicions were right, that the man running Lenard's Haulage was the man he suspected. And if his suspicions were correct, and Leo Darnel was the man who owned the place, the ledgers were evidence. Evidence that would secure the future and that of his family.

He listened to the retreating tread of the security guard before removing the ledgers from their resting place and hiding them under his jacket. He waited until the security guard had finished doing his rounds before making a move, knowing the old fella usually went down to the canteen to make a pot of tea round about now. In minutes, he was down the stairs and out of the front door undetected. All he had to do now was deliver the files where they would do some good, and then get the hell out of Liverpool.

* * *

'She reminds me of an old schoolmistress we once had,' said Lucy, reading the morning newspaper reports about the life of the new

Queen's grandmother, Queen Mary, who had died in her sleep at Marlborough House the week before.

'She had a good innings,' said Evie, not unkindly, half listening to the wireless as she set the table for dinner. Danny was there, relaxing in a chair and was listening too. 'Family Favourites', the request programme linking families at home to Forces overseas, was playing on the BBC light programme when Evie went out to the back kitchen and added the fluffy part-boiled potatoes into sizzling hot beef dripping that had been melting in the oven. She managed to buy the dripping from the butcher yesterday, after waiting in the queue for over half an hour.

Fats, butter and many other things were still on ration, eight years after the end of the war, and she, along with the rest of the country's housewives, was fed up with the situation. Who'd have thought rationing would last longer than the war did?

Evie put the roasting dish into the oven and thought of her younger brother Jack, and she missed him being away from home. She had hoped to receive some news from him, but there had been no word since just after Christmas and she was becoming more worried by the day. Danny said she should expect a sack full of letters to come all at once and Evie thought he was trying to stop her from fretting.

'Evie, come here, quick!' Danny and Lucy sounded excited, and Evie tucked the tea towel in the waist-length apron she had made from one of her mother's old frocks and hurried into the kitchen. Her eyes wide in wonder.

'What's the—'

'Shh,' Lucy pointed to the wireless, and whispered 'listen...'

'Here is a mention from Corporal Jack Kilgaren of number two Reckoner's Row, who is serving with his unit. Jack is from Liverpool and would like me to say hello to his sisters, Evie and Lucy, and also to his future brother-in-law, Danny, who will be marrying Evie at the end of June...'

'How do they know?' Evie gasped.

'... Jack would like me to play this song for all of you.' The announcer gave a little giggle and then said, 'Evie, he wants you to pay particular attention to the beautiful words of Frankie Laine, singing "I believe"...'

The two girls let out ecstatic squeals and hugged each other!

'We got our names on the wireless!' Lucy cried. 'Good old Jack.'

However, Evie was speechless as she listened to the beautiful, heart-rending words that offered hope, and her faith in Jack's arrival home seemed a little bit stronger.

'Do you think he'll be home before the wedding?' she asked Danny, who held her close when he saw the tears trickle down her cheeks.

'Let's hope so.' Those three words were the only comfort he could offer right now, because he didn't have any idea how long Jack would be stuck out in the paddy fields, engaged in a war in a place he never knew existed until Jack joined the army two years ago and was sent there.

20

MAY

'There you are, I didn't think you would make it home in time!' Lucy sounded excited as Evie walked up the narrow lobby and entered the kitchen and saw the table festooned with bunting, paper flowers and tins of red, white, and blue paint for the Coronation party next month, and Evie's heart sank. There was something she had forgotten. But what was it?

'I've been making some decorations to stop me from getting too nervous,' Lucy said, busy clearing the Coronation decorations into a carboard box. 'I've already set Rachel's hair in the salon, and she's been sitting under the dryer for ages reading magazines while I did all the tidying up.' Lucy's words tumbled from her lips like pebbles on a still pond and gave Evie a good indication her younger sister was extremely nervous.

Then she realised! Today was Lucy's hairdressing competition. She had forgotten all about it. Evie only intended to come home to see if there was any post, given that she had taken on extra accountancy work to boost the coffers, and a good thing too, because life would be unbearable in this house if Lucy suffered the disappointment of her big sister not being there to cheer her on.

'We have to be at the Adelphi Hotel for half past six. It's half past four now so we will have to get the bus around half past five, so we won't be late, but that's rush hour, everybody will be trying to get in or out of town and—' Lucy looked panic-stricken.

'Slow down,' Evie interrupted, knowing she had been practising for this evening for months. 'You didn't think I'd let you go into town on the bus on the most important evening of your career, did you?' How could she have forgotten something as important as the apprentice championships – Lucy's big chance to gain a good reputation in the eyes of the hairdressing elite. 'Don't look so scared,' Evie told Lucy, trying to reassure her, 'you will be the star of the show.'

'Oh, don't say that, Evie, I'm nervous enough as it is.' Lucy looked close to tears and Evie knew how much this meant to her sister, who could talk the leg off a table and was now quieter than she had ever seen her before. Evie had experienced those very same feelings when she sat her final exams, knowing her future depended upon the results.

'Is Rachel excited?' Evie asked, wondering if Lucy could manage a bite to eat before the competition.

'She's acting like a Hollywood starlet.' Lucy gave a wry smile, she didn't begrudge her friend her moment in the spotlight, knowing Rachel, being the eldest of her siblings rarely got any attention at all. 'We are allowed to shampoo and set the hair before the competition because we only have an hour on the floor to dress the hair.' Lucy was busy checking her box containing all the tools she would need for the job, terrified she would forget something. 'I've decided to put Rachel's hair up, like a Greek goddess – she can't wait.'

When Evie brought up the subject of food, Lucy thought she was going to be sick.

'But you will be starving; these things go on until late.' But no matter how much she tried to persuade or cajole Lucy into eating, she was having none of it.

'The food won't go down,' Lucy said, 'and even if it did, it would reappear just as quick!'

A few moments later, Evie appeared in the doorway of the kitchen. 'I've made you some potted meat sandwiches and put them in a brown paper bag. You might fancy them later.'

Lucy looked aghast, not able to believe what she had just heard, and said: 'You will not take a brown paper bag of potted meat sandwiches to The Adelphi, our Evie.' Lucy shook her head at the thought. 'Not even if they were wrapped in gold lamé. I would die of shame!' She was horrified. 'This is one of the biggest hotels in Liverpool, we're talking about.'

'I'm sorry for being so thoughtless,' Evie said in mock servility, but Lucy would not be pacified.

'You may have seen it on your travels, crystal chandeliers and deep-pile carpets. The likes of which we don't see every day... Soft music and waiter service – and you want to bring potted meat butties in a brown paper bag!' Lucy left the room with an exaggerated and determined 'huh'!

Evie smiled and shook her head, gazing at the closed door her sister had just exited like a force-nine gale. Less than a moment later, it opened again, and her repentant sister said in a voice full of remorse, 'I'm sorry I bit your head off, Evie, it's just my nerves getting the better of me.'

'I understand completely,' said Evie, giving Lucy a reassuring hug. 'Think no more of it.'

'I brought you home a sample sachet of the new shampoo and conditioner Madam wants us to try. It's on the side of the sink.'

'Thank you, I'll save it for Sunday, when I wash my hair,' Evie smiled and gave her younger sister another hug, while Lucy looked sheepish.

Eventually she said in that soft Irish lilt evoked by many years of evacuation on a family farm, 'I'm sure it's just the nerves that are making me as jittery as a monkey on a hot griddle.' Then her eyes opened wide, and her face lost its colour. 'Rachel told me Madam Bouffant is going too! I do wish she hadn't told me. Here, sit down while I tidy your hair up, you can't go to the Adelphi looking like you've just been dragged by your hair through a hedge.'

Evie hid her smile, knowing Lucy liked to show off her talents to the untrained eye, but it was nerve-wracking to be judged by her peers and experts whose job it was to criticise every turn of the comb.

* * *

'That's lovely,' Evie looked in the mirror over the fireplace while Lucy showed her the back of her head through the smaller mirror she was holding. 'Danny will fall for me all over again. You are so talented, Lucy, you are going to win tonight for sure.'

'Oh, don't jinx me,' Lucy cried. 'Now I know how actors feel when they are going on stage.' She stopped suddenly and grabbed Evie's arm and said dramatically: 'That's it! I've got stage fright.'

'Well, if you don't stop washing those brushes, they will have no bristles left. That's the third time you've washed them since I came home,' Evie said.

'They examine your tools before you start,' said Lucy, 'and if they find so much as a single hair, they knock points off you, and a lost point could mean the difference between a glittering career or failure.'

'I'm sure you'll be fine,' Evie tried to placate Lucy. But she was having none of it.

'Fine will not cut it, if you pardon my expression,' said Lucy, who, an hour later was piling her rollers, brushes, combs, Rachel, and a harassed older sister into Danny's flat-backed wagon.

She hadn't expected a Rolls-Royce to take her to the competition in a posh hotel, but nor did Lucy expect to be stuffed into the passenger seat of Danny's dusty wagon with a gearstick gouging the flesh on her thigh and that was before the engine began to splutter and cough.

'It's all going wrong,' Lucy felt a lump in her throat, 'this isn't how I imagined the competition to be.'

'Remind me to book you a coach of gold, next time, Cinderella,' Evie said. Rachel laughed, her head full of rollers all set under a silk scarf Lucy had bought especially for the occasion, which was tied in a triangle at the back of her head as they clambered from the dying wagon, that only just got them to the hotel before it groaned to a halt completely.

'You go on ahead,' said Danny. 'I'll have this fixed in no time.'

'You're not coming in to watch Lucy?' Evie's voice rose to a whispered shriek and Danny gave her a calming kiss. 'I think Lucy's nervousness is catching,' she smiled and let Danny get on with fixing the engine – again.

'Would you look at this!' Rachel gasped when they stepped into the plush competition lounge of the hotel. 'Me mam would lay an egg if she saw this!'

Around the edge of the dance floor, now turned into the competition arena for the apprentices, fancy tables were set out on a carpeted area, where the audience would be seated. Evie, Connie and Mim had come along to cheer Lucy on and had a front-row view. Their presence made her serrated nerves twang.

Giving a nervous smile, Lucy arranged her kit on a white cloth. Spotless combs, immaculate brushes, new clips, all set out in the pleasing formation she had been taught by Madam Bouffant. Standing behind Rachel's chair, she looked into the mirror to see her best friend give her a reassuring nod of her head as the apprentices waited for the instruction to begin. When it came, Lucy took a deep breath. 'Here goes,' she whispered.

An hour later, after Lucy's deep concentration was afforded to twisting and shaping Rachel's tresses, her fingers working their magic transforming her hair into a cascade of frothy curls and interwoven plaits the width of shoelaces. With seconds to spare, Lucy stood back to check she had fulfilled the brief and make sure everything was as good as she could make it.

'Please put your combs down now,' the order came over the tannoy and the apprentices, as one, placed their tools on the white linen cloths. 'Apprentices, please leave the arena.'

Lucy felt her heart skip a beat. She had done all she could do. Now she would have to wait while the judges did their summing up.

'Go and get a cup of tea,' Rachel told Lucy, who took a deep breath and nodded.

The apprentices streamed out of the hall and Rachel sat with the other models while the judges came over to check what seemed to be every hair on her head, the area around Lucy's workstation, her combs, brushes, gown, and everything else that was needed in the execution of the competition.

It seemed to Lucy that the judges would never decide who was going to get through this competition, because they took so long – or at least that's how it felt – before the apprentices were summoned back to the hall.

Suddenly the crowd hushed, and somebody tapped the microphone. And out of the corner of her eye, Lucy noticed Madam Bouffant standing at the back and she was sure her heart was going to hammer right through her ribs.

'In third place,' said the master of ceremonies, 'the prize goes to Linda Braithwaite from County Hairstylists.'

Everybody clapped as a tall, slim girl went up to collect her rosette and a cheque for twenty-five pounds.

Lucy looked at Rachel through the mirror and her jangled nerves refused to settle down even when she gave Lucy a reassuring smile.

'In second place, we have Diane Rufus from The Golden Mane.'

Again, there was a round of applause and Lucy felt her heart sink. She thought she had a good chance of getting a third or even a second, but it was not to be, and she wanted the ground to open up and swallow her. Everybody she knew had come to cheer her on and she hadn't even secured second or third place. She was torn to pieces as her anguish soared. Her family and friends had had a wasted journey. Evie would pat her arm and tell her there was always next time. Whatever possessed her to think she was good enough to enter the Coronation Cup? Who did she think she was with her high hopes and big ideas?

'Lucy! Lucy, it's you!' Rachel hissed through the mirror and, as if waking from a deep sleep, Lucy looked round to see everybody looking back at her.

'Me?' she mouthed and then she heard the announcer's voice.

'It seems we have a shy apprentice, but there is no need for such modesty, this girl will go far, and she has the talent of more seasoned professionals.' The audience gave a gentle laugh. 'Would Miss Lucy Kilgaren come and collect the Coronation Cup for her Apprentice of the Year Award?' The applause was deafening when Lucy stepped from behind Rachel, whose smile was wider than the Mersey. When she tried to recall the details later, Lucy's mind was blank.

'I've won a hundred pounds!' Lucy gasped, turning to her sister and waving the cheque under her nose. 'Evie, a hundred pounds!'

'What are you going to spend it on?' Rachel asked and Lucy's mind went blank again as they all huddled round her.

'I don't know,' she said. 'I might open my own salon – when I've finished my City and Guilds that is. And I can now afford to study for my masters. I can specialise. I can do anything!'

'You most certainly can, our Lucy,' said Evie, stepping back when the local paper came to take Lucy's photograph, and as she did, Evie saw someone disappear into the crowd and out of the door, but before he did, he turned and looked directly at her.

Evie would know those eyes anywhere. And she was sure she was not mistaken. He may have changed the colour of his hair and grown a beard and moustache, but she would never mistake her father's marine-coloured eyes, so like her own and Lucy's. A moment later, he was gone.

* * *

It was almost ten-thirty when Danny dropped the girls off after the competition and took the wagon to the yard for the night. Both girls were so happy, nothing could burst the bubble of joy. Until they lit the gas mantle and heard the noise upstairs. Footsteps on the bare wooden floorboards above.

Lucy put her hand on Evie's arm, her body tense. Looking up to the ceiling, they heard the floorboards creak again.

'You don't think...?' Lucy whispered, gripping the Coronation Cup she had won in one hand, and a cheque for one hundred pounds in her other. She turned towards the door leading to the lobby and the stairs, where heavy footsteps could be heard descending.

'I don't know,' Evie breathed, picking up the poker from the hearth. Why would her father come back here? He'd know the police would be watching the house, surely? 'Whoever is up there is going to rue the day they broke in though,' Evie hissed as they silently moved towards the door. Her heartbeat hammering, her mouth dry. 'I'll hit them with this poker.' Evie, raising her hand quickly, opened the door and lurched forward, bumping headlong into a six-foot soldier standing in the darkened passageway.

'Well, that's a nice welcome home, I must say!'

'Jack!' Both girls squealed with excitement to see their brother.

'I thought I'd get a hug at least.' He laughed and it took a moment for the two girls to let the reality of his return sink in. But when it did, the kitchen was filled with more excited squeals of delight, happy tears and so, so many questions.

'Why didn't you let us know you were coming home? We would have been here to meet you, but Lucy was in a hairdressing competition, for the Coronation Cup. And she won Apprentice of The Year,' Evie said, looking at her brother whom she hadn't seen for the last two years. 'We want to hear all your news,' she added, holding Jack at arm's-length after almost squeezing the life out of him. 'You've changed so much in two short years!'

'I'm glad you think they're short, it seemed quite a while to me.' Jack had grown into a man with muscles and was no longer the gangly youth of yesteryear.

'You're all grown up and handsome,' said Lucy. 'War has been the making of you!'

'I can see you haven't wasted any time in the growing up department either,' Jack said, not wanting to go into detail about the Korean war and the atrocities he had seen. 'I've brought you both a present.'

'Is this it?' Lucy asked, picking up a package, tied with string, on the table.

'No, that was on the lobby floor when I came in.'

'It's looks like it's for me ' said Evie, thinking it must have come via her Post Office Box.

'Are you home for good? Have you left the army now? Is your National Service over?'

'I forgot she did that,' Jack said to Evie and gave an easy-going laugh, his eyes sparkling against his golden tan. 'She always asks ten questions where only one would do?'

'Nothing changes around here,' Evie laughed, and the three of them spent the rest of the night talking, reminiscing and making plans for the future. They were all back together again and Evie could not be happier.

When her brother and sister went up to their rooms later, Evie told them she would stay down here and clear up. She picked up the package that had been delivered to the post office box address from the table, knowing it to be a business ledger. Undoing the string around it, and removing the brown paper wrapping, Evie was suddenly wide-eyed when she saw who the files belonged to. These were the Lenard Haulage files. Sitting heavily at the kitchen table, she began to flick through the pages. And something told her these could not possibly be the only set of accounts.

Because, according to these files. Lenard Haulage was running on a shoestring, had only a small yard, with a couple of doddery old horses, was barely earning enough to pay the wages of the proprietor, and could only afford one elderly, part-time clerk who was not worth her salt.

Evie felt her hackles rise. Only this afternoon she had discovered that Susie Blackthorn had been working for Lenard Haulage. Her only comfort was knowing that Susie could never deal with figures. She had no head for them. And that was why she sent the ledgers to a post office box.

Knowing the size of Lenard Haulage, as Evie did, she knew they would not miss the cost of an outside accountancy service.

21

'Hello, Dan,' said Angus when Danny walked into the Tram Tavern, the following evening, 'the usual?'

'Maybe later,' said Danny. 'Lucy wants to celebrate her win yesterday and wondered if you had anything besides pale ale?'

'I'm glad she won,' Angus said, reaching behind the bar to the little bottles displayed, 'and tell her I'm sorry I couldn't be there, but that's the way it goes when you run a pub.'

'I'll tell her, Angus, but I'm sure she'll understand.'

'This drink is new,' said Angus. 'It's called a perry, and fizzes like champagne, but it's not champagne, and the ladies love it.'

The bottle looked tiny in Danny's huge hands, and he read the label.

'Here, I'll give you a few of these fancy glasses I got with the promotion.' Angus handed Danny a long-stemmed wide-bowled glass, 'See what they think.'

'What's in it?' Danny asked, his curiosity piqued.

'Fizzy pears, the ladies love it.'

'In that case, I'll take a few more and some crisps to help them celebrate.'

When Danny got back to number two with bulging pockets, Jack was coming in from the back kitchen.

'I'm sure the girls don't want us here, spoiling their night talking military strategy.' Danny wanted to know all the details of his time in Korea, which he knew Jack would never discuss in front of Evie or Lucy. 'Angus said there's a pint with your name on it when you're ready.'

Jack's face beamed. 'Well, what are we waiting for, Danny me old mucker.' Jack nodded his head sideways in the direction of the tavern, and Danny laughed, knowing their antics were being keenly observed by the women.

'Great minds think alike. Let's have a catch-up and wet our whistle.' Danny took numerous little bottles out of his pockets, along with the fancy glasses that made Evie, Lucy, and Rachel coo with delight. It had been a long time since they had something to celebrate, and they were looking forward to tasting this latest innovation as Evie opened the packets of crisps and emptied them into cereal bowls.

'This is posh,' said Rachel, who loved the Kilgarens like her own family and spent almost as much time in their house as she did in her own. And now that Jack was home, she imagined she might spend a lot more time here. Jack was a dreamboat who wouldn't be out of place on the big screen at the Rialto.

* * *

Angus and Danny filled Jack in with all the latest goings-on around the dockyards and railways. Jack was much happier here in the tavern than trying to put his older sister's mind at rest about his last two years in Korea, where he had seen men killed, maimed and seriously injured fighting a war that had nothing to do with British

soldiers, as far as he could see, but who had been sent there to do their bit.

'There are some characters, I can tell you,' Jack laughed. 'We had one guy, Filchy, they called him, because he couldn't keep his hands to himself.' He was leaning on the bar, one foot crossed over his other leg, enjoying the company of like-minded pals who had all served their country in their time. 'If it wasn't nailed down, Filchy would have it and be away on his toes quick-smart.'

'Not much different to Civvy Street,' said Angus. 'There's one black marketeer, naming no names, mind, who relies on warehousemen turning a blind eye while he and his gang nab food or cigarettes from the docks or the railway sidings.'

Danny nodded to Jack, knowing exactly who Angus was talking about.

The men exchanged stories of their military career, and Jack told them he had no intentions of becoming a regular soldier after what he had seen over the last two years, and although he and Danny had only nipped into the bar for a quick pint, they were so engrossed in their conversations they didn't see the time fly and were still there two hours later.

'I see another warehouse got knocked-off last night,' said Angus, and the other two nodded. 'I'm sure we all know who's in on that one.'

'No names, no pack drill,' said Jack saluting, a little bit sloshed due to the amount of welcome-home drinks that had been bought for him by the locals. All the time he was in the army fighting for his country, being shot at and evading being blown to smithereens, spivs like Leo Darnel were heading an unruly shower of villains who were creaming off a nice lifestyle for themselves by looting and thieving everything in sight.

'Pilfering reached a crescendo, as you must have heard,' said Angus, 'which was why I was appointed an undercover inspector

for the Ministry of Food.' Angus kept his past quiet usually and only spoke on a need-to-know-basis.

'Really?' Danny said. He knew Angus was 'something' in procedures but wasn't sure exactly what it was, and he hadn't asked either, knowing when – and if – Angus wanted him to know he would tell him.

Both Danny and Jack knew undercover inspectors were a force to be reckoned with, tough and relentless, they had to be, to confront the criminals who worked alone or in packs like Darnel's mob. You sure as hell didn't want to get on the wrong side of undercover detectives at any time.

'We knew of a factory,' Angus said, lowering his head so his whispered words could not be read from his lips, 'where a van drove up to the warehouse two or three times a week, and then drove away again loaded with food, cigarettes, meat, booze, you name it. Stuff that isn't always readily available because of the rationing, that is still in force.' The three men, in unison, gave their disapproving opinion about the rationing, eight years after the war had ended.

'I've been asked a few times if I want to "offload" goods,' Danny said, his brow furrowing, 'even though, it will do my pocket no harm at all, I'm not getting involved in that game – you never know where it will end.' He liked to keep his nose clean. Stay on the right side of the rails and not get mixed up in anything dodgy.

'I can't say our Evie would be impressed either,' said Jack, knowing his sister was as honest as the day was long. 'She won't stand for any funny business.'

'And quite right too,' said Angus, raising his glass, quickly followed by his two companions. 'Darnel is getting too big for his boots, roping in smaller concerns to give the notion of being legal and above board.'

'Legal, my eye!' Danny scoffed. 'If he goes straight, I'll eat my big toe.'

'Apparently, if the smaller businesses don't comply, he wipes them out altogether,' Angus said. 'The wagons drop the goodies in hotels and restaurants further afield. It's happening all over the country. Most thefts are not quite so bare-faced, but with the Coronation coming up they have no shortage of clients who are willing to pay over the odds.'

'I've had my share of offers, too,' Danny said, accepting another pint Angus placed on the bar. Evie told him they had been getting lots of phone calls recently. 'Wagon drivers are being persuaded to turn a blind eye.'

'Especially by this one haulage contractor who is posing as a legitimate business,' Angus said, casually looking about the pub, making sure nobody was earwigging the conversation.

'I've been getting some very generous bids for the yard,' Danny said, grateful for the chance to offload his worries to Angus and Jack. 'Every time I tell Lenard's I've no intentions of selling my business, the price goes up.' He noticed Angus and Jack were paying full attention. 'But I will never sell to the likes of Lenard's, I don't trust them.'

'You want to watch yourself with that lot,' said Angus, 'they don't take any prisoners.'

Danny assured the gathered company that he was well able for anything that came his way, and looking at his watch he could not believe how quickly the time had passed.

'So, the wedding?' Jack said. He had heard enough talk about skulduggery, and after two years spent in conflict, he was on the look-out for a bit of good news.

'It will be a quiet affair, unfortunately.' Danny would love to give Evie the wedding every girl dreamed of, but the way the business was going, he knew they couldn't run to a lavish party. He'd said as much to his sister, Grace, when he spoke to her on the telephone yesterday. Given the current situation, with work drying up, he'd told her, feeling disconsolate about the matter, they couldn't possibly afford it. 'Evie, my beautiful, headstrong, talented girl agrees passionately.' Danny knew the beer was doing the talking now, because words like 'passionately' brought him troubling thoughts concerning Evie.

'She's always had her head screwed on right,' Jack said proudly, wiping all thoughts of passion from Danny's mind – and rightly so. He didn't have much longer to wait. Just six long weeks.

'She keeps us all on the straight and narrow,' Danny said, 'and will not be intimidated by bullies.'

Angus's eyes lit up when Connie brought them a plate of freshly made ham sandwiches, which were quickly devoured by the ravenous men.

Returning to the subject of Darnel and his antics, Angus said: 'A little bird tells me a warehouse full of bedroom suites and dining-room suites was offloaded by a certain transport manager. And none of your utility stuff either.'

Danny cogitated on what Angus had just said, knowing Ada had bought a new bedroom suite a few months back. She had showed him it, so proud she actually had something new for the first time in her married life, and he worried that she might have succumbed to an undercut priced bit of furniture. He didn't want to see her get into trouble, knowing she had not been hostile to under-the-counter dealings in the past.

The rewards of the black market were substantial for those in control and Danny knew the black market in furniture was thriving.

'The transport manager of Lenard's has taken on more drivers,' Angus said on his return from collecting dirty glasses. 'He can't get enough drivers. I overheard them talking in the bar. The receivers are ready with the cash and they're not stingy either apparently.'

'Some people are never satisfied – they always want more,' Danny said, knowing his own business was losing out to Lenard Haulage hand over fist. He could not possibly compete with a fleet that big.

'There has been an ongoing police enquiry, and you'll never guess?' Angus busied himself behind the bar, emptying ashtrays and collecting beer-stained bar towels. 'There was even one of Lenard's men in that big posh shop in town, Ruby's Emporium.'

'Go on,' said Danny, all ears now. He had wondered when the slick set-up would start to crumble, knowing there were more dodgy dealers in Lenard's than you could count.

'A report in the *Evening Echo* said he was sentenced to six months' hard labour.'

'I remember when their yard was raided before Christmas and shut down, it was like a well-stocked grocers' shop,' said Danny, shaking his head.

'Gin, whisky and brandy by the caseload, crates of tinned milk, cream. Imagine how much that lot was worth on the streets.' Angus warmed to his conversation and Danny, nodding, knew now he had been taken into Angus's confidence, the older man could not hold his tongue. 'Cigarettes, soap, you name it, chocolates, tinned salmon, tinned sardines, tinned fruit, salt, meat, cakes, and what did Lenard Haulage get – nothing. They got off scot-free. How they wriggled out of that one I'll never know.' Angus knew more inspectors had been hired to combat pilfering. 'Police raided an old air-raid shelter down Queen Street,' Angus gave a low chuckle, 'the whole hoard consisted of a packet of stolen biscuits, three bars of toffee and a tin of peaches. And there wasn't one of the little blighters over the age of nine.' They all chuckled. 'The little sods found a hole in the railings, where railway wagons had parked for the night in the siding, and staged a smash-and-grab raid.'

Danny knew that two major sources of pilfering goods was the railways and the docks, and if Lenard had his yard, which was almost on top of the docks, then it would be easier to get the stolen goods away. Danny began to understand the urgency. With the Coronation coming up next month, orders for food and suchlike would be in demand, and Lenard Haulage would need premises near the docks, to work from, and to store their ill-gotten gains.

'And another thing I heard...' Angus said, but he was interrupted when the bar door flew open, banging noisily against the wall, and the desperate-looking figure of Bobby Harris bounced in. Angus, like a bullet from a gun, lifted the wooden flap and was out from behind the bar in a blink, quickly followed by Jack and a few of the less inebriated men who elbowed their way towards Bobby, aware the lad was plainly scared by the way his eyes searched the room, his body rapidly zigzagging, looking for somebody.

'Danny? Where's our Danny? Danny!' Bobby did not see Danny at first, his wide eyes searching the gathered throng of men. 'Evie said our Danny's in here!'

'Aye, I'm here,' Danny said, moving through the throng towards the young man whom he still considered his brother. 'What's the matter?'

'Danny, you'd better come quick – the yard is on fire!

22

Skidding down the back alley, the air was filled with smoke that nipped at his lungs and Danny saw the orange glow flickering on the gable wall of the house he had been living in for the past three years. He could hear the terrified whinny of the horses and saw a long line of neighbours were already sloshing buckets of water over the flames. He was at the yard in moments. His worst fears realised when he saw the terrified horses were still in their stables.

The padlock had been broken and the large double gates swung open in the late-evening air. When Danny tried to get inside the yard, he was driven back by the heat. Time and time again, he tried to get to the stables and free the terrified horses. He could hear their hooves crashing against the stable wall, bucking and snorting as the pungent smoke filled their huge nostrils, the terror clearly visible in the whites of their staring eyes, but still he was beaten back as buckets and the bowls of water were passed along the line from Ada Harris's house, Meggie's kitchen, and the canal too.

'No, lad!' called Henry, hurrying along the line to the yard, his wife Meggie at his heels. 'You can't go in there, you'll be cooked alive!'

'I have to save the horses, Pop!' called Danny, pulling his dark jacket over his head, and trying once more to dodge the rising flames.

'Danny, don't do it!' Evie screamed, hurrying across the debris.

'Here, take this,' Bobby called. His head covered with a soaking-wet sheet, he threw a saturated blanket to Danny, who also covered his head and shoulders, and lowering his head he led the way into the yard. He didn't have time to tell Bobby to stay well back; he was too worried about getting his horses out of the yard alive.

In moments, the air was filled with the sound of fire engines and Danny, his mouth dry and his head a mass of jumbled questions, breathed a little easier. But not for long when the sound of a woman's scream rent the evening air.

Looking over his shoulder through the smoke that was beginning to stealthily seep into the stables, Danny's body momentarily froze when he caught sight of Susie Blackthorn cowering in an empty stable. His jaw slackened. Susie was the last person he expected to see.

'What the hell...?' Danny asked. His eyes streaming with the fumes of acrid smoke, he squinted, peering through the flames to see more clearly. Susie slumped against the stable wall. Surely, she wouldn't be so vindictive as to set light to the stables. That was just plain wicked. 'Did you...' he began, but Danny could not ask the question that was forming on his lips. Surely, she would never stoop so low as to jeopardise the horses.

'I saw someone running from the yard,' Susie cried, her slurred words coming out like a ricochet of bullets above the cacophony of splintering wood, panicked voices, crashing water and the firemen ordering everyone to stay well back.

'Did you recognise him?' he asked as Susie hauled herself up out of the hay and leaned forward, her eyes streaming with tears, and she was obviously drunk.

'Susie, I have to save the horses.'

'Oh, we must save the poor bloody horses. Mind the horses are saved!' Her eyes were slits, as she craned her neck, 'Susie can burn in hell.' Her voice grew louder, hysterical. 'I waited for you to offer a morsel of affection, but you never wanted me. I wrote every day when you were in the army. Thrilled when I would get a cursory reply.'

'Susie, you have to get out of here!' Danny tried to take hold of her arm, but she shook him off, determined not to move.

'Why should I?' Her ruby lips curled in contempt. 'Mighty Danny Harris... Or is it Skinner these days?' Her hand was on her hip and she seemed oblivious to the danger as she stumbled forward on a drunken lurch. 'Danny Skinner & Son... I can see it... Until your little empire went up in smoke.'

'You did this?' Danny's voice was laced with accusation. He would never have believed she could be so ruthless. But now he was not so sure. The flames began to lick the wooden post of the stable and he knew if it reached the hay they would be done for.

'I was here before anybody!' Susie stabbed his chest with her forefinger. 'I was here before you... And before her.' Susie lowered her voice to a whisper. 'We were all fine until *she* came, Danny.'

'Susie, you're not talking sense.' He stepped forward as Susie, once again, withdrew from his reach.

'You know very well what I'm talking about. You know!' Her voice reached a crescendo of seething self-pity. She had been drinking gin, he could smell it on her even over the smell of smoke. When he grabbed her arm to lead her to safety, her inebriated glare turned hostile. 'We were content until *she* came and ruined everything. She's nowt but a jumped-up charlady, a scrubber, a nothing! She came from nothing. And she will always be – nothing!'

Danny saw her face clearly as the dancing flames illuminated her face, distorted with anger and self-pity. He wondered if she had been put up to this by Harry Caraway, but he knew she would never admit to it. His pulse was racing so hard he could hear the blood pounding in his ears.

'You jilted me for her.' Susie was obviously driven by the belief she had been wronged.

'I never made you any promises, Susie.' Danny was still trying to get her out of there, with one eye on the rising flames, aware that people were doing everything they could to get the horses out of the stables. And he knew she was talking rubbish. No matter how much she tried to entice him, Danny would never risk the consequences of one single night with Susie. 'I'll tell you this much.' Danny's words were almost drowned out by the noise of cracking timber as the flames began to lick the stable doors. 'Evie is the only girl for me.' Danny suddenly realised that if Susie Blackthorn were a man, he would be lying face down and spark out right now.

'I tried to get you a good price on this place,' she said, her arms spread out towards the stables, 'all you had to do was sell up. Harry was willing to pay over the odds.'

'But why?' Danny asked, immediately suspicious of her part in all of this. His voice was measured, aware of horse's hooves clip-clopping in the cobbled yard outside.

Lightning-fast, Susie passed him, and he reached out to stop her, to hold her back from the fire still blazing, but she was too fast and in seconds she disappeared through the smoke towards Reckoner's Row.

'This is all your fault, Danny Harris, don't you ever forget that.' Susie's words were forced between her teeth as she ran towards her own home.

If Danny hadn't scorned her, she would not have looked twice at Harry Caraway, who had seduced her with flattery, fine words, and had cast a spell over her. She would never have got through those bloody ledgers he gave her to work on. The ones she sent to an outside accountancy service, who promised complete discretion. A post office box number, where confidentiality was their byword. . But, she admitted to herself, maybe she had been a little foolish to go into the stables with a lit cigarette when she heard footsteps in the yard.

* * *

When the fire was completely out and the damage surveyed, Meggie, Evie and Ada brought out cups of hot tea for everybody whose sooty faces showed bright white teeth as they accepted the much-needed drink in the cold night air.

'Do they have any idea how the fire started?' Evie asked Danny, who had been talking with the leading fireman.

'They have secured what they can for tonight and will be back tomorrow to thoroughly examine the place.'

'What about the office?' Evie asked. 'Is it serviceable.'

Danny shook his head, he looked shattered. 'I don't know,' he answered. 'Luckily, none of the horses were injured, although they are still excitable. It took a while to calm them down when we took them to the stables along Derby Road.' Danny would get to the bottom of what happened tonight and swore he would fix it.

'Best take Evie home and then come and get your head down, lad,' said Henry.

Danny nodded, feeling suddenly drained. He had his suspicions who caused the fire. But he was saying nothing, not until, he was sure. He didn't want to give anybody the heads-up just yet. He was no fool. This shocking destruction had all the marks of a disgruntled rival. One who wanted to see him on his knees and sabotaging all he had built up over the past three years. Danny's affable nature had been tested to breaking point, and now he wanted answers.

'One thing I am sure of, though,' said Danny with a determination he had not felt for a long time, 'whoever did this had better pray I don't get to them before the law does.' Not one for violence after what he had witnessed during the war, Danny knew there was an exception to every rule.

The stables and outbuildings were so badly damaged it was impossible to work from Skinner's yard and after the investigations were completed, Evie offered her front room as an office, while Danny, Jack and Bobby got to work in the yard. The office was unusable, needing a new door and windows, which were smashed in the heat of the fire. Luckily, the filing cabinet was saved, as was the desk, although not much else.

'I wonder what Susie was doing at the stables?' Evie said to Lucy as they moved the office furniture into the parlour as a man in overalls installed a new telephone there and connected it to the exchange.

'Who knows what goes on in her tiny mind, it's not like there is anything of worth in there,' Lucy answered

'But there is something of worth in the filing cabinet,' Evie said in answer to Lucy's suggestion there was nothing worth pinching, 'the Skinner files would be worth a fortune to Lenard Haulage. They have the names of every client we service.' It also held the names of the new accounts, which Evie had been working on.

Evie rang every business they had ever dealt with, to let them know Skinner's was up and running, but she was surprised to discover that many of them were not as enthusiastic as they might have been. Some of them sounded quite distant, even vague about when they would be employing the service of Skinner & Son again.

* * *

'It's going to take weeks to get this lot sorted,' said Bobby as they removed charred wood from the yard, but Danny and Jack were not listening to any of that defeatist talk.

'You have two of Her Majesty's finest soldiers on the job,' said Danny, unloading a pallet of red bricks, 'we know a thing or two about constructing solid buildings and I did a deal with the bloke in the brick yard. These stables are going to be stronger than they've ever been.'

'I wish I could do something to help,' said Henry Skinner, mooching about the yard.

'You can be our can lad,' said Jack, who had been given his first job by Henry, which seemed like a lifetime ago. 'Then there's the horses to check up on at the temporary stables in Derby Road, you won't have a minute to call your own.'

'That's more like it,' Henry flashed a beaming smile. 'Us dads like to be useful.'

* * *

'Penny for them?' Danny said when he returned to see Evie, who turned from the window and tried her best to look cheerful. 'Come on, spill the beans, I can see something is bothering you.'

'I never could hide anything from you, Danny,' she said, weary with the worry of it all. If things carried on at this rate, she told him, she could not see her and Danny being able to afford a wedding, not even a small one.

'Something will turn up.' Danny was ever the optimist, but before she could stop them, Evie's eyes filled with tears that ran in rivulets down her cheeks. 'Hey? Hey, come on, it's pre-wedding nerves.' He looked so concerned she wanted to run and hide, but that would only make things worse, she knew.

'There isn't going to be any wedding,' she spluttered as salty tears covered her lips. 'You won't want to marry a girl who can't keep things in order.'

'What kind of things?' he asked, guiding Evie to her chair behind the desk. 'C'mon, we've always been able to share our worries. I don't know how I'd have coped in the army if it hadn't been for your crazy letters full of gossip and bad jokes.' Evie managed a crooked smile when he said, 'I looked forward to every single one of them.'

'The business is not in very good shape, and since the fire, it's worse than ever,' she sniffed. 'I didn't tell you the whole truth of it, but I'm sure you must have suspected.'

Danny was quiet for a while, then he went out to the back kitchen and put the kettle on.

'There's nothing we can't solve,' he said a short while later, bringing two cups into the parlour and settling down at the oppo-site side of the desk, while Evie picked up the unopened envelope from earlier that day.

'Look,' she said in despair, 'another bill no doubt.'

'Jack wanted to invest,' Danny said quickly. 'He told me he's got a bit put by – there's not many places to spend your money out in the paddy fields and—'

'Yes, he told me in his letters that he used to draw portraits of the lads, and they would buy them from him to send home to their girl, their wife, or their mother. The money could be an investment?'

'I told him we would sort it out,' said Danny, who had his own ideas for the yard, and didn't want to be beholden to anybody, not even someone as trustworthy as Jack. 'We couldn't possibly. He will need the money for his own future, and it might take a while to get things back on track.'

Evie took a letter from the envelope. Her eyes dull and all hopes of her wedding flying out of the door. Then, only a moment later, her jaw dropped, and her eyes widened. She looked across the desk to Danny.

'I have spent all day wondering how we are going to wriggle out of this vat of treacle,' she told him. 'I wondered how we were going to pay another bill.'

'Did you find an answer in that letter?' Danny asked, looking to Evie, her expression had suddenly brightened. She waved the contents of the envelope in the air and Danny's hopes soared. He had absolutely no idea what the letter was about, but he was pleased to see a smile on her face.

'You know I've always been careful with money,' Evie said, and Danny nodded, knowing she had pulled them out of many a scrape in the past. 'I believe in belt and braces, which was what was so annoying, when I couldn't make the income cover the outgoings. But there was one thing I made sure I paid every single week, and that was the insurance on the business and the outbuildings.'

'And...?'

'And this is a cheque for the damage that was done in the fire.' Evie could not believe their luck had changed so quickly.

'That's fantastic news,' Danny said, delighted things were making Evie smile again. 'At least you will be able to pay the bills and—'

'And with this amount, we will have enough left over to buy a second-hand wagon.' Evie jumped up from the desk and, coming towards Danny, she sat on his knee. 'I know this isn't the thing to do,' she said, making Danny's temperature soar, 'but it is certainly a day of celebration in more ways than one.'

* * *

Later that week, Evie heard a noise and went out to the narrow lobby to see a brown paper package lying on the polished linoleum-covered floor. The clunk she heard had obviously been the parcel being pushed through the letterbox. Turning it over, she noticed there was no name or address, nor any stamps. The parcel had been delivered by hand.

Opening the front door, Evie peered down the street, allowing the spring sunshine to flood into the narrow hallway, but she could see nobody who might have delivered the package, only children playing and neighbours decorating their houses for tomorrow's celebrations. And, distracted, her heart fluttered when she caught sight of Danny sauntering up the row like he owned every house.

'Someone has just posted this through the letterbox,' Evie told Danny as he slipped his hand round her slender waist.

'Not me,' he answered. Pulling her towards him, he gave her a long lingering kiss, right there on the doorstep. Evie did not resist his kiss, she couldn't even if she wanted to, which she didn't. They were getting married at the end of June and she could hardly wait.

'Are you coming in for a cup of tea?' Evie asked and felt a stab of disappointment when Danny shook his head and shrugged his broad shoulders.

'I've got to pick up a consignment from the docks and take it to Manchester.'

'That will take all day,' she said, and Danny nodded.

'If we are saving for the wedding, I can't refuse any jobs at all.'

'This one isn't in the book,' Evie said, knowing all the jobs came through her. 'It's not illegal, is it?' Evie asked. She was having nothing to do with dodgy dealings.

'Don't be daft,' Danny laughed. 'I'm not going to ruin the good reputation of Skinner's, am I?'

Evie agreed that the idea was ridiculous. But over the last few months so much had happened, she didn't know what to think.

'Thank goodness, Jack and Bobby are such good workers to keep the working parts of the yard going.' Danny, never one to see a glass half-empty, always looked on the bright side. He gave her a kiss on her cheek before going back to the yard to pick up his wagon.

Evie sighed. They could only go so far down before they bounced back up, she thought, knowing if optimism was local currency, they would be richer than Grace. Clasping the package close to her body, she watched every step that Danny took as he headed down Reckoner's Row towards Skinner's Yard, swelling with pride, knowing very soon she would be his wife. Mrs Evie Skinner. The name had a good solid ring to it.

Leaving the front door open, she went back into the parlour and unwrapped the package. There was nothing unusual about it; these types of parcels were being delivered all the time. The post office box number had turned out to be quite lucrative and she was surprised at the amount of very successful businesses that looked so poor on paper. Her body tensed, and her breath hitched a little when she pulled the contents out and saw the name written in block capitals across the front.

'Lennard Haulage Accounts,' she said, breathing hard when she realised their significance. Flicking through the pages, her jaw dropped, and she swung round when she heard the door open behind her. 'Lucy! You frightened the life out of me,' she told her sister as adrenaline zipped through her like fireworks exploding on bonfire night. 'These are the original account books from Lennard's,' Evie exclaimed, trying to contain her excitement. 'I *knew* those first set of accounts were bogus,' said Evie, engrossed in the lines of figures which she was going to enjoy working on so much.

'Lenard's Accounts?' Danny said, causing the two girls to turn sharply, they hadn't heard him coming back into the house, and Evie's forehead pleated into a silent question. 'I came back to ask if you wanted to go to the pictures tonight.'

Evie had been so excited, but her excitement dissipated to nothing, like a fresh painting left out in the rain. Danny knew little about the extra work she had taken on to support his business and keep a roof over their heads.

'There's something I have to tell you,' she said, wondering how the hell she was going to explain to Danny why she was doing the accounts for his biggest rival.

'I'll leave you to it,' Lucy said, heading for the door.

The scant work Danny had been doing kept the yard going and the horses fed. But even that was diminishing by the day. When she'd phoned one of the most loyal firms Skinner's had dealt with for years, she had been told in an almost apologetic tone that they had been offered a better deal. Danny was not in the least pleased, as Evie knew he would not be.

'I can't have you bailing me out,' Danny explained. 'If the business isn't working, I will have to try something else.' His hands were in the pockets of his brown corduroy trousers, and he stared out of the parlour window, knowing Skinner's yard which, in years gone by, had been a bustling hive of activity was like a ghost yard these days. The only work being done was restoration work, and if he didn't get some more work soon, even that would come to a halt.

'*We* will have to try something else,' Evie insisted, 'and guess what I have here in my hot little mitt? The accounts of Lenard Haulage!' Evie stabbed the hard-backed ledger with her forefinger.

'I received some accounts before and according to those they were limping along, with only a clapped-out wagon that is constantly in need of expensive repairs. Run-down stables... Horses to feed, clean and care for...' Evie saw Danny's expression change, and he showed an increasing interest in the contents of the accounts as she read out the list. 'And listen to this pile of cheek! Those accounts recorded that the only office employee is an *elderly*, inexperienced clerk who has no knowledge of bookkeeping whatsoever.'

'Sounds dodgy to me. Accounts for the taxman to see?' Danny's cheeky grin lit up his incredible blue eyes.

'I didn't want to tell you about the extra work, because I know how hard you work to keep everything together – but business has been decreasing rapidly. We had to do something.'

'You mean *you* had to do something?' Danny's words were momentarily laced with disappointment, 'but you did it with the best of intentions and for that I love you even more – if that were ever possible.'

'We are honest and loyal, Danny,' she said, 'doesn't that count for anything these days?'

'My thoughts, exactly,' Danny sighed and put his arm round Evie. 'That's why we are so good together, we both have the same values, but there is one thing you have that I can't match,' Danny said, and Evie worried momentarily that he was going to voice his regret that she went behind his back to keep the business afloat. 'You have much better legs than I do.' He smiled that heart-stopping smile and Evie laughed with relief, playfully slapping his hand.

'I would never have expected a little gem like this to fall into my lap, though.' Evie breathed, knowing that this latest ledger told the true story of who, and what, Lenard Haulage was all about. 'I offered total discretion when I put the advert in the paper,' Evie explained, 'and I know how hopeless Susie is when it comes to figures – the only figure she's interested in is her own. I also know she will always get somebody else to do her work for her.' Evie could have danced. 'But this is beyond my wildest dreams; I didn't expect her to outsource Lennard's accounts.'

'Thank you for being so damned lazy, Susie,' Danny laughed. He still had his suspicion that Susie started the fire, but he had no proof, and it wasn't the kind of thing he could go around accusing somebody of, unless he had solid knowledge. 'I never thought I would ever say that.'

'Obviously, she doesn't know who is offering the accountancy service,' Evie said, taking the seat behind her desk and picking up the original accounts ledger that Susie had sent through the post office box address, 'otherwise she would never have sent this pack of lies.' She was quiet for a moment and then, pointing to the second ledger, said: ' It doesn't explain how these got here though.'

'Or she may have been struck by a stab of conscience and decided to do some good for a change?' Danny said. 'I'm sure she must have some good points.'

Evie raised a well-shaped eyebrow and said, 'You'd waste most of your day trying to find her good points, I'm sure.' Then in her usual brisk way she waved her hand to Danny. 'Right, I must get on, I have work to do,' Evie's words pushed Danny towards the parlour door, 'and so do you.'

'Pictures? Tonight?'

'Maybe,' Evie said and a moment later she was alone, engrossed in rows of figures, and as each moment passed, she became even more excited. This new ledger was explosive in the wrong hands. Whoever was responsible for the illegal goings on at Lenard's was going to be in serious trouble.

24

JUNE

Connie, Evie, Ada Mim and Meggie, along with the rest of the Reckoner's Row women, were sitting at long tables in the tavern, the morning before the long-awaited Coronation of Queen Elizabeth the 2nd. They were busy making red, white and blue crepe paper flowers and the floor was a mass of cardboard boxes containing the decorations they had been making for months which would festoon Reckoner's Row. The kerbstones had been painted red, white and blue and everybody was so excited for the actual day of the Coronation.

Connie's daughter, three-year-old Annie, had been chosen as Reckoner's Row's very own queen and there was going to be a ceremonial crowning after the real service. Everybody was looking forward to the celebrations and the preparations for the big day had brought a harmonious atmosphere of anticipation.

'Ada, come and see this!' Angus popped his head round the door, interrupting the low buzz of female conversation, and all eyes turned to Ada, who shrugged, not knowing what he was alluding to. 'There's a man at your door says he has to deliver a television set.'

Her brows pleated and she looked from one to another of the

women, all dressed alike in flowered pinnies and bright turbaned headscarves, their quick-working hands now still.

'A television set?' said Ada. 'I haven't ordered a television set.' She looked puzzled and put away her decorations in her box and hurried to the door, quickly followed by the rest of the women, who didn't like to miss a bit of something going on in the row.

'Have you come into a few bob, Ada?' said Mim with a smile.

'I wish I had,' said Ada, who knew television sets were out of reach of most people's purses, especially round here, and those who were lucky enough to have a set in their house rented it from the Rediffusion shop. She hadn't ordered a television. The thought hadn't even crossed her mind.

Hurrying down Reckoner's Row, the smell of baking in prepara-tion of tomorrow's celebrations filled the air: cupcakes, biscuits, sausage rolls, meat pies, jam tarts, while freshly made jellies and trifles would be brought out on the day by a small line of women. In the small, tightly packed street lined with three-up, three-down terraced houses that had no bathrooms and only an outside lava-tory, the delivery of a brand-new television set was something to behold.

'On whose authority did you do that for?' asked Ada, getting her words tangled as she was apt to do when she became overexcited. 'I didn't order a television set,' she told the two delivery men who looked like they were carrying a cupboard, 'and if you think I'm going to sign for an expensive weight around my neck, you've got another thing coming because I most certainly am not!' On the last word, she gave a single, determined nod of her head.

'We've just been ordered to deliver it, Missus,' said the taller of the two delivery men, looking very red in the face. 'Do you mind if I put it down for a minute, it's very heavy.'

'Only if it's not going to cost me,' said Ada. Eyeing the walnut veneer casing and the fourteen-inch screen, she already had a covetous gleam in her eye, imagining it sitting on the sideboard in the front-room bay, knowing it would look a treat and could be seen by anybody who passed her window. She held her hand out when the other delivery man, dressed in muddy-brown coloured overalls, handed her an envelope.

'It has already been paid for, here is the docket and all the particulars.'

Ada opened the envelope and took out a card from her daughter, Grace.

Dear Ma,

Grace had written,

Now you can watch the coronation from your armchair, love Grace, Bruce, and baby Niamh xxx

'It's from our Grace!' Ada was delighted, and she couldn't praise her daughter highly enough. But when she looked at the receipt for full payment of the television set, Ada's eyes nearly popped out of her head at the price. 'Sixty guineas!' Ada gasped. 'That's a whole year's wages.'

Ada heard the whispered words and sharp intakes of breath from the other women who were standing down by the gate and she turned towards them. Her eyes a mixture of surprise and pride.

'Didn't I tell you I had the best children in the whole world.'

'Often,' whispered one neighbour and although Ada heard, she didn't retaliate as she usually would. She was so happy with her new television set.

'You must all come and watch the Coronation here tomorrow,' she said on impulse, 'it is going to be wonderful.' The set would have pride of place in her parlour, she told the delivery men, who took it into the front room and, removing the aspidistra from the sideboard, placed the set on the lace cloth. Just where everybody could see it.

'Hiya, Ma! It came then.' Bobby's face was beaming with pleasure when he came into the parlour. 'All we have to do now is put the aerial on the roof and we have television!'

'The roof?' Ada looked horrified. 'You will not be going up on to the roof!'

'No, Missus,' said a workman dressed in baggy navy-blue overalls, who followed Bobby into the front room without invitation, 'you have to leave that kind of thing to the professionals. We're insured, you see.'

Ada nodded, forgetting to scold the workman for coming into her house uninvited. Insurance meant everything. Because she was in no position to fix the roof if Bobby put his foot through it. Not once did she think of the consequences of him falling off it.

Ada's pride swelled her body. She would invite the whole row in to watch the Coronation on her very own television set, the first in Reckoner's Row. For the first time in months, she managed to forget about the locked box sitting in the gas cupboard next to the bay window.

* * *

The following morning, Evie collected the post that was still being delivered to the yard, hoping some of the letters might be tenders for work instead of bills. While Danny, Jack, and Bobby had done their best to build the new stables, she knew the whole yard needed a complete overhaul to bring it up to date as the office was still unusable, and Evie continued to work from her parlour.

Looking out of the parlour window, she was pleased to see the residents were busy putting up decorations as there was going to be a competition for the best decorated street, so Reckoner's Row was bedecked in festoons of patriotic colours of the realm. Everybody was hanging new decorations on their houses after this morning's rain left yesterday's efforts dripping wet. Even the bridge had been decorated with paper chain flowers and streamers.

The morning drizzle had done nothing to dampen the enthusiasm of eager residents from celebrating the coronation of the new Queen and the housewives were thrilled they had been awarded extra rations to ensure plenty of food including home-made cakes, biscuits, jellies and pastries, all set out on trestle tables borrowed from the church hall placed down the middle of the row, while Angus and Danny rolled out the Tram Tavern piano for a good old singsong later.

Settling down to work on the Lenard's folder, Evie's heart missed a beat when she saw the accounts which were much more detailed than the previous reports that came from Lenard Haulage. Her eyes widened as she stared at the name of the managing director, who was not Harry Caraway.

Evie covered her open mouth with the palm of her hand to stem the small squeal that escaped her lips when her eyes scrolled the huge list of figures. Obviously, the managing director wanted to keep track of what his company was earning, even if he didn't want the tax man to know.

'Got you!' she said aloud when she looked at the true figures. The names of all their clients were listed. They had started off paying a paltry introductory sum for the haulage, which Lenard's was offering. Then, gradually, when Lenard's had gained their trust, the sum became larger, probably unbeknown to the firms who were calling on their services. The invoices would be much higher at the end of the month than they were at the beginning with daily interest added, even though the same work had been done on all occasions.

Evie could not be more astonished if she had been hit with a shovel. Looking again at the name of the managing director, Leo Lenard! The name loomed large. Lenard was an anagram of Darnel. Evie wasn't stupid, so why hadn't she seen it sooner? How could she have missed it?

All the pieces began to fit in place. So many questions answered. But she could say nothing for the moment. She must be sure. If Darnel was behind this company, it was little wonder Danny was losing work. Darnel would do everything in his power to ruin Danny, because, most of all, he wanted to destroy *her*.

'Well not today, Mister,' Evie said, determined she was going to make him pay for the heartache he caused all those years ago. Now Evie knew who was responsible she intended to present her findings to the proper authority without further delay.

'You burned my books, and I swore I would get even. Now I am going to make you pay, in more ways than one.'

25

'Get down from there, you dozy mare.' Ada Harris marched along Reckoner's Row still in her carpet slippers. Her arms, as thick as ham shanks, were folded across a matronly bosom, and she was clad in the matriarchal uniform of a full-length flowered pinny covering her best dress. Glaring up to the first-floor window, Ada began to wave when Evie Kilgaren came out into the street to see what all the shouting was about. The brightly coloured turban covering Ada's salt-and-pepper hair seemed to take on a life of its own, her head bobbing about as she covered the cracked paving flags at an Olympian pace. 'You'll break your bloody neck if you fall off there,' Ada called, in no mood for this carry-on today. She calculated the drop if this silly girl, standing on the edge of the first-floor window ledge, slipped and fell. 'There'll be blood and sand all over the pavement.'

'Blood and sand?' Lucy asked Evie, who nudged her sister and made a shushing noise to silence her. 'What's Susie doing?'

'I don't think she's cleaning the windows,' Evie said, guarding her eyes with the flat of her hand across her eyebrows, as the glare from the June sun was brighter than it had been of late.

'I can't get down,' Susie moaned, holding on to her shivering body like it was coming away at the seams. She had already tried to drown herself in the canal, but her instinctive desire to live prevented her from letting the water cover her head, and she kept bobbing up, gasping for air. Harry Caraway had disappeared, leaving no forwarding address, and dumping all blame at Susie's door. And not only that, she thought, but he had left her with more than a fraudulent, money-laundering company, he had left her with an unborn child and no possible chance of marriage. What else could she do? Deciding it might be better to throw herself from the bedroom window, she had clambered onto the parlour's bay roof under the window, before real-ising she was not so keen on heights either. They scared her witless.

'You won't kill yourself if you fall off that,' one of the Gilmore brats had the temerity to inform her. 'The bay roof isn't high enough. You might break an arm or a leg, or a fingernail.' They hooted with laughter, finding the whole episode hilarious. *Bloody cheek!*

The thought of six weeks in plaster of Paris put paid to Susie's idea of throwing herself onto the street below. She would have stuck her head in the gas oven – but the gas went out just after her mother had gone shopping and left no money for the meter.

'Why are you dripping all over the parapet?' Ada called. It was a stupid question, but she knew Susie responded to straight talking. Common sense had never been the girl's saving grace, and Ada could see Susie was not listening to the coaxing tones used by other women of Reckoner's Row. Huddled like silver grey pigeons, cooing, and nodding their heads while bovine arms enfolded empty breasts, suckled dry by years of childbearing.

'I can't get down,' Susie whimpered with a hint of impatience in her voice.

'What do you mean, you can't get down? You got up there quick enough.' Ada's pragmatic, native Irish inflection told Susie the older woman was in no mood for being bothered by hysterical harpies on the day their new Queen was crowned. 'You'll get down if I have to come up there and drag ye down.'

The obvious warning in Ada's voice caught Susie unaware. She had expected a bit of persuasion, a bit of sympathy for her plight. Hoping Danny would come along and beg her not to do away with herself. Maybe even promise to marry her. But that was never going to happen. Evie Kilgaren would never make a show of herself like this, and that's the kind of girl Danny needed.

'Get in, and stop acting so daft, before I come up there.' Ada's determined expression told Susie she meant every word. 'I'm having none of your *hystericals* today,' she said, making a beeline for Susie's open front door.

'I'm coming down now.' Susie knew that she had gone too far this time. Women who had suffered through world wars, dock strikes, and the misery of defective housing caused by enemy bombs swayed before her with pity in their eyes.

'She must be desperate to even think of doing something so unholy,' said Meggie Skinner, who had suffered desperation first-hand as the women of Reckoner's Row paused in replenishing cake plates and filling waxed paper cups with lemonade to made a quick sign of the cross. A familiar sight from Catholic women who journeyed from their homes in Ireland to settle in the narrow, cobbled streets nestling in the silhouette of the Mersey dockyards and warehouses.

'Desperate for attention if you ask me,' said one woman and Susie scanned the row, as her frozen bare feet inched back towards the window. Suddenly, she slipped, and her flailing arms could find no purchase, she felt her feet slithering beneath her.

'Jesus wept!' Susie's feet headed towards the edge of the bay, her arms rotating, trying to regain her balance. Suddenly, she didn't want to fall off the bay roof any more.

'Come on, get yourself in here,' said Danny, who had seen Susie's performance and slipped through the door, taking the stairs two at a time. His no-nonsense tone was met with relief, when his hand shot out to grip Susie's arm, and she felt herself being hauled through the bedroom window. Her legs and the top of her feet scraping across the sandstone windowsill, taking the skin from her flesh, but the relief of being on the firm floor of her bedroom far outweighed any pain she may have experienced. Too embarrassed to look Danny in the eye, she ran to the back room and locked the door, until she heard him descending the stairs.

'See to her, Ma,' Danny said as he headed to the door, allowing Ada to enter the house with her chin held high and her shoulders back.

Danny had called her Ma, in front of the whole row. With a gleam in her eye, Ada turned to see the reaction of her neighbours and the satisfaction she got from their surprised expressions and hasty whispers brought a smile to her face.

'When me mam gets back from shopping in Stanley Road, there'll be hell to pay.' Susie told Ada, through the locked bedroom door when she tried to persuade the silly girl to come out. 'Mam and Da don't like to draw attention to themselves,' Susie whimpered.

Unlike you, Ada thought but kept her opinion to herself.

'Why don't you come down to my house and we'll have a nice cup of tea, like old times.' Ada's tone was much more sympathetic now. She knew first-hand what it was like to be on the edge of desperation. She knew what it was like to keep a secret that could not be told to another living soul. The weight of it was cripplingly heavy. 'You can tell me all about it.'

'I can't, Mrs Harris,' Susie said as tears ran freely down her cheeks, 'I can't tell a living soul.'

'Well,' Ada's voice was coaxing, 'I don't suppose you have to say anything. I know only too well what it is like to be an outsider in my own community.' The only child of a single, free-spirited mother, Ada was just a girl of fourteen when she had to fend for herself after her own mother died. Her only security was hard work, family, and to be one step ahead of death.

'Who says I'm an outsider!' Susie unlocked the door and swung it back against the wall. 'I never said that. I've lived in this row all my life; how can I see myself as an outsider?' Her tone was challenging, and Ada knew she had to tread carefully. This girl, as an only child, had been the centre of her elderly parents' world. Her father worked long hours for the gas company and her mother was always off doing charitable works for the church. Hardly a day went by as Susie was growing up when she was not cluttering up Ada's kitchen.

* * *

'I've done a terrible thing, Ada,' Susie said as she sat at the older woman's table. The house was empty except for the two of them.

'Everybody does something they are ashamed of at least once in their life,' said Ada, 'even if it was only buying a bit extra from the spivs, knowing there are many who cannot afford their exorbitant prices.' Ada shuffled in her seat. Hadn't she, many a time, been guilty of such a crime?

'I've got to get away from Reckoner's Row,' said Susie, reluctant to tell Ada the true reason, that she had been helping Harry Caraway to all but ruin Danny's business using the stolen accounts from Skinner's. But, it was she who decided to do more now that Harry had disappeared and had given two young idiots the nod. They were now locked up in Walton Gaol awaiting trail for setting the stables on fire and Susie worried that they might yet tell the police about her involvement. She only meant for them to let the horses go. Or put sugar in the engine of Danny's flat-back wagon. Not set fire to the place. That was going a step too far. But she couldn't possibly tell Ada all that, suspecting Ada would skull-drag her back to the bedroom window and throw her off the ledge herself! 'I made a right show of myself,' she told Ada. 'You know only too well.'

Ada nodded.

'I said some terrible things to Danny that I never should have said.' She scraped her cup along the saucer, making a grating noise that set Ada's teeth on edge. But she let it go wondering what Susie had said to Danny to make her so eager to leave the place where she was born and reared. For wasn't it Ada herself who had brought Susie into the world, when her mother took bad in the middle of the night, and a midwife could not be reached in time? Susie had been born with a caul over her face, and Ada had secreted the membrane about her person, salted it to dry it out and sold it to a sailor for twenty-five pounds. The superstitious Ada believed he wouldn't drown at sea, and it worked, because the sailor was now happily married and had three children.

'We all say things we don't mean with a drop of the hard stuff inside us,' Ada cooed, feeling benevolent, knowing she was going to be the first with this nugget of information to share with Mim Sharp in the tavern.

'I told him that I loved him.' Susie lowered her eyes and pulled at the skin on the back of her hand. 'I told him that Evie was not the girl for him... And that she was nothing but a charlady... A scrubber who would never amount to anything.'

'Is that so?' Ada's voice lacked pitch or tone. Here she was giving her best hospitality to this spoiled, self-serving madam when others would not give her the time of day. Where had Susie been when Ada had been disgraced by *poor Bert,* as Susie called him, she was nowhere near this house, that's for sure. She had been *conscientious* by her absence, thought Ada, mismatching her words again.

For a long time, there was no sound in the kitchen except for that of the ticking clock, and Susie realised what she had just said, and wished the ground would open up and swallow her. She had just made things worse.

'Well, let me tell you something for nothing, Susie.' Ada's words were low and steady, belying the rage that was rising inside her. 'My Danny was brought up on the earnings of a charlady – a scrubber, as you so thoughtlessly put it – and it didn't do him any harm, in fact, it did him the world of good because he has never looked down on anybody in his life.'

'I didn't mean to—' Susie began, but Ada cut her off mid-sentence.

'I know quite well what you meant.' Ada had no intention of letting this ungrateful wretch worm her way out of what she had already said. Not this time. 'And you are right, Susie, I do think it is time you left Reckoner's Row and found out what that big wide world has to offer.'

'Could you have a word with Grace's husband for me? Ask him for a job on one of his ships? I'd be ever so grateful.'

'I am sure you would be,' said Ada, 'for haven't you always had people doing your bidding? Haven't you always fluttered your over-made-up eyelashes and to hell with the consequences?'

'I don't know what you mean.' Susie stared blankly back at Ada. She had said she was sorry. What more did the old trout want?

'Of course, you don't,' Ada said in her sweetest tones, 'and do you know why you don't know what I mean, because I'm just a charlady and you would never listen to anybody so low. As far as you're concerned, we can all go to hell in a dustcart.'

'Handcart,' corrected Susie, giving Ada cause to offer a withering scowl and Susie knew she had to make amends. 'Look, Ada, you are the only woman I would ever tell this to. You are like a mother to me, better than a mother to me.' *Steady on, girl*, she thought. 'But the thing is, you have always been very kind to me, like Danny. And I mistook his kindness and attention for love – and because I believed he loved me, I loved him, too.'

Ada listened, knowing she was being soft-soaped. Susie had never done one thing that did not benefit her.

'I thought he would get fed up with Evie and ditch her for me, and we would live happily ever after – but life is not like that, is it?' She shook her head as if replying to her own question. She thought he was going to be rich. He had his own business. He was going to be someone. But when he started losing business and he had next to nothing, she didn't want to stick around to see the end result. 'I know now that I don't love Danny as he deserves to be loved,' she hesitated, waiting for some admonishment from Ada, but none came. 'I loved him like a brother I never had. He will always have a special place in my heart.'

Ada's temper cooled. For hadn't she loved Danny like her own son, even though she was not allowed to show him any favour which he so rightly deserved, especially when Bert was in the house. When Meggie visited every Friday night to pay for Danny's upkeep, she too was not allowed to show any favouritism. As far as Bert was concerned, Danny was a commodity. A way of earning money to keep him in baccy and betting slips. Bert didn't like Danny because he was not his. Ada closed her eyes.

Initially irritated by Susie, Ada felt something akin to compassion for the girl's predicament. 'I will speak to Bruce and Grace when they come back home later,' Ada said on a sigh, and her body tensed when Susie jumped up from her chair and hugged her.

She had never expected such a response from this girl who was so self-centred, yet, Ada understood now, Susie's ego was the shield she hid behind, to protect herself from yet another one of her life's many setbacks and frustrations.

'Also,' said Susie, 'I don't think, after all she has put me through, I could watch Evie Kilgaren walking down the aisle, thinking she has got the better of me.'

'I doubt she would think such a thing,' said Ada, finishing her tea.

'Why not?' Susie asked. 'I would think that.'

'That says it all, Susie.' Ada stood up to let the girl know the conversation was over when she picked up the cup that was still half-full and put it on the wooden tray.

26

When did it all go wrong? thought Ada as she stared at the black screen of the new television set, suspecting her life had been mapped out before the Great War. Before she was even married. Bert had an uncanny ability to make her feel sorry for him. But that was no reason to marry somebody. That was the last reason she should have married him. She knew with certainty she never loved him and, if truth be told, he didn't love her either. They were two lonely souls in search of freedom. Bert had been scratching around looking for companionship and wanted to settle down – Ada was sure he would have settled down with anybody. While she was eager to get away from a demanding aunt who was looking for cheap labour and found it in Ada who skivvied from morning 'til night in her aunt's lodging house. Marrying Bert and taking care of him seemed like a good idea at the time.

Although, he didn't take long to revert to his indolent ways. Bert did not exert himself if he could get away with somebody else doing the work. Never fond of putting himself out meant he didn't hold a job down for long, using his war wound to shirk all responsibilities. Without the merest stab of conscience, Bert could doze on the sofa until the pubs opened, then he would drink and gamble without using a penny of his own money. When she had a few coppers, he would steal them from her purse and spend what little house-keeping she had managed to earn. He would break the lock on the gas meter in the blink of an eye and be out of the front door so fast she wouldn't even notice until it was too late. She screamed at him until she was blue in the face, but he didn't take any notice. She called him a bum and a scrounger, a waste of God's good air, and all he would do was turn on his heel, walk out of the door and that was the last she would see of him for the next few days or even weeks, by which time she would have calmed down and he would turn up with a bunch of wilting flowers he had pinched from a dead man's grave.

Bert didn't have scruples; she knew that then as she knew it now. He never felt that searing panic squeeze a stranglehold on her heart when the rent was due. Or lie awake at night staring at the ceiling, worrying where the next meal was coming from before having to go cap-in-hand to the money lender or begging for more hours scrubbing out the tavern.

Although, to give Bert his due, he was a fine actor. For the sake of appearance when the parish priest came on a Friday to collect the parish fund money, he would adopt that sorrowful expression, confess to feeling so ashamed coming home from the Great War a burden on his sainted wife who had to go out cleaning to earn an honest crust.

Then, much later, he managed to get a proper job as a night-watchman, looking after the warehouses on the docks. It was like putting a fox in charge of the henhouse. Bert thought all his birth-days had come at once when Leo Darnel picked him out as a new best friend...

A knock at the front door made Ada jump. But she was grateful for the interruption that urged her to give her arthritic knee a bit of exercise and stop remembering the old days with Bert.

'Hello, Danny,' she said, glad he called in regularly these days. 'Come in and have a look at my new television set.' She stood aside to allow Danny into the long hallway.

Entering the house he grew up in, Danny inhaled that familiar scent of furniture polish and fresh bread that Ada baked every day. It was as memorable as the nose on his face and immediately he was back home.

'Did you get your new hat yet, Ma?'

'I was waiting to see what colour Meggie chose,' Ada said. 'I don't want to upstage the mother of the groom now, do I?'

'Mam won't mind what colour you wear,' he said.

'You've a lot to learn about women, Danny boy.'

'I wanted to come and give you a few bob,' Danny said, giving a low whistle when he saw the new television set taking pride of place on the table in the bay. 'I know you,' Danny said, 'you'll have the whole street in here and put on a spread while they're watching the Coronation.'

'A few ham butties, that's all, 'Ada answered.

'A few? Knowing you as I do, you won't put on just a few ham butties.' He slipped the money into her apron pocket, and she chucked him under the chin the way she used to do when he was a child who had done something she was proud of.

'You didn't need to do that, lad.' Her words were soft, barely audible, and all those years of struggle were etched on her face in every line. 'Our Grace sorted me out with a few bob and...' she paused, not wanting to tell him that the lavish, overpriced food, provided by the spiv, had also been paid for by her daughter, 'and, with our Bobby working, I'm not short of a few bob, now.'

'Well, treat yourself to something nice, on me.' Danny was glad, she would not be struggling to buy herself a new wedding outfit.

Bert Harris had bled her dry for years while he was alive, it wasn't right he should do it after he was dead too. 'Is something the matter?' Danny asked. Even though the room was toasty warm and comfortable, Ada looked uneasy.

'It's these last few months, the funeral, the... the...'

'The, what? Tell me. There's nothing that can't be solved.' He watched her closely for a few moments as she was about to say something and then stopped. 'C'mon, Ma, spit it out – like you always say, it might be a gold watch!'

It was when Danny called her *Ma* that changed Ada's mind. Why shouldn't she tell him about the box? She couldn't keep it to herself forever. And if Bert had killed Rene Kilgaren, Danny had a right to know.

'I've got something to tell you, and you're not going to like it...'

* * *

Like Bert, the box was rough round the edges. There was nothing special about it. Just a rough-sawn carton made out of orange box wood, with a hinged and padlocked lid. Ada took it from the gas cupboard and placed it on the table beside the aspidistra while Danny watched with interest, wondering what was in it.

'This was the only thing that Bert left when he died,' she said, taking the key from her apron pocket and hesitantly turning it between her fingers, as if unsure about using it.

'So that was his whole life, in one box?' Danny asked and Ada nodded.

'Not much to show, is it?'

Danny shook his head. The box looked like it hadn't been opened for years, the padlock rusted and dull.

'That landlady should have been reported,' Ada said between gritted teeth, 'and her dosshouse wanted fumigating. I saw bugs crawling under the wallpaper, fleas hopping on the bed – I was lousy by the time I got home and couldn't wait to strip off and get the tin bath in from the back yard.'

'I hope you stripped off *after* you got the tin bath in from the backyard and not before,' Danny grinned, his blue eyes twinkling the way Ada remembered, and her face burned, realising what she had said. Then, laughing at the absurdity, she gave him a half-hearted clout with her tea towel.

'You always were a daft eejit,' she said, laughing and then she stopped and her expression changed . 'The proof of how Rene Kilgaren's died could be in that box,' Ada blurted the news out before her brain even registered what she was going to say. She knew she had to tell him. It was the least Danny deserved, after having to put up with an old rogue who thought of nobody but himself. Ada saw Danny's face grow solemn; all signs of amusement had disappeared.

'What are you telling me?' he asked, and Ada shrugged. 'He didn't...' Danny's stomach sank to his shiny black shoes.

'I don't know, lad, I'm only telling you what he told me,' she said. 'Bert told me that Frank Kilgaren didn't kill Rene and to look in the box for the proof, but I can't, I am too scared that might be the case.' She heaved a sigh and she looked at the box, backing away as if it might attack her. 'I put it in that cupboard and tried to forget all about it, but every time I put a shilling in the meter, the bloody thing seemed to mock me. Just sitting there, giving off a whiff of doom.' Her facial expression was one of disgust. 'He said it had been his insurance.'

'What did he mean by that? What insurance?' Danny was certain this box was not going to contain good news, some kind of legacy to make Ada's life better. That wasn't Bert's style.

'I don't think he meant the kind of insurance you get from paying the clubman from the Co-op every Friday,' Ada said with the authority of her years. She had lived alongside the docks long enough to know that if you play with fire, you get your fingers burned, and Bert was the type of man who would be drawn to heated skulduggery like a magnet – especially if he had a gold-grade insurance policy. 'He said it would shed some light on the night Rene Kilgaren died.'

'Do you honestly think he knew who killed Rene?' Danny saw the fearful look in Ada's eyes and could tell she did believe such a thing. 'Do you think *he* did it?'

'That's what I'm frightened of,' she said, close to tears, 'I can't tell anybody... I was going to leave the box in the cupboard until I could get rid of it. Tie a brick round it and heave it into the canal like poor Rene.'

'A bit ironic, don't you think?' Danny said, his tone sombre, and Ada looked at him with a quizzical expression in her eyes, not knowing what he meant by that comment. Danny shrugged and shook his head. 'Do you want to find out what he meant? Find out the real identity of Rene Kilgaren's killer once and for all?' he asked, knowing Evie had voiced her doubts over the years, telling him that her father adored her mother to distraction, and she admitted she never truly believed he would hurt her. Until he actually admitted he killed her.

He watched Ada go and sit over by the window. 'Bert seemed to know a lot of information about some things,' Ada said, 'and I've got this feeling in my bones.'

'Well, you never could ignore your bones, Ma.' Danny realised a bit of levity might not be called for, but it was his only defence against Bert Harris's dark deeds. Ada could not be blamed for Rene's death, although Danny knew she would carry the burden of shame if Bert had anything at all to do with it. Looking at the key sitting in the palm of her hand, Ada picked it up and handed it to Danny.

'If we don't find out what the old bugger was talking about now, we never will,' Ada said on a sigh, obviously ready to learn what secrets her husband had harboured for all these years, knowing she would never have the courage to open the box alone. Danny was the only one she trusted. Feeling a menacing deluge wash over her, Ada felt strongly her life would be changed forever once he unlocked the box. 'I can't open it,' Ada told Danny and picked up the box, 'you take it with you and if there is anything I need to know you can tell me later.'

'If you're sure, Ma,' Danny said as some of the old familiar feelings rekindled in his heart, which was big enough to feel love for both his mothers. 'I'll take the box and let you know if there is anything you should know about.'

Ada nodded and he saw the look of relief in her eyes as he slipped the key into the top pocket of his black Crombie overcoat.

'I'll see you tomorrow, Ma,' he said and bent down to kiss her cheek, something he had not done for three years. Yet it came as naturally as if he did it every day like he used to do. 'Are you sure you'll be all right?'

'Of course, I will.' Ada's pragmatic tone belied the soft warmth that shone from her eyes. She had her lad back. 'Now you go and do what you have to do, and I'll see you in the morn.'

'Aye, see you tomorrow, Ma,' Danny said.

'Aye, son,' Ada said. 'See you tomorrow.

* * *

Danny took the box to Angus. Sitting at the edge of the bar, he stared at it for a long time, knowing when they unlocked it, the contents of the box might give some answers as to why Bert Harris kept hold of it for so long. Was it his security? Or was it the answer to what happened to Rene Kilgaren the night she died? And were the two things connected? Danny wondered if he really wanted to know what was inside. Was it wise to dig up old memories? Would the answers ruin his relationship with Evie?

No! Never. Nothing could ruin his love for the girl he had adored since he was a schoolboy and she was a shy young thing who barely lifted her eyes from the ground, reminding him of young foals he had seen on the edge of Dartmoor when he was training wet-behind-the-ear recruits.

There were so many questions buzzing round inside his head that he had no answers to. What if, like Bert told Ada, Frank Kilgaren had been wrongly imprisoned for a crime he didn't commit? But why on earth would he admit to killing his wife if he hadn't done it?

When he and Angus went upstairs to the living quarters of the tavern, Danny took the key out of his pocket and put it into the rusting lock, finding it stiff and difficult to yield. Eventually, after a few drops of oil, he managed to easily open the rough-sawn box.

Lifting the home-made lid, Danny and Angus ignored the protesting hinges, assuming the box had not been opened for years, and was surprised to see an oblong shape wrapped in newspaper. Peering inside, he saw a pillowcase, inside which was a blood-stained female shoe. And an envelope with Ada's name on it, hand-written in a childlike scrawl. Danny recognised Bert's handwriting immediately and he slipped the envelope into his pocket. Some things were not for the eyes of strangers. .

'Rene's shoe?' Danny asked, and Angus shrugged, shaking his head.

'There's certainly a few good fingerprints,' said Angus. 'Look here, on the heel, a perfect print, and if I'm not mistaken, I would say it was a thumb print. Leave it with me, I know someone who owes me a favour, he's quick and discreet,' said Angus, taking the box, 'I will see what I can find out.'

'Whatever you do,' said Danny, 'don't tell Ada. If she needs to know anything, I feel it's my duty to tell her.'

'I hear you loud and clear,' said Angus, 'but don't worry, if this shoe has a story to tell we'll be the first ones to know.'

'Thanks, Angus, much appreciated.' Danny tapped the peak of his cap and left the tavern with the envelope in his pocket. His next stop was home, and a quiet word with his stepfather, Henry Skinner.

* * *

'What do you think, old man?' Danny asked Henry, a level-headed gent, who was the salt of the earth.

Henry scratched his head. 'It's not our place to open this envelope when it hasn't been addressed to us,' Henry said, 'but, on the other hand, if it contains something sensitive – or even a confession – do we want Ada upset once more by that old rogue?'

'You're right, as always, and seeing Ada doesn't even know of the existence of this letter... No, I don't think we should open it. If she wants us to know she will tell us.'

'I doubt that very much,' said Henry. 'If I know anything about my cousin, she can hold onto a secret.'

Danny looked thoughtful as he stirred his tea. Henry was right. There were many mysteries wrapped up in a riddle as far as Ada was concerned. Look how long she kept it from him that Meggie was his mother and not his aunt as he had grown up believing. He decided then and there to open the letter. Depending on what it said he could either tell Ada the contents or keep it from her.

'Here goes,' he said to Henry, opening the letter.

My dear Ada,

I cannot tell you how sorry I am for the way I treated you during our married life together, and if you are reading this now, I have already gone to meet my maker. But first of all, before I go, I must clear up one injustice that has caused so much heartache and pain.

The truth of the matter is, I was there on the night Rene Kilgaren was attacked. I saw everything from the shadow of a derelict house that had been bombed during the war.

I had been drinking and playing the piano in the Tram Tavern when I saw Rene dancing with a chap who looked like her husband, but he'd been dead for years. I could see she was in a playful mood, but she kept looking over to a man sitting in the booth at the far end of the bar. I couldn't see who he was at first but then he leaned forward and I saw it was Leo Darnel and he was watching Rene. A short while later when the man she was dancing with went to the Gents', I could see clearly, he was definitely her husband, Frank Kilgaren...

Danny put his head in his hands and let out a sound akin to a groan. He could have sworn Frank Kilgaren would not kill Rene. The man was head over heels in love with her. He adored her and even kept their children, Jack and Lucy, in Ireland until he could afford to bring them all home together.

Leo Darnel was watching every move Rene made from his seat in the booth, and when her eyes followed her husband to the Gents', Darnel shattered an empty gill glass with his bare hand, cutting it badly and spraying glass all over the table.

Rene went over and gave him a tongue-lashing and she grabbed her coat and bag and left the bar in a right fury, then Darnel got up from the table and followed her, I could see his left hand needed a few stitches, but he never did get it sewn up.

I had been playing the piano and decided to call it a night after Connie called for last orders. I'd drunk enough and wanted to go home and get my head down after my supper. I was going down the jigger when I was caught short.

I stopped in the alleyway and heard two people arguing. I recognised the man's voice to be Leo Darnel and the other voice was Rene's. I could hear them coming closer and she was telling him to leave her alone, she didn't want to see him no more. Then she told him that her husband was going to take her and the kids to Ireland. I was shocked by that news, I can tell you.

I wanted to finish what I was doing and get out of there, but I couldn't. I wasn't interested in a couple having a barney. Then I heard them getting closer and I didn't have time to get down the alleyway when I saw Darnel dragging Rene by her hair down the jigger, and she lost her shoe.

The ground was white with hailstones and freezing cold, I can tell you, but that made no odds to Leo, he threw the shoe over the wall opposite the back of the tavern, into the bombed-out house in Summer Settle.

Then he was gripping her round the throat and when he heard me, he dragged her further down the middle jigger in Reckoner's Row and I went through the broken back gate to get the shoe so I could give it back to her. But I doubt she would have wanted it, covered in Darnel's blood.

It looked like Ada wasn't the only one who liked to mind other people's business, thought Danny as his eyes scrolled the words.

She was whimpering, like she didn't want to go down there, and he was pulling her, telling her she was an ungrateful bitch. And he would make sure nobody else had her. Not even her own husband.

By the time I got down to Reckoner's Row, Rene was nowhere to be seen and Leo Darnel was standing on the canal bank looking down into the water.

I never did see Rene again after that and so I kept hold of the shoe in case he saw me and wanted to make summat of it. It would come in handy as evidence. But I kept it as insurance.

The next part of the letter made Danny's jaw drop. But he wasn't surprised as much as amazed at the downright cheek of a man who had no scruples whatsoever.

The tables have turned now, and Leo Darnel won't be threatening me or harassing me for the money I borrowed. The interest on the loan trebled every day. I will have no chance of ever paying back what he says I owe. I was at me wits' end, that's why I had to get the money from old man Skinner, but I did intend to pay it all back, Ada. On my life.

Then I told Darnel I knew what happened the night Rene didn't get home. He never knew where I hid the shoe. And when I moved lodgings, after being driven out of Reckoner's Row, the landlady told me he had turned the room upside down one day, and wouldn't leave until she threatened to call the bobbies.

In the end, Leo Darnel squashed my debts and even offered me a job in 'the firm', but I turned him down. I don't need to work when someone as rich as Darnel gives me money every week to keep shtum!

So, you see, Ada, it weren't my blame that Henry Skinner got screwed for money, it was all Darnel's fault. He was the one what made me do it in the first place.

This is the truth, the whole truth, so help me God.

Albert Sidney Harris. August 1950

'The conniving old bastard,' Danny said to Henry, He was pleased he had decided to open the letter because, knowing her as he did, the contents would upset Ada. And boy would this upset her. She would probably tear the letter into a thousand pieces, but this would be the evidence that Frank Kilgaren needed to show he did not kill his wife.

'Bert Harris only ever did things to suit himself and this letter is proof of that,' Danny said in disgust

'He would rather see an innocent man imprisoned in an asylum for the rest of his days,' Henry said, 'than give this vital evidence to the police.' 'I remember Father O'Leary calling to the house on a Friday to collect parish fund money,' Danny told Henry: 'Ada always gave the priest half a crown, even if it left her without another penny to call her own. "Rather the church gets it than Bert Harris," she used to say.' Danny continued his tale as Meggie brought in a tray of tea things and Henry listened attentively.

'Bert would tell the priest how bad he felt, how useless a man he was when his wife had to come home from work, cook clean, and look after the children, and I would see Ada seethe with pent-up rage, knowing everything Bert said was his version of the truth and nobody else's.'

'He'd always been self-serving, had Bert,' said Meggie who rarely spoke ill of anybody.

'Bert even managed to squeeze out a few crocodile tears for good measure.' Danny replied. 'The sorry little act always worked in his favour and the priest would pacify him by calling him a hero and tell Bert not to feel ashamed, he had served his country.' Danny slowly shook his head. 'Then the priest would give Bert a few bob from the Parish Fund and was hardly out of the front door before the old goat was hotfooting it to the tavern – not to be seen again until the money had run out.'

Danny put on the black donkey jacket and the flat cap he wore for work, knowing what he had to do. Ada was going to have to know the contents of this letter, but first of all he must give it to Angus, to have it examined by the forensic chap he knew. This was more proof Frank Kilgaren did not kill his wife.

* * *

'Interesting,' said Angus, obviously deep in thought when he opened the envelope and read the letter. 'Birdy's retired,' he said of his friend in forensics, 'but there is another chap, loves this kind of thing – right up his street. Leave it with me, Danny.'

Danny nodded, knowing that Angus was very discreet. If Danny had taken the letter to the police there would have been all kinds of awkward questions, information may have got out and got as far as Evie, when all the time she could be spared the worry and the heartache if this turned out to be a false alarm, and the ramblings of a scheming old man who wanted to get into his wife's good books in the hope of being allowed to return to Reckoner's Row. And then realising he had more power if he kept hold of the evidence.

* * *

Danny gave Ada the news about the letter and the shoe, and, up to her elbows in home-made jam tarts and fairy cakes she was making for tomorrow's celebration, she took the news in that practical way she had about her. Not seeming the least surprised.

'Bert told me the day I went round to see him that Frank didn't murder his wife. It was his last confession, so to speak.' Ada bustled about the kitchen like a demented bluebottle, wiping her floury hands on her apron, filling the kettle, taking cups and saucers from the shelf, ladling tea into the brown earthenware teapot. 'He didn't tell me who had killed her, though, that was the problem.'

'Here, let me do that,' said Danny, taking the tea caddy from her hand, but Ada was having none of it. She had to keep going. Keep herself busy. Try to stop her mind working overtime.

She let out a long sigh. 'I was worried sick Bert might have been the one who killed Rene.'

'By the sound of it, he believed the killer was Leo Darnel, and I should have a better idea by tomorrow.' Danny answered, wondering if he was giving Ada too much information and knowing how she liked a good gossip. However, she seemed to have turned a corner, because these days she was much more inclined to listen rather than to tell, and that could only be a good thing. He doubted she would say a word until the truth came out.

'I couldn't unlock the box - in case Bert had done it.' Ada looked suddenly weary, and Danny wondered if the last few years had taken their toll. 'Although I never had him down for being a murderer.'

'You didn't have him down as a blackmailer either,' Danny said, and she shot him a glance that was full of shame. 'But why would you?' Danny said quickly. 'He was devious to the last breath, and he kept so much hidden from you.'

'What the eye doesn't see the heart can't grieve over.' Ada pulled the skin on the back of her hand and the tea she had poured into her cup grew cold. 'I didn't want any upset with your wedding coming up, and I didn't want to be like Pandora, opening the box to allow the evils of the world to escape. I did it for you and Evie,' Ada said, her eyes filling with rare tears, and she quickly wiped them away with the pad of her hand, obviously annoyed at letting her true feelings show.

Danny knew that for all her bluff and bluster, prying into other people's business, and being the local gossip, those things hid the real person she truly was. Those things were a front, to disguise her genuine, charitable nature and push down the heartbreak and hardship she had suffered over the years.

'Will you be telling Evie?' Ada asked, and Danny felt his heart race, he wasn't sure. The question was not one he could easily answer. How would she react? Danny's thoughts wouldn't line up. Then he realised why an answer wouldn't emerge, because he was shying away from telling Evie the bad news. But was that a basis for a good marriage? He doubted it. Bert and Ada had kept secrets from each other all their married lives and in doing so it destroyed them. Danny could not bear for that to happen to him and Evie. And if it was proven that it was Darnell who had murdered her mother, Evie would be upset that he hadn't told her about Bert's box and what had been discovered in it.

'Yes, of course I will tell her,' Danny's rational tone had a serrated edge and was low. His gaze did not meet Ada's, as he looked anywhere but in her trusting eyes., He did not want to see the look of disappointment, suspecting he was being disloyal to the woman who raised him. 'We can't start our new life together with a huge lie hanging over our head like the sword of Damocles.'

'You and your big words,' she pondered, giving a gentle laugh, 'I haven't got a clue who this Damocles fella is, but if he's got a sword, I'd stay well clear of him, if I were you.'

Danny's eyes met Ada's and he let out a long sigh of relief when she said, as if he were still a child; 'Good lad. I wouldn't expect anything else.'

* * *

'The dried blood on the shoe did show a perfect thumb print,' Angus told Danny the next morning, when he got the results back from his pal in forensics, 'and none of them belonged to Rene.'

'Just as Bert said,' answered Danny as second thoughts poked at him like a sharp stick. 'What about Leo Darnel?'

'This goes no further,' Angus said in his deep Scottish burr, 'not even to Evie?'

Danny nodded. She would know soon enough, of that, he was sure.

'The fingerprints definitely belong to Darnel,' said Angus. 'He probably thought he would get away with his foul deeds when he threw the shoe over the wall of the derelict house.' Angus leaned towards Danny and lowered his voice to a whisper. 'It matched the thumb print on Rene's throat, which came from a left hand and also belongs to Leo Darnel.'

'What about Frank?' asked Danny, knowing Evie was worried sick about the outcome of her father's escape.

'Frank is not only right-handed,' said Angus, 'but he is riddled with arthritis – he couldn't strangle a new-born kitten.'

'The date was on the letter written by Bert when he left Reckoner's Row and it could only have been written by someone who actually saw the crime, would have known what happened that night.'

'But that was three years later,' said Danny, 'how do they know when the shoe was found?'

'The shoe is wrapped in the *Evening Echo*, which also contains blood from the shoe. It was dated the night the big freeze gripped the country and froze everything solid, including the canal. Darnel could not have timed it better.'

'Poor Evie,' said Danny, 'now she will have to go through the whole thing again.'

'Not necessarily,' said Angus, 'there is enough evidence to set her father free.'

'But why was he presumed guilty?' asked Danny, his brow furrowed.

'When he was arrested, he said he was the cause of Rene's

death, which he believed he was, because when she left the tavern, he didn't follow her, he thought she had run out on him. If he had followed immediately, he would most certainly have seen Rene being attacked.'

For Danny, the news was a lot to take in. Angus explained that according to forensic evidence, Rene had been dragged under the water by her heavy winter coat and the belt was caught on an old pram, holding it fast when the big freeze came that night.

'Let's hope they catch Frank, and tell him the good news, before he does something stupid,' said Danny. He knew Frank Kilgaren had a fiery temper and he would be biding his time, waiting for Darnel to slip up and then he would pounce.

27

Connie couldn't leave the bar unattended when the pub cleared of customers who had gone to Ada's house down the bottom of the row to watch the Coronation on her new fourteen-inch television set. With all the running around she had to do for the street party, Connie had completely forgotten to apply for a licence and could not put the television on in the bar, much to the disappointment of the customers.

But if the tavern stayed this quiet, she might close and nip upstairs to watch it until the street festivities began. However, before she got a chance to lock the tavern door, two strangers came in and ordered a pint each, so that put paid to her watching the new Queen being crowned.

The two men sat at the table near the bar, and by the look of it they had no interest in listening to the broadcast on the wireless, their heads were almost touching as they carried on their animated conversation regardless of the historic ceremony and Connie thought it was most disrespectful. Like talking in church. It was not the done thing to hold a conversation while Her Majesty was on the wireless, so she raised the volume.

A familiar tingle at the back of her neck told her to be on her guard when she glanced over to where the two men were seated. They had both been sitting on that pint for nearly an hour and the dark brown liquid still hadn't reached halfway down the glass.

Busying herself behind the bar while listening with deference to history being made. The country had a Queen. A young and beautiful Queen she was too, with a dashing husband and two cherubic children. Connie felt her cheeks grow hot when she recalled her mother saying only this morning that she noticed many similarities between her daughter and Queen Elizabeth. 'Queen of the Tram Tavern,' Mim had said. 'Dashing husband and two children – one even born on the same day as the little princess, Anne.'

Connie, straightening bar towels, made sure all the labels on the bottles were facing outward, before cleaning glasses for the umpteenth time, making sure they sparkled. Not the kind of thing a new monarch would be interested in, she was sure. Connie was annoyed at the only two customers in the place who had no intentions of buying another drink, by the look of things, and were making her miss the Coronation ceremony on the television.

Connie noticed the two of them did not engage in conversation as she would have expected them to. They kept themselves to themselves and made no attempt to move on somewhere else when she said she would have loved to watch the ceremony. Then her thoughts turned to something darker...

A woman on her own with a till full of money would be an easy target for two young whippersnappers who were obviously new around here because she didn't recall seeing them in the pub before today.

Nevertheless, did they think she was born yesterday? Most of the money was taken out of the till at regular intervals, and certainly before Angus went outside to join the happy residents of

Reckoner's Row. Watching the two customers closely, Connie knew the cash had been securely locked away in the safe beneath the bar.

She could see they were keeping their eyes to business. The taller of the two, who she silently named the lanky fella, was watching the outside door leading into the bar, while his pal looked to the other door that led to the private staircase. She could tell immediately they were up to something, and it didn't take a genius to know what it was.

They weren't local she was certain, making her highly suspicious and immediately on her guard, her landlady antenna working on overdrive. Her mother was upstairs with her two children, and there was not another person in the bar. Not one familiar face. Nevertheless, she would only have to yell or scream or throw a glass through the window and she would have a street-full of people racing to help her out. Her Angus was only a loud screech away.

Connie knew everybody from around here, and they knew she wasn't a soft touch. But these two were strangers. This was a busy dock road public house and the safe was under the bar, where she was now standing. If there was anything she had learned from years growing up in a dockside alehouse, and nursing soldiers while the enemy tried to blow you to Kingdom Come, it was that she must hold her nerve.

One of them, the lanky fella in a flat cap and a donkey jacket, got up from his seat and walked towards the bar, while the other one headed towards the 'gents' situated next to the door marked 'Private' leading to the rooms upstairs. Connie's senses heightened as she heard the click of the latch behind her and the hairs on the back of her neck stood on end.

'Not that one, luv,' Connie called. Knowing this pub as well as she did, Connie didn't need to look behind her, keeping her eye on jack-the-lad on the other side of the bar who was looking past her to the till. Angus would have put this chancer on his arse as soon as look at him, but he wasn't here. The thought caused a cold shiver to shoot down her spine, but Connie knew she could not show fear.

'Open the till and you won't get hurt,' said the man standing in front of her, his voice low, controlled, and Connie stared at him for a long moment. Then she saw the glint of the knife in his hand and her hackles rose. *Bloody cheek!*

Nevertheless, she said nothing. Listening intently to the movement of the man behind her. He had no intentions of going to the gents', and she quickly realised that her instincts had been right. These two were a couple of chancers, thinking they were in line for some easy pickings. A woman on her own and all that loot in the till, they would assume, just sitting there ripe for the taking.

Connie looked at the knife and she looked into the eyes of the man holding it. He couldn't be any older than eighteen or nineteen. She knew hard men when she saw them, men who could put you down as soon as look at you. And slowly, as her eyes travelled from the peak of his dipped flat cap to the leather gloved hand carrying the slightly trembling blade, she knew these two were miles from that. Her instincts gave her strength, and she knew what she must do.

'You don't need to flash that thing around in here, love,' she said in a calm voice, eyeing the knife, now more annoyed than ever that she was missing the Coronation ceremony, 'someone might come in and see it.' Her voice was steady, belying the tremble that threatened to overtake her body. Her heart jackhammering against her ribcage. She had to play this cool. Young men could be like savage dogs when backed into a corner. 'You can take the money,' Connie said, as if the man behind her was not even in the bar. Aware he had moved from the door marked Private. His hands on the wooden bar flap, ready to lift it open. 'I'll do whatever you want,' she said, turning to the shorter man, 'you don't need a weapon. I'm just a woman working on my own.' Connie knew she had seen more bloodshed and misery that these two could ever imagine, and even saying the words *just a woman* made her blood boil. But she had to be careful.

She heard the creak of the hinge as the shorter one made to lift the wooden flap and her head whipped around. 'Nobody comes behind this bar uninvited.' Connie shot him a venomous glare. 'Don't even think of it.' Her voice ice cool.

Connie noticed his eyebrows arch and she matched his direct gaze, silently relieved when he took his hands from the bar even though the calm, authoritative words that slipped from her ruby-coloured lips did not match the alarm bells ringing in her head.

But despite her reservations Connie was sure she could handle these two. This was her territory. Neither of these two fools knew a bolt secured the bar flap, and it was already locked in place, which would certainly cause them problems and slow them down if either of them tried their luck. Connie knew it would take some strength to prise the strong bolt from the chunky oak bar, to get to her or the till.

Her instincts told her these two were idiots, a pair of nobodies, but they would probably do anything they needed to do, to get what they came for. She had to play for time. When the royal ceremony was over, the bar would be heaving with locals who would want to raise a glass to the country's new Queen.

These two were too thick to realise they could be defeated, and they could get hurt. Maybe not immediately, but certainly in the not-too-distant future when news got out that they tried to rob the landlady of one of the most popular pubs in the port. Her tavern was the beating heart of this community, the regulars, mostly tough, hard-working dock labourers who would laugh in the face of these two, treated the tavern and its staff with the greatest respect.

'Come on, lads,' Connie said, her tone persuasive, 'there's no need for violence. I'm no heroine, you can take the money and be away on your toes in no time.' She smiled with all the élan of a first-class hostess, and from the corner of her eye she caught sight of them sharing a glance of uncertainty.

Like a lioness scenting her prey, Connie suspected these two were new to this game, and this was a daring act they had not attempted before. Their eyes darted round the bar, jumpy now and probably a little unhinged at her relaxed composure. Most likely they would have expected her, *a mere woman*, to panic in terror at the sight of the knife. Perhaps scream for help. Maybe even faint clean away like those witless women who acted out parts in films on the pictures. But that wasn't her style.

Connie watched the clueless clots trying to make up their mind if they wanted to be tough guys, like Dirk Bogarde, who starred in *The Blue Lamp,* which she and Angus went to see the other week on the pictures. *And look where that got him*, she thought. *Swinging on the end of the rope, that's where.*

Connie had spent too many years watching Mim and her late father calming an explosive situation, keeping an orderly house. The Tram Tavern had one of the best reputations along the dock road for gritty determination and facing down bigger and harder men than these two tough-guy-imitators. They had no idea who they were trying to threaten. Connie wasn't the innocent these two took her for. She had stood up to Leo Darnel more than once, and there were not many who could say that. With every passing moment, her courage increased until, at last, the taller of the two put the flick knife down on the bar, and, pacified by their submission, she smiled and let out an exaggerated sigh, letting them suppose they had the upper hand.

'Why don't we all have a drink, just to show no hard feelings?' Connie asked, turning to the smaller, edgier of the two.

'Why not the whole bottle?' he replied in a cocky tone, obviously miffed his mate had put down the knife.

And as Connie looked over his head, she noticed a man peering from the door of the ladies. He put his finger to his lips and made a silent shushing signal, and there was something familiar about him that gave Connie a strong back-up. She unfurled her hands and rested them on the bar.

'Why not, indeed!' Connie's dark eyes twinkled, her smile wide and bright. 'Let me just go and get a new bottle for you. After all, I wouldn't want you to feel you have been short-changed.' She turned her back on the two of them and sauntered down to the other end of the bar, aware the shorter one was trying to open the bar flap as her high heels clicked against the linoleum-covered floorboards. Bending to retrieve a cheap bottle of rum, she clocked the baseball bat, which Angus kept near the till. Just in case. Unseen by the two jokers eager for free booze, using her foot she began gently pushing the solid bat towards the two men at the other end of the bar, her hips snaking sensuously, while waving an unopened bottle in the air. Unbeknown to the two adolescents a shadowy figure watched the unfurling episode in the dimness of the unlit corridor leading to the ladies'. Reaching slowly to the shelf above, she heard a sharp intake of breath caused by her shapely figure, no doubt. Before she passed two glasses across the bar, she poured a generous amount of rum into each and noticed how the eyes of the smaller man greedily devoured the fiery alcohol, impatient for his to be filled and she knew she had found his weak spot. But before she could do any more, she clearly heard the door of the ladies' creak.

'That glass is cracked,' Connie said, swiping the short glass from his hand to divert attention from the door. 'Let me get you another.' She threw the glass in the bin and the sound reverberated round the empty bar and Connie hoped the noise drowned out the creak of the door hinges. Every nerve in her body screamed. *Please, don't let them turn round!*

The smaller of the two, startled, made a grab for the knife.

'Who's that?' he asked, and Connie shook her head determined not to panic.

'Who's who?' she asked. 'I didn't hear anything.' Her voice was dispassionate and she looked for all the world like a woman who didn't have a care in the world. There was the creak of squeaking hinges behind them, and all eyes turned.

Connie propelled herself towards the bar and lurched beneath for the baseball bat, and before she had time to realise what was happening, the stranger from the ladies' lavatory opened the door wide, sprinted across the bar room floor, grabbed the bat and floored the two trainee- gangsters like he was slogging for a home run. Crack!

The impact of the contact across the tall one's shoulders caused him to fall forward and bang heads with the short fella! They both went down like skittles just as the pub door opened and Angus came into the bar.

'Do you want to have your picture drawn by Jack Kilgaren?' asked Angus. 'He's very good and has sold a lot of portraits for the...' He didn't manage to get the word *army* out when he saw the two horizontal figures lying on the floor as the dark-haired stranger with a beard and moustache dropped the baseball bat, rushed past him and hurried out of the tavern.

'He saw the tall one going for the knife, and moved quick as lightning,' Connie told Angus. 'If he hadn't swung out, I don't know what could have happened.' She had a very good idea that didn't bear dwelling on.

'You could have been killed or maimed,' Angus said when Connie explained, 'leaving our children without a mother, leaving me without a wife.'

'Leaving Mim with an excuse to cry for the rest of her days, you mean?' Connie suspected she knew the face of the man who protected her from these two and if she wasn't mistaken, she would have sworn the man was Frank Kilgaren.

'Oh please,' said Angus, horrified. 'That thought doesn't bear dwelling on.' He reached for the baseball bat. 'But I'll take this, someone might do themself a mischief.'

His darling wife was standing over the two chancers when the police came into the bar and arrested the offenders, but Connie was not going to tell them what really happened and put anybody on the wrong side of the law for defending her and her property.

'She was like a lioness protecting her territory,' Angus told the police, prouder than he had ever been, his heart swelling with love and adoration for this strong, beautiful woman who could hold her own in any situation.

Everybody in the tavern wanted to know what had gone on, while they had been watching the New Queen being crowned, not realising their own landlady had also been watching a bit of crowning.

In minutes, word spread, and Evie, along with the residents of Reckoner's Row, clamoured round the bar. But Connie, true to form, took the whole incident in her stride, telling them it was nothing. She did what she had to do, that's all. How was she going to tell Evie that her father had been here all along?

'Pint of bitter, was it?' Connie asked, like she had two prone bodies on her tavern floor every day of the week.

Then, as she and Angus crossed behind the bar, he bent and kissed her on the cheek and Connie smiled. All was right with the world now the excitement was over.

'We won't forget today in a hurry,' Connie said, 'and news has just come on the wireless saying Edmund Hillary and his Sherpa, have reached the top of Mount Everest.'

'What a day!' Angus exclaimed. 'And it's not over yet.' He slipped the bat under the bar and started to pull pints.

At that moment from outside there was the sound of raised voices, and when the regulars went to see what was happening, they saw Frank Kilgaren being held down by two burly dockers. One of the policemen ran to the police box on the corner, to summon more help.

As Evie stared open-mouthed at the fracas and saw her father being led away, she was even more surprised when Jack came to her side and said:

'He's the man in my picture,' He flip the pages of his sketchbook until he found the picture he was looking for. 'I thought he was a delivery man.' Jack did not recognise the man whose hair had been tinted black and now sported a beard and moustache when he drew him delivering a package to his own house.

'So he was the man who delivered Lenard's, I mean, Darnel's account ledger!' Evie's words were barely audible. Only this morning, Danny had told her about the box and what it contained. Her mother's shoe held Darnel's fingerprints. There was a letter from Bert Harris – and everybody knew dead men can't lie. There had been no sign of her father being at the murder scene and the evidence in the box pointed only to Darnel. And, now believing the spiv had killed her mother, everything fell into place. Her father, Lucy's good shepherd, had been wrongly arrested and the spiv, along with Bert Harris, had cause to encourage the lie. Evie felt a wave of shame wash over her. She had been quick to believe he could have killed his own wife. And she had been wrong. 'I didn't recognise him.'

'It was me,' said Lucy. 'I coloured Da's hair, so he didn't get caught.'

'You did what?!' Evie could not believe what she was hearing. 'You helped him.'

'He didn't kill mam, Evie, he said so.' Lucy had every faith in her father and she went on to say. 'I could not believe my own father

would even think of doing such a thing to the woman he loved.'
And although Evie didn't have Lucy's romantic notions of her
parent's marriage, she no longer believed he was capable of murder.

* * *

'These silly men bumped heads,' Connie said sweetly, noticing her
youngest, Angel taking great interest in the strange men being
bundled outside and into a police car, then turning to her five-year-
old son, Fergus, she said, in that conspirative, chummy tone she
always used when she wanted him to do something he would
rather not do, 'Would you do me a good turn, Fergus, and help
Grandma, Mim, get the sandwiches from the kitchen and put them
on the table outside?'

Fergus nodded. He would do anything for his beloved mam. He
took his young sister's hand and the hand of his grandmother and
went towards the kitchen, where Connie had prepared lots of delicious treats for the party. As they got to the door leading to the
kitchen, Mim turned, her brows furrowed, and Connie gave a slight
shake of her head, letting her mother know everything was in hand,
and that she was perfectly safe now. Mim understood, knowing
better than to ask questions in front of the children.

'It's a wonder Ada hasn't come in for a gill to see what went on,'
said Connie, who knew her mother's best friend was not slow in
coming forward when there was a bit of gossip to share. And she
also suspected Mim would want to disclose every detail of the hold-
up, which would be all round the dockside in no time at all.

'She will be too busy watching the new television her son-in-
law, Bruce, sent from Cheshire.'

'Of course,' said Angus. 'Normally you can't scratch your head
round here without Ada jumping to the conclusion you've got nits.'

He laughed when Connie gave him a disapproving shake of her head, knowing his wife thought fondly of her mother's best friend.

'Let's just enjoy the rest of the day,' said Connie. 'Evie was telling me that Jack has gone back to work in Danny's yard.'

Angus nodded his head. Although he would not tell his lovely wife that Danny had confided he was getting threatening letters, demanding he sell the haulage yard at a knock-down price. After such a busy day, Angus did not want to worry Connie with the information he had been given, with regard to Rene Kilgaren's demise. That would keep for another day. First of all, he would have to speak to Danny.

* * *

Angus took out a wad of paper from his inside pocket and asked Danny to follow him upstairs while Mim watched over the bar.

'Rene's autopsy notes,' said Angus and Danny cast his eyes over the evidence.

'Darnel paid Bert well, to keep his mouth shut.' Angus explained, 'I saw them both most Friday nights, heads down, envelopes being slipped across the table.'

'Darnel does not have one decent scruple to his name,' said Danny. 'If Bert hadn't been useful to Darnel, I imagine he would have been dead long ago.'

'Thick as thieves they were,' said Angus, careful his words were not being overheard.

'So why wasn't Darnel at Bert's funeral?' Danny asked and Angus shrugged.

'He was no longer useful if he was dead. So, Darnel, being the callous villain he is, didn't bother himself with details like funerals.'

* * *

'You got it then?' Susie said, coming out of her front door behind her father, who was carrying two heavy-looking suitcases to a waiting black cab parked behind a removal van.

'Sorry?' Evie asked, and Susie nodded to the ledger Evie had under her arm. The proof of Leo Darnel's years of skulduggery. These accounts, which had been delivered anonymously, gave the true version of his dodgy dealings over the years, and could put him behind bars for a very long time.

Susie, dressed in the latest style as always, looked like a film star in a pink pencil-slim skirt that clung to her shapely legs and matching jacket, showing off a perfect hour-glass figure, which was sure to turn a few heads.

'Going anywhere nice?' Evie nodded to the waiting black cab, and she was surprised when Susie told her she was leaving Reckoner's Row.

'I am going to see the world.' She pushed her handbag further up her arm. 'Like Grace did.'

'I hope it works out for you,' Evie said. And she meant it.

'Anything has got to be better than this place,' Susie said as she walked towards Evie. Reckoner's Row did not suit her, and nor did she suit Reckoner's Row. Susie's view of her hometown was not pleasing to her eyes and probably never would be. 'I need to go and see what I've been missing all these years.'

'What did you mean, when you said, I got it?' asked Evie, nodding to the package of accounts she had been working on.

'I deliberately left the office door and filing cabinet unlocked,' Susie said. 'I had to redeem myself from some of the damage I had caused, and this is the only way I knew how.' Although Susie had wanted to get back at Harry she had started to feel guilty about what she had done to Danny's business.

'You mean, you delivered Darnel's accounts and they didn't come via the post office?' Evie asked.

'Not me this time,' Susie smiled, 'but I know the man who did. He was very grateful and eager to help, for money of course, I asked him to do me a favour and steal the files from the filing cabinet and deliver them to your address.' Susie paused, plucking at the skin on the back of her hand. 'I am sorry for all the hurt I caused, Evie. I truly pray that you and Danny are happy together.'

'Thank you,' was all that Evie could say.

'I wanted Danny to whisk me away and treat me like a princess, but that was never going to happen.' Susie made a weak attempt to laugh, but it was flat and dull and unconvincing. 'I didn't love Danny – I loved the idea of him.' She looked away and then she said, 'I'm truly sorry.' And, leaning forward, she kissed Evie's cheek.

Susie stepped into the taxi, and it rumbled out of Reckoner's Row. And, still stunned by the show of friendship, Evie knew Susie would have to learn to stand on her own two feet, before she finally got to know peace. Because if she didn't find the independence she craved, Susie would always need someone to lean on.

28

Ada pulled the white cotton sheet tight and tucked perfect envelope edges under the mattress, before adding the heavy grey blankets, which she had bought after the war, from the Army and Navy stores, and were still as serviceable as the day she purchased them.

Stripping off the pillowcase, she put on a clean fresh white one. Even though Danny's head no longer rested there, she liked to keep his bed fresh. Picking up the bundle of sheets and pillowcases that had not been slept on, she sighed, and something outside caught her eye. Looking out of the window, she moved the crisp, white net curtains to one side and looked over to Skinner's yard. The man, whom she had called her son, for the past twenty-five years, was working hard to build up the haulage business, which he had bought for just £1 from her cousin Henry.

'Danny has grown to be a fine man,' Meggie said when she called later. The two women had made their peace and enjoyed a harmonious friendship. Different as chalk and cheese, Ada was loud where Meggie was quiet, and Ada was never happier than when she had her nose in everybody else's business, whereas Meggie, although friendly and welcoming, was more private. But these days neither was in competition, because they knew the woman Danny had chosen, the woman he wanted, and the only woman he loved and trusted with his heart and soul – and her name was Evie.

'And for all that, I take no credit,' Ada answered. Even though she had raised him, she had been well paid for the service. Meggie made sure he had shoes on his feet, food in his belly, and an insatiable hunger to do the right thing by her son. 'You were the one who worked all the hours you could to make him what he is today.'

The two mothers waved when they saw Evie coming out of the refurbished office, to show Danny some paperwork, both smiling at how good they looked together in the June sunshine.

'They are made for each other,' Ada said, 'like you and Henry.'

Evie, trim in a serviceable, calf-length black skirt, white blouse and pale blue cardigan that set off her corn-coloured hair was as efficient as ever and looked very businesslike, until Danny caught her round the waist, and she melted into his arms, giggling like a carefree schoolgirl. Meggie's face softened as memories of a time long gone surfaced, when she had felt exactly the same way as Evie must be feeling right now. She had never seen a couple more perfect for each other.

'Here,' said Ada, 'did you hear about the Lenard Haulage place?' She knew Meggie wasn't interested in gossip, but she'd want to hear this. 'It got shut down. Apparently, it was being run as a cover for Leo Darnel's dodgy dealings.' She nodded as if to confirm her explanation. 'Mind you, I always said he was no good. He'd rob the eyes out of your head and spit in the holes, that one.'

'Really?' said Meggie, who knew Ada had lived quite comfortably from the ill-gotten gains of Leo Darnel in the past. But that was all water under the bridge now. And the least said... Meggie knew that living so close to the docks there would always be a market for a bit of this, or a bit of that.

When Darnel's despicable schemes and that he killed Rene Kilgaren were made public and splashed all over the front of the Sunday newspapers, the residents of Reckoner's Row rallied, to see Frank Kilgaren released from his wrongful incarceration.

* * *

Skinner & Son had plenty of work when Lenard's was closed down by the authorities. Darnel, along with a few of the so-called *managers,* had been arrested for fraud and money-laundering. Then there was the new evidence he had killed Rene, which sealed his fate when the judge placed the black cloth on his head and told Darnel he would hang by the neck until he was dead.

Business had picked up for Danny and the honest men he employed. The insurance money had paid for the modernisation of the yard, built a new office and, much to Danny's delight, Jack was now a partner in the business. The money he invested allowed Danny to buy the bulk of Darnel's ex-service wagons, sold off at a knock-down price.

Evie showed Danny and Jack that Skinner's was finally out of the red, and the order books were looking very healthy indeed.

'All because you had the good sense to keep up with the insurance payments,' Danny said when he saw the way Evie had turned the business around. 'I am the luckiest man in the world to be marrying you, Evie Kilgaren,' Danny told her, and Evie felt ten feet tall.

'I've come a long way from the gutter,' she said with a smile. These days she could hold her head high, proud of a job well done, knowing in days gone by, she had walked with her head down, unable to meet the gaze of her neighbours, because of the shame of being poor, neglected and believing she was worthless.

But not any more. Now, she believed she could conquer the

world. And why not? Evie had done everything she could to keep her family, and her man, safe, comfortable and, above all, loved. She had brought about Leo Darnel's downfall, as she vowed she would do six years ago, when he disgraced her that summer afternoon, in Reckoner's Row. The day he left her lying in the gutter. The last time she ever saw her mother alive. Now he was going to pay the price for his wicked ways, and she would not lose one moment's sleep worrying about his demise.

She had worked hard to drag herself out of that gutter. Proving that, by working hard, and searching for answers, she had found a way of life that suited her. Evie didn't want vast riches, although security was important to her and to her family.

The things that held her back before, being closed-minded, and feeling unworthy of success, were no longer a problem, because she was open to change, along with the business. They would grow together.

29

'She's all lace curtains and orange boxes that one,' Ada said, arms folded and head nodding when she saw a new family moving into the Blackthorn house. The Blackthorn's had moved away the same day Susie left. 'Outside show and inside poverty, she comes from Beamer Terrace.'

'Ada, don't you think it's about time you went in and started getting ready,' said Mim, who had called to collect the silver tray and fancy knife for cutting the wedding cake, 'otherwise they'll be starting without you.'

'Well, let's hope that wagon's out of the way before the wedding cars arrive,' Ada said, taking no notice of Mim, as usual, but busy watching what the new family had in the way of furniture. 'Blimey, there's enough beds. How many kids has she got?'

'No doubt you'll find out soon enough,' said Mim, holding the tray under her cardigan, as she sauntered off along Reckoner's Row. 'Nice day for it,' she said in a neighbourly voice when the harassed-looking woman, who looked about thirty years old, pushed back her frizzy dark hair from her perspiring brow.

'Aye, I suppose so,' the woman answered, and Mim, taking in

every detail with the sweep of her dark eyes, thought that the new woman could do with a good pan of scouse, she was so thin.

'I'm Mim Sharp, by the way,' she said, when the other woman did not offer to introduce herself. 'I used to run The Tram Tavern, with my husband, before he was killed during the war.'

'I'm sorry to hear that,' said the woman, 'about losing your husband, I mean, not about you running the pub.'

'I knew what you meant,' said Mim, sensing this woman did not want to talk. 'My daughter, Connie, runs it now, with her husband, Angus – he's a Scotsman, as you might've gathered. So, have you come far?' she asked as a line of children ran indoors and started flicking the light switches on and off.

'Pack it in, you lot!'

Her voice is bigger than she is, thought Mim, and nodded when the other woman said, apologetically, 'We've never had electricity before. We come from Beamer Terrace, just by the electrical works near the docks – my husband worked there before...'

'Before?' asked Mim, but the woman shook her head and turned to go inside.

'I must get on, I've got beds to put together and boxes to empty.' She went up the two steps that led inside the house and turned, 'I'm Mollie, by the way, Mollie Applewhite.'

'Here,' said Mim, 'your husband wasn't Denny Applewhite who got blown up when there was a gas leak...' Mim's voice trailed. Denny Applewhite was a bit of a ducker and diver. Word had it, that he had his gas illegally connected to the mains supply, and when he went to light a cigarette, he took the roof off his house and his walls caved in. Although she wasn't sure about the rumour that bits of him were stuck on the walls and doors. 'I'm so sorry for your loss,' Mim said. 'We had a whip-round in the tavern and sent a wreath.'

'I remember,' said Mollie, 'thank you for that. Well, I must get on.'

She was about to go into the house when Mim said in that friendly fashion so familiar to the dockside area, where nothing was secret for long: 'If there's anything you need, you know where we are.' She supposed the woman would not ask for anything, she didn't look the needy type.

'Thank you,' she said, as she walked up the hallway, laid out exactly the same as every other house in the street.

'I meant to ask,' Mim called up the lobby, 'will your delivery wagon be here long? You see, there's a wedding at number two today, and the wedding cars need to get in.'

'What time's the wedding?' Mollie asked in a dull, toneless voice.

'One o-clock,' Mim answered.

Mollie informed her that as it was only half past eleven, and most of her home had already been unpacked. 'The wagon would have well cleared out by then.'

'Thank you,' Mim said sweetly, thinking Mollie was a right sourpuss.

'Well, what do you expect, Mim?' said Connie as she flicked the pristine white tablecloths onto the T-shaped formation of wedding tables. 'The woman has lost her husband, and by the look of it, she's got a gang of kids to bring up single-handed. I doubt a widow's pension will go far.'

'Aye, I suppose you're right,' said Mim, who went and poured herself a large gin. 'To keep me going,' she said, when Connie raised a shapely eyebrow.

'As long as it doesn't send you over the edge,' Connie replied, 'I'm going to need all the help I can get this afternoon.' Her son, Fergus, was Evie's page boy, and her little Annie was a bridesmaid.

* * *

'Up or down?' Lucy asked as she took the last roller out of Evie's hair.

In her new self-assured way, Evie lifted her tumbling curls, turned her head to examine her profile and decided. 'Up, I'd say,' she smiled, letting her curls fall onto her shoulders. Lucy was coming on in leaps and bounds at the salon.

'Good choice.' Lucy loved nothing more than arranging intricate bridal styles. Since her win at the Adelphi Hotel, they had been getting quite a lot of bridal appointments at the salon, and Madam was thrilled because she always charged a bit more. Now she had the pleasure of producing a spectacularly elegant creation for her very own big sister. 'What do you think?' Lucy said through a cloud of hair lacquer when she'd finished. Stepping back, she admired her handiwork, and swelled with pride when Evie hugged her.

'I won't get my beret over it though,' Evie said, eyeing the simple ivory felt hat that would go with her simple two-piece costume of slim skirt and matching jacket. She had bought it in the sale at Henderson's in Church Street, not wanting to pay too much, as she and Danny were saving so they could expand the business.

'Don't worry about that now,' said Lucy.

There was a knock at the front door, which was closed for the first time since Leo Darnel lodged here. But this time it wasn't closed to hide from the police or the rent man, it was closed to stop the gawping street kids from edging up the hallway to see if there were any treats going spare.

'I'll go and see who that is,' said Lucy. 'It's too early for the cars, and the flowers have already been delivered, so I wonder who it can be?' Lucy felt the excitement buzz through the house, and the kitchen was alive with female chatter, as some of the neighbours had volunteered to help with the wedding breakfast. The aromas sailing through the house from the kitchen made Lucy's mouth water.

'We're doing Coronation chicken,' said Mrs Maguire, who bustled into the lobby just as Lucy reached the front door. And their jaws dropped in unison, when they saw a trolley full of boxes, ready to be delivered.

'Miss Evie Kilgaren,' said the delivery driver, 'and Miss Lucy Kilgaren.'

Lucy's eyes widened when he started to unload the boxes, from one of the leading couture houses in London.

'For me as well?' cried Lucy. 'Take them straight upstairs,' she said, 'the front bedroom.' She hurried on ahead. 'Are you decent?' Lucy called, and she heard Evie reply in a voice filled with curiosity.

'Of course, I am decent, come in!' Evie, sitting at the oval dressing-table mirror, in her woollen dressing gown and slippers, was not expecting a line of box-carrying delivery people to invade her bedroom. When all the boxes were brought in and deposited on the queen-sized bed, the two delivery men doffed their caps and left. 'What's all this?' Evie asked, when the door clicked shut, before noticing the mischievous eyes of her younger sister, who was wearing the widest smile.

'Shall we open them and find out?' Lucy asked, her voice full of glee. She was itching to get the lids off, to see the creations within.

'I didn't order these.' Evie looked a little pale, and when she lifted her gaze, she said to Lucy, 'You know about this?' Evie didn't want her sister sending her hard-won competition money on fripperies that would only be worn for one day.

'I didn't order them,' said Lucy, eager to open all the boxes, 'but I know who did.'

'Danny?' asked Evie, knowing they had been saving hard to buy more wagons. Since Darnel had been arrested, his company liquidated, enabling Danny to get Darnel's wagons cheap, Skinner's Haulage had continued to expand so that Danny now needed to buy more wagons to keep up with the orders which were coming in thick and fast.

'Look,' said Lucy, releasing the snug-fitting lid. 'You remember when you said how much you adored our new Queen's Coronation dress?'

'It isn't...?' *Don't be so stupid, Evie*, she thought, *the Queen of England is not going to lend you her Coronation dress to get married in.* The idea was ridiculous!

'No, it isn't,' said Lucy, 'but this is the next best thing. Let's get it out of the box and you'll see!'

'But who...? What...?'

'It's a wedding present, from Danny,' Lucy said. 'He wanted to do something, that would bring a smile to your face.' Lucy helped Evie remove the dress from the forest of tissue paper, and they both gasped when Evie held the exquisitely beautiful wedding gown. The creation took the breath from both of them.

Slipping the shoulders of the dress over the padded, white, silk hanger supplied, Evie hung it on the door of the wardrobe, so she could get a better look at it.

For a long while, Evie could do nothing, except stare at the wonderful creation, her mouth open, but no words would come. Completely dazed, she believed she must be dreaming. Any moment now she was going to wake up and see her ivory-coloured two-piece hanging in place of this glorious wedding gown. And when she did wake up, she was sure she would cry.

'Try it on,' said Lucy.

Evie knew she had never had a dream so lifelike in all her born days. She turned to Lucy. 'Pinch me, go on, pinch me, I am having a fabulous dream, but I need to get ready for my wedding.'

'You're not dreaming,' Lucy said, her voice quivering with excitement. 'So come on, let's get it on you.'

'What if it doesn't fit?' Evie was beginning to worry she still may not be able to wear something so beautiful.

'Of course, it will fit,' Lucy said, 'I measured everything so carefully. I sent your details to Grace, who said you are both the same size. Grace said she loved it so much, she is thinking of getting married all over again.' Lucy laughed, and Evie wondered how her devious little sister could keep this so quiet. 'Obviously, I was worried it wouldn't arrive on time, Danny expected the dress to arrive yesterday, and I nearly told you a couple of times.'

'Isn't it heavenly,' Evie gasped when Lucy helped her slip the gown over her head without disturbing one hair, and as it slid over her slim frame, Evie marvelled at its gorgeousness. The sweetheart neckline, and handmade lace sleeves, fitted like a second skin, giving way to the structured bodice of duchesse satin, which moulded itself to Evie's torso, shaping her slim hips with a billowing full skirt of ribbed silk that made her small waistline look tiny, giving her the perfect silhouette. Every time she looked at the gown, she saw something different. Her eyes took in the smooth fitted sleeves, infused with gold thread and she realised. 'This must have cost a fortune!'

She gasped when she took out the veil of the same soft handmade lace with its matching pattern. In another smaller box, there was a single strand of real pearls that adorned her slim neck and was finished off with matching pearl earrings. While on her slender feet she wore open-toed duchesse satin shoes.

'Oh Danny,' Evie whispered, hardly able to take her eyes from her reflection in the full-length mirror. 'This must have cost the same as a wagon.'

When she finally managed to drag her eyes from her refection, she realised Lucy had a box too, and so did Fergus and Annie!

In no time at all, Lucy was a vision in pale, mint-coloured taffeta and tulle, the ballerina dress had matching-coloured satin shoes, and the crescent-shaped headdress saddled her head of titian curls to perfection.

'You look like a princess,' Evie whispered, as tears threatened to spill down her cheeks, and Lucy handed her a handkerchief.

'And you look like a queen,' said Lucy, 'and you will knock Danny's eyes out when he sees you walking down the aisle.'

'Stop it, you have me blubbering all over again,' said Evie, hardly able to breathe for the excited hammering of her heart. She could not wait to be Mrs Danny Skinner. Her biggest wish had come true.

'I hope you two are decent,' Jack called before coming into the bedroom. But he didn't get far when the sight of his two beautiful sisters dressed in their finery gave him cause to gasp in amazement. 'Wow, you two scrub up well,' he said, and the two sisters rolled their eyes.

'As compliments go, that's the best we'll get from our Jack,' Evie smiled, aware they were all trying so hard to keep the atmosphere light, and she noticed when Jack looked out of the window, he pinched the bridge of his nose with finger and thumb – like he was wiping away a tear.

'I see we've got new neighbours,' Jack said, admiring one of the most beautiful girls he had ever set eyes on. 'I must introduce myself later.'

Evie smiled, knowing Jack's confidence had soared since his spell in the army.

* * *

'You've made my day, allowing me to walk you down the aisle, you know that don't you?' Frank Kilgaren had been exonerated when the evidence proved he had not killed his wife.

When he saw the announcement in the newspaper telling him

his daughter was engaged to be married, it spurred him on to make his plans to escape and prove his innocence. Frank now realised his children were adults. He had missed out on so much of their lives, and he had so much more to give. Why should he pay for the sins of a crook? Especially when that man had been Darnel. Frank knew the time had come to dig out the truth, and even though it had taken him three months of painstaking sifting through the evidence, while acting as a dumb odd-job man for Lenard Haulage, and keeping his head down, it had all been worth it.

'It's every girl's dream,' Evie answered, proud her father was the man who was going to give her hand in marriage.

'I've just thought of something,' said Lucy, 'isn't the best man supposed to make off with the chief bridesmaid?' She had a playful, mischievous gleam in her eye, knowing Bobby was Danny's best man.

*** * ***

When her car arrived, Evie took her father's arm and pride shone from his eyes.

'Don't forget these,' her father said, handing her the bouquet of pink and white roses. The aromatic perfume filling the house. 'I wish I could make time stand still,' Frank said, looking round the room. 'This house was crying out for a happy occasion.'

Evie, swallowing the happy lump in her throat, nudged him gently with her elbow. 'It was,' she said. 'Shall we go?'

'My pleasure,' Frank said, looping his arm, allowing Evie to slip her hand through.

When they opened the front door, Evie got another surprise to see a black and cream Rolls-Royce taking up what seemed to be half the street.

An appreciative neighbourly murmur, accompanied by a round

of applause followed them, as Evie and her father stepped inside the luxurious car.

Danny's heart leapt as the organ sounded. When he turned at the altar rail, his gaze rested on the light etched in Evie's eyes. He knew, he was the luckiest man in the whole world. And from this day on he would be blessed, because he had Evie, who would always be at his side, through sunny days and rainy nights. But those rainy nights would be unlike any other he had known up 'til now. From this day, they would be together, forever.

Her pace was slow. Regal. And he felt the complex storm of emotions surge up inside him, which he would never be able to name. When his gaze rested on her beautiful face, he felt invincible. Proud to be the man to capture her heart. They had longed for this glorious moment.

Danny knew the exact moment the love for Evie coursed through his veins. He saw her walking down Reckoner's Row towards the docks, with a baby on her hip, holding the hand of her younger brother. And he knew immediately, she was the girl for him.

There wasn't a colour more vibrant, a perfume sweeter, a touch gentler, or a melody as intense as his love for this wonderful woman whose eyes sparkled like they were sprinkled with diamonds when she finally reached him. And, for a while, they were the only the two people in the church...

Meggie, magnificent in a fetching fuchsia dress and coat ensemble, with matching feathered hat, took her place beside Henry.

'Did I tell you?' said Ada, resplendent in a lavender, two-piece, with matching hat, shoes, and gloves, to her best friend, Mim, who was sandwiched between Connie and Grace. '*Our* Bruce has given Danny and Evie a first-class cabin on one of his ships, for their honeymoon.'

'Only a few times, Ada,' Mim answered drily, rolling her eyes heavenwards as the bridal march faded, and the Mersey Mothers sat down in the front pew. 'But you don't use the same words every time... So that's a blessing.'

MORE FROM SHEILA RILEY

We hope you enjoyed reading *The Mersey Mothers*. If you did, please leave a review.

If you'd like to gift a copy, this book is also available as an ebook, digital audio download and audiobook CD.

Sign up to Sheila Riley's mailing list for news, competitions and updates on future books.

http://bit.ly/SheilaRileyNewsletter

Why not explore the rest of the *Reckoner's Row* series.

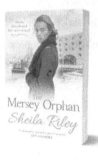 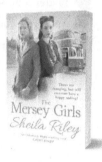

ABOUT THE AUTHOR

Sheila Riley wrote four #1 bestselling novels under the pseudonym Annie Groves and is now writing a saga trilogy under her own name. She has set it around the River Mersey and its docklands near to where she spent her early years. She still lives in Liverpool.

Visit Sheila's website: http://my-writing-ladder.blogspot.com/

Follow Sheila on social media:

       f facebook.com/SheilaRileyAuthor

       y twitter.com/1sheilariley

       O instagram.com/sheilarileynovelist

       BB bookbub.com/authors/sheila-riley

ABOUT BOLDWOOD BOOKS

Boldwood Books is a fiction publishing company seeking out the best stories from around the world.

Find out more at www.boldwoodbooks.com

Sign up to the Book and Tonic newsletter for news, offers and competitions from Boldwood Books!

http://www.bit.ly/bookandtonic

We'd love to hear from you, follow us on social media:

facebook.com/BookandTonic
twitter.com/BoldwoodBooks
instagram.com/BookandTonic